# Clare Chambers

# BRIGHT GIRLS

HarperCollins *Children's Books*

First published in Great Britain by HarperCollins *Children's Books* 2009
HarperCollins *Children's Books* is a division of HarperCollins*Publishers* Ltd
77-85 Fulham Palace Road, Hammersmith, London W6 8JB

www.harpercollins.co.uk

1

ISBN: 978-0-00-730727-2

Printed and bound in England by
Clays Ltd, St Ives plc

**Mixed Sources**
Product group from well-managed
forests and other controlled sources
www.fsc.org Cert no. SW-COC-1806
© 1996 Forest Stewardship Council

FSC is a non-profit international organisation established to promote the
responsible management of the world's forests. Products carrying the FSC
label are independently certified to assure consumers that they come
from forests that are managed to meet the social, economic and
ecological needs of present and future generations.

Find out more about HarperCollins and the environment at
**www.harpercollins.co.uk/green**

To Christabel and Florence

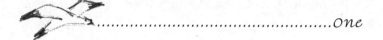

# The Arrival

There was no one to meet us at the station, which didn't surprise me. My only distinct memory of Auntie Jackie, along with various hints dropped by Dad, had convinced me that she wasn't a hundred per cent reliable.

Rachel and I stood on the forecourt with our luggage, in the evening sunshine, scanning the cars as they pulled in to collect or deposit passengers, our attention continually drawn away down the hill to the horizon and the blue wedge of sea. Living in Oxford, almost as far from a proper beach as you can get in Great Britain, we had only been to the coast on a handful of occasions, and the seaside still seemed something full of mystery and promise.

"Would you recognise her?" I asked, when the crowd of commuters had melted away and no one had come forward to claim us.

Rachel nodded. "Old people don't change that much," she said confidently. (Auntie Jackie is thirty-nine.)

After about five minutes, a man approached us. This often happens when I'm out with Rachel. "Are you all right, ladies? You're looking a bit lost." He was wearing an open-necked shirt, white trousers and flip-flops, revealing horribly craggy male toes. A pair of mirrored sunglasses, which replaced his eyes with blank discs of sky, made him look more unsavoury still.

"We're fine thanks. We're just waiting for a lift," said Rachel, giving more information than I felt was strictly necessary.

"You look familiar," he said to her, undeterred. "Are you off the telly?"

She laughed and shook her head. "'Fraid not."

"Oh well." He sauntered off, with the swinging arms and sucked-in stomach of a man who thinks he's being watched.

"Creep," muttered Rachel.

"Did you see his feet?" We both shuddered.

A minute or so passed. "We could phone, I suppose,"

said Rachel, who was generally reluctant to waste her credit on practical matters. "Only my battery's a bit low." She had been firing off texts almost constantly since we'd got on the train at Victoria, so this was hardly news.

From the chaos of her bag she produced a piece of paper on which Dad had written Auntie Jackie's address and phone number, and passed it across to me. My phone was, of course, topped up and fully charged for just this sort of eventuality because I am the Sensible One.

I thumbed in the number and it rang and rang unanswered. "She must be on her way."

We sat at the bus stop to wait, our feet propped on our suitcases, determined not to waste the last of the day's sunshine. Although it was after six it was still warm and Rachel rolled her skirt up as far as it could go and still be called a skirt – to soak up the maximum amount of dangerous UVB.

We'd set off from home before lunch and I was surprised how tired I was, considering that I'd been sitting down almost all day on one train or another. I suppose it was that two-hour interlude in London, lugging my suitcase the length of Oxford Street while Rachel was bargain hunting in the summer sales. Her case was one of those zippy new ones on wheels – an eighteenth-birthday present which she'd considered thoroughly uninspiring at the time, but was rather pleased with now that she'd seen my struggles. Mine was an ancient family heirloom which obviously predated the invention of the wheel, as it had to be carried everywhere – all twenty kilos of it. I was seriously considering ditching it at the end of the summer and posting my clothes back home in Jiffy bags. That's if we ever got home of course.

"Oh, this is ridiculous. Let's get a cab," said Rachel. A bank of bright cloud had boiled up over the rooftops, throwing our bench into the shade, so there was no point in further sunbathing. "You've got the money, haven't you?"

Dad had handed me a bundle of notes as we said our goodbyes on the station platform that morning. I resisted the temptation to count them straightaway, in case it looked grasping. "I'm giving it to you to look after because Rachel would spend it before you were halfway to Brighton," he said. She had overheard this and protested, so he'd relented and given her fifty quid of her own, which she had blown in Topshop at Oxford Circus.

"What if she turns up and we're not here?" I asked. I didn't want to get off on the wrong foot.

"Well, it's her fault for being so late."

She set off at a brisk pace towards the taxi rank, wheeling her case, while I staggered behind. The driver sprang out of the car and almost fell up the kerb in his haste to help her put the bags in the boot.

"Where to, ladies?" he asked.

"Cliff Street," I said, consulting Dad's scrap of paper again, wondering how far away it was, and how much of that precious £100 it would cost.

"Here on holiday, are we?" he said over his shoulder as he swung out into the traffic. Rachel and I exchanged significant looks.

"Not exactly," she replied. We were both remembering Dad's instructions: *Don't tell anyone in Oxford where you're going, and don't tell anyone in Brighton why you're there. You don't need to lie. Just be vague.*

"Oh, I don't mind lying," Rachel had volunteered cheerfully. "That's the fun bit."

# Two

# The Neighbours

The inside of the cab smelled strongly of pine air-freshener, and the radio was tuned to drive-time on one of those easy-listening stations that refuse to play eighties music because it's too modern. I meant to pay attention to the route so I'd know how to find my way around, but after a right and a left I lost concentration because a thought had just struck me. If there was no one at Auntie Jackie's to answer the phone, then presumably there would be no one there to answer the doorbell either. This complication didn't seem to have occurred to Rachel, who was sitting back, admiring the view, thoroughly at ease in her favourite form of transport.

29 Cliff Street was a tall, terraced house with railings

outside and a basement window below the level of the pavement. Once white, it was now streaked with grey – not unlike a cliff in fact. There was a general air of shabbiness about the street, which made me feel quite sad. While I produced a ten-pound note from the mugger-proof zip pocket of my trousers, the driver unloaded the cases and carried them up to the front door – a piece of chivalry worth every penny of his 50p tip.

As I'd predicted, there was no one at home. A Post-it note had been stuck over the doorbell. BROKEN, PLEASE KNOCK it said in ink so faded that it suggested a long-standing problem. Rachel rapped forcefully on the knocker, and when this produced no results, shouted, "Hello?" through the letter box, snapping one of her fingernails as the flap sprang back, which didn't improve her mood. "If only we didn't have these stupid cases, we could go back into town and sit in a café," she said, nursing her squared-off nail. She gave the knocker a last, defiant rap and the whole thing came off in her hand. "Oh, great."

As if in response to this disturbance, the front door of the neighbouring house opened and an elderly woman appeared on the step. She was wearing a flowery dress and an inside out cardigan, and holding a tray of flapjacks which, for some mysterious reason, she tipped into the paper recycling box beside her. As she straightened up with some effort, she caught sight of us over the dividing wall. "Hello? Are you looking for Janice?" she said. Then, before we could correct her, added, "She went out in the car about an hour ago. She was going to get some shopping and then pick up some visitors at the station."

"Well, we are the visitors," said Rachel. "She didn't turn up so we got a taxi. But there's no one in."

The woman peered over the wall at our cases. "Oh. Did you knock loudly? Charlie might be in – he sleeps during the day."

Rachel and I exchanged looks. This was the first we'd heard of any "Charlie".

"We shouted through the letter box and everything," I said.

"Oh dear, well, you can't wait out on the doorstep. Come in here and have a cup of tea until Janice gets back."

If I wasn't such a polite person, and so desperate for a drink, I would have said no thanks, but the old woman had already turned back into the house so there was nothing for it but to follow, carrying our bags down the steps on to the pavement again and back up through next door's gate.

I could sense Rachel beginning to simmer. Unless she had a cast-iron excuse on her eventual return, Auntie Jackie was likely to get an earful.

Our hostess was waiting in the long hallway, beckoning us down a flight of stairs to the basement. "Leave your cases by the front door," she sang out before hobbling ahead on feet so swollen it looked as though someone had filled her tights up with sand. "I'll get my grandson to carry them round for you later."

She was already filling an aluminium kettle from a rubber-snouted tap when we came into the room, which was exactly like a mock-up of a 1950s kitchen from a museum of domestic life. There was a free-standing stove and an enamel round-cornered fridge the colour of very old teeth. Beneath our feet the brown and orange checked lino rose and fell in a series of ripples, crackling slightly where we trod. A Welsh dresser looked ready to collapse under the weight of mountains of crockery, teapots, china ornaments, candlesticks, figurines, polished stones and bits of driftwood. From among this collection the old lady selected a porcelain urn, and ignoring the rising shriek of the kettle, measured out four teaspoons of black dust into a teapot.

"You must have one of my flapjacks," she said, prising

the lid off a biscuit tin which proved to contain nothing but a pile of used envelopes. She looked at them, mystified, for a second or two before laying the tin aside with a shrug. "How about a ham sandwich?" she said brightly.

"No, thank you. Just tea would be lovely," said Rachel, gesturing urgently towards the billows of steam pouring from the still-wailing kettle.

The old lady dived for the hob and snapped the gas off, and the room fell silent again. When she had tipped what was left of the boiling water on to the tea leaves, she wrenched open the fridge door and produced a sliced loaf and various cellophane packages, and began buttering bread, very fast, deaf to our protests.

Her task done, she turned back to us, beaming, holding a plate of limp sandwiches cut into eight triangles, the white bread still bearing the dimpled impression of her fingers. "There we are." She looked at us expectantly.

"Thank you," I said, helping myself to the least mauled of the triangles, and glaring at Rachel until she followed suit. The ham tasted slightly fishy. Perhaps it wasn't ham, I decided. Perhaps it was some form of beige, pressed fish. I ate two of the sandwiches, while Rachel nibbled delicately at the crust of her first one, and wondered how many we could leave on the plate without giving offence. I knew Rachel had no intention of sharing the obligation fifty-fifty: she tended to have sudden crippling attacks of vegetarianism on these occasions. The tea, at least, tasted recognisable, even if it was served in bone china cups so tiny they must have come from a teddy bears' picnic.

"I wonder if we ought to have left a note on Auntie Jackie's front door," Rachel was saying, using this as an excuse to lay down her sandwich. "She won't know we're here."

"Oh, yes. Perhaps we'd better go and see if she's back," the old lady agreed, as the two of us leapt to our feet. "It's been lovely to meet you," she said to me as we made our way along the corridor, and added confidentially, "I know your mother, you know." And I now realised what had been dawning on me, oh so slowly, all the time I had been in the house: she was completely and utterly mad.

As we reached the front door, it was pushed open by a guy of about nineteen who was holding a bicycle which he had evidently just carried up the steps. He had curly hair and thin oblong glasses and was dripping with sweat. We stood aside to let him pass into the house. He propped his bike against the wall and wiped his forehead on the edge of his T-shirt.

"Hello, dear," said the old woman. "This is my grandson, Adam," she explained. "These girls have come to visit Janice."

"Jackie," said Adam, not loudly enough for her to hear. He gave us an apologetic look.

"I said you'd carry their cases round for them later."

"Oh, there's no need," said Rachel quickly. "We can manage. We've carried them halfway across London already."

*Well, I did*, I thought. *You wheeled yours*.

"It's no trouble," said Adam.

"If we could just have a piece of paper, we could leave a note to say where we are," said Rachel, fishing in her bag for a biro.

"Why don't you just borrow the spare key," said Adam, selecting one from a row of hooks on the wall beside him. Rachel and I looked at each other.

"Do we have a key to Janice's?" his grandmother said. "I didn't know we had a key."

"She gave it to us because Charlie kept locking himself out."

The old woman looked blank. "Who's Charlie?"

This bewildering exchange was interrupted by the *whoop*

of a siren which grew to a crescendo and then stopped as a police car pulled up at the kerb, lights flashing. The passenger door opened and a woman in a strappy sundress clambered out, showing rather a lot of leg. Her chunky calves were laced almost to the knee into high, cork-heeled espadrilles. She had long plum-coloured hair plaited into dozens of thin braids and gathered up into a sprouting ponytail high on her head. A pair of heavy chandelier earrings dragged at her earlobes. She flew up the steps towards us, blethering apologies.

Auntie Jackie.

# Auntie Jackie

"You got here. Thank God!" Auntie Jackie advanced on Rachel and me with arms outstretched and crushed us against her in an uncomfortable three-way hug. "I'm so, so sorry I wasn't at the station. I went to Asda to get something nice for your dinner and on the way back some lunatic jumped the lights and smacked into the side of me. My car's a wreck. Luckily there were witnesses. Anyway," she went on, releasing us at last, so we could uncrick our necks, "you're here, safe and sound, and that's the main thing." She stepped back and looked us up and down, her eyes resting admiringly on the expanse of smooth tummy exposed by the ten-centimetre gap between the end of Rachel's vest and the start of her skirt.

"Your dad was right," she sighed. "I'll be beating the men off with a broom." She seemed quite capable of it too, if that hug was anything to go by.

"You look so much like your mum," she said, turning to me, and for an awful moment I thought she was going to cry, but she contented herself with a last bruising hug. All this while, the policeman had been busily unloading plastic bags of groceries from the boot of his car and carrying them up to the door of number 29. I wondered if all Brighton's policemen were this helpful.

"There you are, lovely lady," he called out when the job was done and he was about to drive off. Auntie Jackie went haring down to the kerb and leant, head and shoulders, through the driver's window to speak to him. In fact, from where I was standing, she looked as though she was giving him a kiss, but she couldn't have been. Could she?

Without waiting to be asked, Adam disappeared back inside his house and emerged with our suitcases, one in each hand, and carted them next door.

"Adam's at the university," Auntie Jackie said, as if this was some rare and marvellous feat. "So he knows all the fun places. Don't you, Adam?"

He nodded placidly.

"Thank you for looking after them," she went on, as she kicked a path between the piles of Asda bags to let us into the house.

He didn't seem to take this as his cue to go, but stood, loitering awkwardly while Auntie Jackie unlocked the door. I wondered if he was waiting for a tip. Then just as I turned my back to follow Auntie Jackie and Rachel inside, he tapped me on the shoulder and said in an urgent whisper, "My gran didn't give you any food, did she?"

"Yes," I said, a trifle uneasily.

Adam went white. "Oh my God," he said. "She always does this."

I didn't have a chance to enquire what he meant as Auntie Jackie was calling from deep inside the house, so I picked up a few of the shopping bags and went inside, and when I turned round, he was gone.

My room was in the basement, along with the kitchen and a tiny, airless shower room. It faced the street and looked directly on to a wall, and, if I was lucky, the passing feet and ankles of pedestrians. It felt strange to be down below pavement level, but the room was large and pretty, with an open fireplace filled with chubby candles, and a sofa bed dressed up with satin cushions. It was home to assorted curiosities including an archery target, a double bass missing all but one string and a life-sized papier-mâché pig. Above the mantelpiece was a painting of a meaty nude, who bore a faint resemblance to Auntie Jackie, showing off a lot of underarm stubble and much else besides. More to my taste was a black and white photo on the opposite wall which showed a group of nuns punting on the Cherwell.

"This is usually the sitting room," Auntie Jackie explained on our tour of the property. "But I've tried to tidy it up for you."

The alternative was a recently decorated room on the first floor, bagged by Rachel because she said she was a fresh air freak and wouldn't feel safe having the window open at night downstairs. Privately I thought it was more likely to be the double bed and the en suite that had persuaded her, but I didn't mind. Not really. Auntie Jackie's bedroom and an antiquated bathroom were also on this storey. The attic room at the top of the house was occupied by the lodger, Charlie, when in residence. He kept odd hours, we were told, because he was a professional musician who worked in the West End, and he liked to practise his trumpet when he got up in the afternoons, but apart from that, and a habit of locking himself out, gave very little trouble and was hardly ever in.

There were more Post-it notes, like the one over the doorbell, dotted around the house, offering warnings and reminders to past and present tenants. NO LOCK said the label on the loo door. DOOR CLOSED = OCCUPIED. Another, beside the oven, advised would-be chefs: TAKE BATTERY OUT OF SMOKE ALARM BEFORE USING GRILL. The most mysterious of all was stuck above a plug socket in the kitchen and said simply: NOT THIS ONE! On making enquiries, I was told that Charlie had once unplugged the freezer for a whole weekend while recharging his motorbike battery, resulting in the destruction of a month's supply of Weight Watchers' ready meals.

The whole of the ground floor was taken up by Auntie Jackie's "business" – *Ballgowns, Evening Wear and Accessories for Hire*. The front room was entirely given over to dresses of every size and colour: rail upon rail of taffeta, silk, velvet and tulle; sequins, feathers and pearls. In the back were chests of drawers containing shawls and scarves and elbow-length gloves, and above our heads, beaded evening bags hung in clusters like chandeliers. In one corner was a curtained changing cubicle, and the rest of the space was occupied by a workbench and sewing machine, for repairs and alterations. Dad, typically, had got it wrong and told us Auntie Jackie worked in a second hand clothes shop, which made it sound one step up from a car boot sale.

The pride of the collection was displayed on a tailor's dummy in a glass case. It was a midnight blue strapless dress which flowed out from knee level into a fishtail of hundreds of tissue-thin layers, all embroidered with sprays of silver stars. I wondered why it had been singled out for this attention – it was one of the least ostentatious of the lot – until Rachel gave me a nudge and pointed to a framed photograph on the opposite wall, and it suddenly made sense. In the picture, greeting a line-up of celebrities and smiling her famous, modest smile, was Princess Diana in that very same dress.

"Is that really…?" I asked Auntie Jackie.

She nodded, amused by our gawping. "You'd have been too young to remember, but Princess Diana auctioned off most of her wardrobe for charity in 1997. I'd just got an insurance payout for a whiplash injury – nearly $18,000 – and I blew the whole lot on one dress. I didn't have the business then – I just wanted it for myself.

My husband was hopping mad: he didn't speak to me for a week. And then within two months she was dead."

There was a solemn pause as we looked again at the holy object.

"Have you ever worn it?" asked Rachel.

Auntie Jackie shook her head. "Sadly, no."

"Because it's too precious?"

"No. Because I'm too bloody fat. Every time I try a new diet I think 'I'll be wearing Diana's dress by Christmas!' but it never happens."

"It must be worth a fortune," said Rachel wistfully. She was probably thinking how much stuff she could get from Topshop if she put it on eBay.

"Priceless," Auntie Jackie agreed. "But I'll never sell it. I could end up living in a cardboard box under the promenade, but I'll still have my dress. They can bury me in it – it'll probably fit me like a glove when I've died of starvation."

"I wouldn't sell it either," I said. Although I'm the Sensible One, I do have a romantic streak.

Auntie Jackie left us to unpack and "freshen up", as she called it, while she put away her groceries and began to prepare dinner. I could hear her clattering around in the kitchen cupboards and singing along to the radio, while I hung my few decent clothes in the wardrobe. In the absence of any empty drawers, I left the rest in the bottom of the suitcase, which I pushed under the bed. Various other items from home – my clarinet, music stand, books, tennis racquet – I deposited around the room as though marking out my territory. It was only now that I came to unpack that I realised how little I'd brought. We had left in too much of a hurry. The last item to be rehoused was a cream shawl, crocheted in softest baby wool, which I used to cover up a depressed-looking armchair. It was the only thing I owned that my mother had made especially for me, which made it even more priceless in its way than Princess Diana's dress.

*Four*..................................................

# Big Sister, Little Sister

Mum died when I was one and Rachel was nearly four.
I don't remember a thing about her of course. I used to
think I did, but then I realised that all my memories
were photographs. Rachel doesn't really remember her
either, which is even worse. All those years Mum spent
playing pat-a-cake with her, and being patient and kind,
for nothing! Nowadays, whenever I see some toddler
kicking off in the supermarket and the mum trying to
negotiate and be all reasonable, I feel like going up to
her and saying, "For God's sake, just smack him! He
won't remember!"

I can't say I "miss" her because you can't miss someone
you never knew, but sometimes, when school work's

piling up, and things indoors are a bit disorganised, and Dad's too preoccupied with his job to notice, I can't help thinking that one parent isn't quite enough. I suppose it must be like being an only child. You wouldn't spend all your time grieving about the brothers and sisters you don't have, but now and then you'd look at those big, boisterous families and feel a twinge of envy.

It's only in recent years that Dad has talked to us about how he coped or rather didn't cope when Mum died. He'd always talked about Mum of course, so that we would know how wonderful she was and never "forget" her, but not once about himself and his own feelings. To begin with, Nanny Chris (Mum's mum) came to stay and look after us while he was out at work. After a while, they had a bit of a falling out because she didn't approve of the way he let us sleep in his bed, and he thought she was too strict about mealtimes and TV rations, so she went back up to Scotland in a strop and we didn't see her for some time.

That was when Mum's sister – Jackie – came. She was only twenty-five – ten years younger than Mum – but she gave up her job in London and left her flat and her friends, and moved into our spare room in Oxford so that she could take care of us all until Rachel started school and I went to nursery. I suppose Dad must have paid her. She wouldn't have done it for nothing.

It all worked well for about a year, and then Auntie Jackie started to make friends of her own and go out in the evenings a bit more. Before long she'd got a new boyfriend and wanted to move him into the spare room with her. Dad was furious and said he didn't want some strange bloke in the house with us when he wasn't around, and they had this huge row and Auntie Jackie walked out. Within three months, she and the boyfriend had got married and moved to Chicago, where he was from, and we didn't see her again for another eight years.

The rest of the family was *outraged* that she had deserted us, convinced that the husband was some sort of gangster and it would all end in tears. Which it did eventually, but nothing like as soon as the family had predicted (and no doubt hoped). After twelve years she came quietly back to the UK, and with her share of the divorce payout, she acquired the house in Brighton and started up her business.

During her time in America she had sent gifts at birthdays and Christmas, and cards signed "from your loving Aunt", and at Dad's insistence we had dutifully replied with bland reports of our progress and copies of our school photographs, but as far as we knew, Dad never wrote to her himself.

There had been just one visit, the year that Nanny Chris died. I'm afraid to say that it was the memory of this that had given me a pessimistic view of Auntie Jackie's reliability.

I am ten years old, standing in the wings at the school concert, sucking nervously on the reed of my clarinet as I listen to Elizabeth Gallup play Minuet in G on the piano. Although I can't see them, I can sense, from the occasional distant cough and rustle, the bulky presence of the audience beyond the stage. Even so, I am surprised by the storm of applause that greets the end of Elizabeth's performance. The hall must be full. I am on next. A lone, metal music stand, like an instrument of torture, glints coldly in a shaft of light from the high hall windows. For a moment I am completely paralysed: my eagerness to perform, to show off and be applauded is brought down by a crippling attack of stage fright.

Something I have known all along, and buried, rises up now: I am not meant to be here, playing in this concert. I am not good enough. It is a mistake.

"Ruth, I've put you down to play a solo in the school

concert," my clarinet teacher said at the start of a music lesson, three weeks ago now.

"I'm not Ruth. I'm Robyn," I said. Ruth is a year older. She has done grades. The teacher faltered for a moment before her smile was back in place. "Of course you are. Robyn. Well, you can play something in the concert too, Robyn. Why not?"

The wooden boards, stripped of varnish and slightly soft, quake underfoot as I cross the stage and balance my single sheet of music on the solitary stand. It is mid-afternoon, the hall is uncurtained and well-lit, and I can see the faces of the audience as clearly as they can see me, clearly enough at any rate to be sure that Dad and Auntie Jackie aren't among them. She is supposed to be here. Dad has taken the day off work so that he can collect her from Oxford station and bring her along. It was a firm arrangement, a promise, and I have been boasting to the whole class for days about my aunt coming all the way from America to watch me. If she doesn't show up, everyone will think I'm a Big Fat Liar, the sort of girl who invents fantasy relatives to make herself look important.

As my damp, nibbled lips close around the mouthpiece of the clarinet, the other buried thing chooses this moment to surface. I have never, in all my practices, even in the privacy of my own room, played this piece all the way through without mistakes.

If I can just get through the first bar without a misfire. I can never seem to recover from an early *squawk*. I fill my lungs and attack the first long note, and it emerges pure and clean. Relief.

From the back of the hall comes the *swish* and *clump* of the double doors opening and closing as Dad and Auntie Jackie creep in late. Heads turn at the disturbance. I falter, *squawk*, lose my place in the music and then, just as I find it, the gust of air admitted by the swing doors comes rolling up the aisle towards the stage like a giant wave, snatches my flimsy sheet of music from the stand and lifts it high in the air, where it swoops to and fro above my flailing hand before wafting slowly down into the audience. I turn and bolt into the wings to general laughter and applause.

I was slightly surprised when Auntie Jackie finally returned to live in England that she didn't get straight back in touch. She and Dad had patched up their quarrel by then and we were her only living relatives, but Dad explained that she probably felt guilty and wouldn't want to make the first approach in case it was rejected. Besides, Brighton was 110 miles from Oxford – hardly a feasible distance for a day trip. He also had a theory that Mum's death had hit her harder than he'd appreciated at the time. He'd been too caught up with his own sorrows to notice anyone else's. "Your mum was always the good, clever, sensible sister who everybody loved. And Jackie was the difficult, wayward one who was always in trouble. She once told me she felt that people were secretly thinking that the wrong sister had died."

"That's terrible. Poor Auntie Jackie," said Rachel, identifying immediately with the naughty sister.

Dad was wrong though. Guilty or not, she did make the first approach: a letter arrived addressed to me and Rachel.

*I know I've been the world's most useless Aunt, but I kept you all in my heart while I was away, and never stopped thinking of you... Now I've had time to settle in and find my feet, I want you to know that I'm here if you ever need me. Blood is thicker than water, I appreciate that now...*

"She's got a good heart," Dad conceded, when he read this outpouring, which ran to two pages of badly spelled scribble. "And if it ever came to the crunch, I know she'd be ready to help out."

When the crunch came, within six months of this casual remark, and we needed somewhere to run to, Auntie Jackie's had been the obvious choice.

# The Bucket and the Bell

That first evening at Cliff Street Auntie Jackie made us a prawn stir-fry with noodles, which we ate in the kitchen – the only communal area now that I had taken over the basement. This proved to be the one edible meal she could make, and she soon abandoned proper cooking altogether.

Unfortunately I couldn't do justice to her initial efforts as about two mouthfuls in I began to feel queasy and had to go and lie down. By ten o'clock my stomach was in spasms, my head was in a bucket and I was puking myself inside-out. Living in Oxford I'd witnessed quite a lot of public vomiting – you really had to watch where you put your feet in Freshers' Week – and I'd always had a horror of being sick. It was such a disgusting spectacle.

"Sorry," I said to Auntie Jackie in between torrents, as she discreetly wiped the toe of her shoe with a tissue.

"You don't think it's the prawns, do you?" she said, passing me a wrung-out flannel so I could mop my face.

I shook my head. I knew the culprit was the fishy ham: traces of the strange, beige film were floating in the bilious slop in the bucket. Besides, I hadn't eaten any of the prawns.

"No, I bet it's those sandwiches," said Rachel from the doorway. "I thought they smelled funny at the time. Thank God I never ate mine."

"Do you think we should ring the doctor?" Auntie Jackie asked her. "Or your dad?"

We had only called him a few hours earlier to say that we'd arrived safe and well. It seemed a pity to phone and retract the good news so soon. The two of them conferred in low voices for a moment and then Auntie Jackie disappeared upstairs.

"Poor old you," said Rachel, stepping just inside the sickroom with extreme reluctance, and covering her mouth and nose. "You'll be all right, won't you?"

I nodded weakly. I was experiencing the momentary relief that follows violent puking. Auntie Jackie returned a few minutes later and shone a torch in my face.

"Ow. What are you doing?"

"Does your neck hurt?" she asked, snapping off the torch.

"No. Why?"

"Just checking you haven't got meningitis. Excuse me. Do you mind?" she lifted my T-shirt and peered at my pale flesh, apparently satisfied.

"You need to drink plenty of fluid," she instructed me. "But sip, don't glug. Do you want me to sleep in here tonight?"

I shook my head. I wanted to curl up quietly and die, without any fuss, and that was something best done alone.

They withdrew to the kitchen, and I could hear the murmurs of conversation and the comforting domestic noises of washing up and tea-making. Just before she went up to bed, Auntie Jackie came in again to bring me some fresh water. In her free hand she was holding a large Swiss cowbell. "This is the nearest thing I've got to an emergency cord," she said. "If you want me in the night for anything, ring this and I'll come down." It let out a soft *clong* as she set it down.

When she had gone, I lay there feeling sorry for myself for a while. There were no curtains on the window and the street lamp outside gave just enough light to pick out the shapes of the furniture. I could see the double bass, and the candles in the fireplace, and the papier-mâché pig sitting on the window seat, and the picture of the punting nuns, which made me think of Oxford, and I wondered when or if it would ever be safe to go home.

# Adam

I stayed in bed for two days, unable to do more than take sips of water and doze, and make occasional shuffling visits to the bathroom next door. At one point during the first night my mobile phone rang, but it was out of reach, hanging on the door handle in my bag. I could hear it buzzing away like a furious insect, but I couldn't summon the strength to fetch it. When I did finally sleep, I had lurid nightmares about a giant pig – as if the ham was taking revenge on my mind as well as my guts.

Rachel made occasional mercy visits to the basement to cheer me up and harass me back to health. She even brought me a copy of *Hello!* and a pen so that I could draw the spots and hairs and wrinkles back on to the airbrushed celebrities. She had already made a preliminary exploration of the town and discovered some promising shops, but was waiting for me (and Dad's cash) to join her for a proper spree.

"I suppose I'll have to start looking for a job," she said glumly. "Next week. When you're better." I wasn't quite sure what my recovery had to do with it. She had promised Dad she would work over the summer, to build up some sort of cash reserves before going off to university. He admitted he didn't have any great hopes that she'd *save* anything, but he figured that every hour she worked was an hour she wouldn't be out spending.

Another regular presence at my bedside was Auntie Jackie, so regular in fact that I never needed to resort to the giant cowbell. I knew she must be popping in, even when I was asleep, because someone kept emptying the bucket, bringing fresh water, and opening and closing the window. The room faced south and in the middle of the day, when the sun was at its height, the uncurtained basement was as hot as a greenhouse. At other times I could hear footsteps overhead, in the "shop" and I knew she must have a client in for a fitting.

On the third day I felt the first stirrings of hunger, so Auntie Jackie brought me a cup of clear soup and a piece of toast, which I tore into cubes and submerged until they were just soft. I'd never tasted anything so delicious. I had retrieved my phone by this time, so I knew that it was Dad who had rung me. He had followed it up with a text – fully spelled and punctuated as always: it must have taken him hours.

> Hello Robyn. Sorry to hear from Jackie that you've been sick. I tried to phone last night, but there was no reply. Roger's room in college is comfortable, but extraordinarily noisy with summer-school students next door partying at all hours. I miss you and hope we can all be together again soon. I haven't been near the house. Love you. Dad xxx

Rachel had also had a message from him – equally long-winded. We'd tried to teach him the basics, but he seemed to have a morbid fear of abbreviations. What normal person would use the word "extraordinarily" in a text?

I sent off a quick reply to stop him worrying.

> Hi Dad. Thx 4 ur msg. 8 some food 2da 4
> 1st time and feel ok. Luv u 2 xxx :-)

I knew I was getting better because the fact that I hadn't showered or washed my hair for three days was starting to bother me. On my way out to the kitchen to return my empty soup bowl I had caught a glimpse of my reflection in the mirror above the mantelpiece – a sight which sent me scurrying to the bathroom to take action. My hair was so greasy it was almost waterproof: I had to use nearly half a bottle of shampoo before I could work up a lather, and the run-off was the colour of ditchwater.

I felt rather light-headed when I'd finished, perhaps because I wasn't used to being vertical, or possibly because the shower was too hot, and I was still sitting on my bed on my wet towel, while the room swayed tipsily around me, when there was a tap at the door.

"Visitor," said a voice. "Are you decent?"

"No," I squeaked, diving back into bed and dragging the duvet up to my neck. Just in time, as the door opened and Auntie Jackie ushered Adam inside. He was carrying a bunch of white carnations and looking embarrassed.

"Hello," he said, trying to peel off the 50% EXTRA FREE label on the polythene wrapper. "I heard you've been ill.

I brought these to say sorry." He held them out, and then realising that I couldn't take them from him as well as hold up the duvet, gave them to Auntie Jackie instead.

"I'll go and put them in a vase," she said, retreating graciously.

It occurred to me that this was the first time in my life that anyone had bought me flowers, but I didn't admit this of course. I just said, "Thank you. But you don't need to apologise."

"Well, I feel slightly responsible," Adam said, advancing into the room, but not going so far as to sit down and make himself comfortable. "My gran's suffering from dementia – you probably noticed. And she tends to be a bit careless with sell-by dates and stuff. So every few days I have to do a sweep of the fridge and chuck out anything dodgy. But lately she's taken to hiding packets of food in other places – like under the sofa – which means it goes off even quicker. It's fine if I'm around because I can warn people, but in your case I got there just too late…"

"There's no proof it was the sandwich that made me ill," I said, to be kind. "It could have been something I ate on the train."

He looked sceptical. "No. I found the empty wrapper in the bin. It was well out of date."

"By how much?"

"You don't want to know."

All the while he was speaking, he was looking out of the window or down at his feet or at the wall above my head – anywhere but at me, which gave me a perfect opportunity to observe him without having to make eye contact. He had a nervous mannerism that I hadn't noticed on our first meeting: a way of twitching his cheeks, as if trying to shrug his glasses higher up his nose. It was quite sweet in a geekish sort of way.

"Why do you live with your granny? Are your parents dead?" I asked. Having some experience of this subject myself, I felt entitled to ask.

"No, they're in Telford," he replied. "Though some might say that amounts to the same thing." The twitch gave way to a quick smile. "I'm only staying with my gran while I'm at university because it's cheaper than renting. Plus, I can keep an eye on her. Sort of."

From above came the tripping sound of footsteps on the stairs and presently Rachel bounced in without troubling to knock.

"I'm ready," she announced.

She was dressed in a white cropped vest, joggers and trainers. Her hair was tied up in two long plaits. It was positively indecent, I thought, the way she flaunted her health and energy while I was still so pasty and weak.

"Where are you going?" I asked, trying to sound politely interested rather than envious.

"Into town and then to play tennis. Do you want me to bring you anything back? Chocolate?" she wheedled.

"Maybe some mints." There was a foul, rusty taste in my mouth.

"OK." Rachel held her hand out. For a moment or two I acted mystified.

"Can I have some of that money... please," she conceded. "I'll pay you back as soon as I get a job."

Still trapped under the duvet by my nakedness I gestured towards my bag on the door handle and watched in dismay as she helped herself to ten, twenty, thirty...

"Bye then."

They sauntered out and a few minutes later I saw their feet passing along the pavement outside. Their mingled laughter floated carelessly down through my open window.

I knew this would happen. Rachel would spend all summer swanning around with Adam and I would be left to amuse myself. I had hoped that there might be a brief lull between boyfriends so that we could spend some time together, the way we used to when we were younger, before she became the Beautiful One.

It seemed to happen overnight, the transformation. One day we were building obstacle courses for the guinea pigs, diving for weights at the Marston Ferry pool, French skipping and practising dangerous stunts on our rollerblades, and the next day she woke up with boobs and periods and didn't want to play any more. She started straightening her hair and wearing thick black eyeliner, and high heels that made her walk like someone with two sprained ankles. She couldn't bear to be separated from her friends for a minute: as soon as she came in from school, she would throw her bag on the floor and get straight on to MSN to continue the conversation that they'd just been having on the bus. It seemed to me that all of her time was spent in one of three pursuits: tarting herself up for parties, going to parties or exchanging post-party gossip with her mates. These various commitments had crowded me out over the years.

When the first boyfriend came on the scene, it was even worse. She was never in except with Him, unless they'd had a row, in which case she would stay in bed eating biscuits and listening to suicide rock on her iPod and generally suffering until he came crawling back.

Once she'd got a taste for them, she couldn't seem to do without a boyfriend. Even when she'd been viciously dumped – a rarity this, as Rachel was usually the first to cool off – and she would rage and storm about having had enough of blokes, this high-minded singleness would only last a couple of weeks. Then her phone would start chirping at unsociable hours, a new name would keep cropping up in conversations and she would revive and blossom again. I couldn't help envying her luck, or whatever it was. I'd never even got close to having a boyfriend and I wasn't anything like as fussy as Rachel. He didn't have to be tall or good-looking – just funny and nice and available, but even that, it seemed, was asking the impossible.

If Rachel hadn't recently split up with the latest specimen – Todd – and wanted to put some distance between them, I doubt she would have agreed to leave Oxford at all. She said she'd tried to let him down gently, but he was obviously much keener on her than she'd realised. Every time she went to the pub or a party there he'd be, moping around looking tragic and making her feel guilty for flirting with other blokes. In short, his refusal to move on was seriously spoiling her fun, to the point that our banishment to Brighton began to seem a convenient solution.

I was secretly pleased that they'd parted because I'd never much liked Todd. Unlike the fit, confident, sporty types she usually went for, he was thin and arty and depressed. On one occasion I had walked in on him in the bathroom because he'd failed to lock the door and caught him peeing in the washbasin, even though there was a perfectly adequate toilet right beside him.

I said, "Whoops, sorry," and backed out, pretending I hadn't noticed. After he'd gone, I bleached the basin and threw my flannel in the bin in case it had been within range, but I never told anyone what I'd seen. Not even Rachel. It was too weird and, besides, my critical insights about her boyfriends were seldom well-received. (Once, in a spirit of sisterly solidarity, I'd passed on the information that a boy she was seeing had been at the Penultimate Picture Palace two rows in front of me with a notorious local slapper, and she hadn't been the least bit grateful.)

After a while I began to wonder whether I had imagined the whole Todd/bathroom episode, or misinterpreted some entirely innocent and hygienic activity. But I knew I hadn't really.

# Seven

# Of Rats and Men

My gloomy prophecies of romance between Rachel and Adam turned out to be a little premature, as she returned from their outing distinctly unimpressed.

"Men are so competitive," she grumbled, throwing herself down on my bed, which I had only just vacated. "I've hardly played tennis in my life and he's some sort of county champion, so of course he's going to win!" Her face was still the colour of corned beef from her exertions on court. "I thought it was going to be a nice, gentle knockabout."

"What about the rest of the day?"

"Oh, that was all right. We went on the pier and walked down to the marina. I did most of the talking. The only subject that really got him going was computers."

"Oh. Did you tell him about—"

"No, of course not." She tutted at my lack of faith in her discretion. "He wouldn't let me win one point!" she burst out, unable to leave the subject alone. That thrashing had really got to her. "I think he's just a bit young for me."

"He's older than you."

"Yes, but *emotionally*. I need a man with more experience… By the way, here you are." She produced a Sainsbury's bag from her holdall and slung it across to where I was sitting on the window seat. On inspection I found it contained a packet of "Taste-the-difference extra-lean steak mince".

"What's this?"

"You said you wanted some mince," she replied.

I looked at her in disbelief. "I said *mints*, you stupid troll. Why would I want a lump of raw meat? I'm just getting over food poisoning!"

"I dunno. I thought you might want to make a burger or something."

"I don't even eat burgers when I'm well!" I stuffed the plastic box hastily back in the bag – the sight of the oozing, pulped flesh was too much for my delicate guts – and threw it back at Rachel.

"I'm sorry," she laughed remorselessly. "You should speak more clearly. You mumble; that's your trouble."

I glared at her.

"Oh, well, no point in wasting it. I'll make spaghetti Bolognese tonight. Auntie Jackie is the worst cook." She lowered her voice, remembering just too late our proximity to the kitchen. "I think she must live on baked potatoes."

A baked potato sounded good to me: bland and fluffy and easily digestible, and not greasy or recently slaughtered.

Rachel stood up and began to prowl around my room in search of diversion, opening and closing the wardrobe and poking about among Auntie Jackie's ornaments on the mantelpiece.

"What's she keeping all this stuff for?" she asked, twanging the one remaining string of the double bass. "I mean what's with the archery target? And this?" She picked up the papier-mâché pig, which was surprisingly light considering its vast girth, and stared into its painted eyes.

"He's called Gunter. She made him at art college."

"What are you going to do all day when I'm at out at work?" Rachel asked suddenly, as if I was the one who was bored and restless.

"Have you got a job then?"

"No, not yet. But I will have soon. And then what are you going to do?" Anyone would think she had done nothing but entertain me since we arrived.

"I'll be fine. I thought I might help Auntie Jackie in the shop."

"You could get a job of some sort. A paper round or something."

"I don't need a job," I reminded her with a smug smile. "Because I'm not in debt."

As I said this, I noticed something out of the corner of my eye; a small brown shape with a pink, thread-like tail suddenly shot out from under the double bass, crossed the carpet in a blur and vanished under the door. It was over before either of us could react with the proper squeals of horror: instead, we just blinked at each other in surprise.

"Was that what I think it was?" Rachel said after a pause.

I nodded, my heart hammering.

"Oh, *gross*. There's probably a nest under all that junk."

I approached the double bass tentatively. I wasn't scared of mice – in their place, which was in cages or clinging to ears of corn on the front of birthday cards –

but I didn't fancy confronting a whole nestful. On the other hand, I wasn't wildly enthusiastic about sharing my sleeping quarters with one - or more. I began to tweak at the pile of "junk", bracing myself for a stampede. As well as the double bass, that corner of the room was home to a rack of ancient LPs, relics of Auntie Jackie's past no doubt, stacked vertically like slices of toast, an Ali Baba basket full of shoes and a box of dressmaker's patterns in paper packets.

I picked one of these up: BUTTERICK 1949. I took this to be a reference to its year of origin. The cover showed a pen and ink drawing of a woman with bouffant hair and impossibly elongated legs wearing a tight-waisted tartan suit. She was standing with hands on hips, wrists bent back to an angle of ninety degrees and looked like no woman you would ever see. The edges of the packet had been well nibbled. On closer inspection I discovered that only the patterns closest to the top of the heap had been spared: those further down had been totally shredded.

I left Rachel sniggering over the evidence of our ancestors' fashion crimes and went upstairs to report my findings to Auntie Jackie, making sure that there were no clients around. Even I could see that an infestation of mice wouldn't be great for business. I found her in the back room performing repairs to some recently returned stock. She was wearing a pair of glasses and there was a row of needles, trailing different coloured cotton, pinned to her chest.

"Someone had a good time at the Young Conservatives' Ball," she said drily, holding up a pale pink taffeta dress. There was a bald patch on the bodice where a whole section of beads had torn loose, an unidentified stain down the front of the skirt and a muddy bicycle tyre track up the back.

"It's completely ruined," I said indignantly.

"Well, she's blown her damage deposit," sniffed Auntie Jackie. "And I won't be giving *them* a ten per cent discount again in a hurry." She folded the dress up and dumped it in a wicker laundry basket. "That's one for the specialist dry-cleaner's." She hauled the next dress on to the bench. "I'm glad to see you up and about. What can I do for you, my love?"

"I think there's a mouse in my bedroom," I said, and went on to break the news about her dressmaking patterns.

"Oh, I'm not bothered about those. I got them in a car boot sale about a year ago. I thought I might do something with them, but I never got round to it." She rummaged in a drawer filled with cotton reels of every colour until she found one the right shade of blue and began to rethread her sewing machine.

"Well, I just thought I'd mention it," I said, hoping for something more concrete in the way of mouse-catching strategies.

"Yes. Glad you did." Auntie Jackie beamed. "Never be afraid to mention things."

"I think you can get these humane traps," I suggested. "I don't really know how they work."

"No need for anything like that," Auntie Jackie replied breezily. "The rat in the kitchen will get it."

# Experience Preferred

The next day Rachel went job-hunting, taking me with her for moral support. She had imagined that a seaside resort in high season would offer dozens of opportunities of which she, naturally, would have the pick. She hadn't taken into account that Brighton, like Oxford, was a university town and therefore, just as at home, summer job-seekers would greatly outnumber summer jobs. As we came down the front steps, calling a goodbye to Auntie Jackie, I noticed a girl of about twelve or thirteen sitting on the wall of the house opposite. She had long, very distinctive copper-coloured hair and skin so pale that it had a bluish tinge, like skimmed milk. She was looking at us in a way that wasn't particularly friendly. As if we had disturbed her, she slid off the wall and walked away up the road at a brisk pace, without looking back

Our first port of call was the Lanes, an area of quaint old streets which contained most of Rachel's favourite clothes shops and where she felt confident of success. Invariably, however, we found ourselves queuing to speak to the manager behind someone else on exactly the same vain errand. "Sorry, no vacancies" was the story everywhere. It was quite depressing. Expensive too, as Rachel somehow felt uncomfortable approaching the till empty-handed.

"You don't *have* to buy something from every shop we go in, before you ask if they've got a job," I pointed out, as I handed over another tenner.

"It looks better," Rachel assured me.

Her visit to the jobcentre, once the more appealing lines of enquiry had been exhausted, had been a rude awakening. All those A*s at GCSE counted for nothing, it seemed, in the brutal world of employment. Experienced Book-keeper wanted. Experienced Chef wanted. Experienced Legal Secretary wanted. "How is anyone supposed to acquire this essential experience?" she grumbled.

By midday, Rachel had been turned down by at least

thirty shops on a meandering three-mile route and my feet were aching, so we stopped for lunch on the pier – one packet of chips between two, to save money. All that rejection didn't seem to have affected Rachel's appetite: I had to race to match her chip for chip. That's the problem with sharing food – the greediest always dictates the pace. The only glimmer of hope had come from a receptionist at a tattoo parlour who had taken Rachel's name and phone number and said she'd call back when she'd spoken to the boss, who was out the back doing some major piercing work.

"If only there was a way of living without money," Rachel sighed, tossing a piece of frizzled potato to a fat seagull which had been stalking up and down the railing opposite us in a hopeful manner all the time we'd been eating. "Birds do all right, don't they. Flying around, no responsibilities."

"What responsibilities have you got exactly?" I inquired.

"Looking after you for a start."

"When have you ever looked after me?"

"I brought you that copy of *Hello!* when you were sick."

"Oh and don't forget the mince," I retorted.

"It's not just about doing stuff," Rachel replied airily. "It's a *feeling* of responsibility that goes with being the older one. It's like I have to set a good example."

Let her think that if it makes her happy, I thought.

I finished the last of the chips and balled up the paper, passing it from hand to hand to clean my greasy fingers, before posting it in a bin.

"Come on," said the responsible role model. "Let's go and play on the slot machines. I'm feeling lucky."

"You've got it the wrong way round," I said, catching her up as she strode along the pier. "You don't need to get more money. You need to spend less. Just stop buying things."

"I know. I totally have stopped. I don't want any more stuff. The only thing is, I need the fare to Oxford."

"Why?" I said, horrified. "You can't go home already. We're not allowed to go home."

"I'm not going to the *house*," she said. "But it's Frankie's eighteenth next weekend. I can't miss it. It's going to be massive." Frankie was Rachel's best friend from school. Her parents lived in a huge house on the river at Iffley and were lavish party-throwers.

"They've probably hired Blenheim Palace," I said. "Or did they already do that for her seventeenth?"

Rachel laughed. "I'll get the train up on the Saturday morning and stay over at Frankie's after the party and come back first thing Sunday morning. Well, maybe not first thing," she conceded.

I felt inexplicably annoyed that she was going off without me. But it would have seemed a bit ungrateful for both of us to abandon Auntie Jackie so soon after our arrival. Besides, I felt safer in Brighton.

The prospect of a party had driven all thoughts of poverty and unemployment from Rachel's mind. "Shall we have our fortunes read?" she said, as we approached a booth advertising the services of a clairvoyant. SORRY. CLOSED FOR THE AFTERNOON read a handwritten note Blu-tacked to the door. Underneath, some joker had scrawled: *due to unforeseen circumstances.*

We were still sniggering over this when a blonde woman in big sunglasses touched Rachel on the arm and said, "Excuse me." She was dressed in a red halter-neck top displaying a leathery suntan, and white trousers which trailed in the dust on the decking. I guessed her to be a bit older than Auntie Jackie, though it was hard to tell as the glasses covered so much of her face.

"I'm sorry to interrupt," she said, picking through her wallet with hilariously fake scarlet talons, before finally producing a business card which she pressed into Rachel's hand. "I'm a scout for a modelling agency in

London," she said. "Have you done any modelling at all?"

Rachel shook her head, blushing faintly.

"Well, people have probably told you this before, but you're very striking. You've got an interesting face. Very… modern." She moved around, looking at Rachel from different angles, while I tried to melt into the background. Rachel gave an embarrassed laugh: she wasn't used to taking compliments from women. "I'm sorry," the woman went on, smiling to show two rows of fridge-white teeth. "I hope you don't think I'm being personal, but when I see a young girl like yourself with a certain look about her, I have to say something. A lot of our most successful girls are people I've just spotted on the street, who'd never given modelling a thought."

"I'm not tall enough to be a model," said Rachel doubtfully. "Or thin enough. It's all size zero and laxatives for breakfast, isn't it?"

"Kate Moss is only five foot eight," the woman replied. "But anyway, there's other sorts of modelling than just the catwalk. You think about it. That's all I'm saying." She indicated the card which Rachel was now holding. "That's the name of someone in Brighton who can do your photos. If you go along to his studio and tell him Mags sent you, he'll do it for nothing." She gave us a last flash of that double-decker porcelain smile before moving on, her trouser hems catching under her heels with each step.

"Ridiculous," Rachel snorted when she was out of earshot. "What a load of old rubbish." All the same, I noticed she pocketed the card.

"Do you think she was genuine?" I said, failing to disguise my bitterness at having been so blatantly overlooked.

"Nah. Probably just escaped from a loony bin," said Rachel, modest in her triumph. "I mean she didn't exactly dress like someone who works at the cutting edge of fashion. Those trousers must have come straight from Primark."

I knew she was saying this to make me feel better, so I laughed, and decided not to point out that the jeans I was wearing came from Primark *Sale*. I didn't share Rachel's addiction to designer labels. If Dad gave me £50 to spend on clothes, I'd spend ten and keep the rest for emergencies. I'd built up quite a sizeable fund over the years; after all, emergencies were Dad's department really.

For some reason – perhaps Rachel's sisterly refusal to gloat – this incident on the pier seemed to bring us closer together, and we walked slowly back to Cliff Street listening to Rachel's iPod, sharing one set of earbuds and a bag of candyfloss. But all the way back, in spite of the music and the sunshine, I had an uneasy feeling – as if there was a worry that I couldn't quite name hovering just out of reach. It was only when we reached Auntie Jackie's, just as one of her clients was coming down the steps carrying a gold ball dress cocooned in polythene, that I remembered what it was: Frankie's party. My heart gave a kick of protest at the thought. In spite of her promises to Dad and the police, Rachel was determined to go back to Oxford, even though there was somebody there – perhaps a whole group of somebodies – who knew our names and where we lived, and hated us enough to try and kill us.

# Oxford

There's a place in Oxford called Jericho which sounds solemn and biblical, but is actually full of cafés and arty-crafty shops and student hovels. Turn down any of the side streets towards the canal and you'll find bicycles leaning drunkenly against every lamp-post and railing, curtains closed until mid-afternoon, wheelie bins overflowing with empty bottles and the pavements strewn with the fall-out from kebabs. If you walk north along the towpath and turn right, you eventually come to a close, a development of six modern houses, all out of tune with the surrounding architecture, but pretty in their own way. One of these – the one that is now dark and abandoned, and under surveillance from a camera hidden in the bedroom of the house opposite – is ours.

Unlike Jericho, our turning is quiet, day and night. The other residents are made up of retired couples, young professionals and an elderly widow. The only noise you are likely to hear at weekends is the whirr of garden-grooming equipment – hedge trimmers, lawn mowers, leaf hoovers – and the occasional *crump* of car doors as people come and go.

Until this summer I never minded being in the house by myself, which was lucky, as Dad and Rachel were not very good at co-ordinating their timetables, and from the age of about twelve it wasn't an uncommon occurrence to find myself home alone.

That all changed one Thursday night in June. Dad was out at a retirement do for one of his colleagues at the Institute, and Rachel was celebrating the end of Frankie's A Levels. (Rachel's friends all seemed to finish their exams on different days and require separate festivities. This was the third in a week.)

I had lined up a programme of activities for myself to fill the empty hours until bedtime. 7–7.30: homework. 7.30–8.00: clarinet. 8–8.30: dinner in front of the TV (jacket potato with bacon, sour cream and chives.) This was one of my favourite meals, outlawed by Dad on two counts: cholesterol and fuel consumption. I had to wait until he was safely out before committing the eco-crime of running the oven on full for an hour and a half to cook a lone potato. 8.30–10.00: MSN. 10.00: DVD of *Pride and Prejudice* which, as it was a set text, also counted as homework.

When the potato was nearly done, I spread a couple of rashers of bacon under the grill and left them spitting fat while I went outside to pick some chives. As well as a small vegetable plot at the bottom of the garden, in which Dad was growing runner beans, hops, tomatoes, spinach, radishes and redcurrants, we had a few tubs on the patio containing useful herbs. Basil for pesto, chives for salad and parsley for disguising garlic breath before an important kiss (Rachel's idea).

It was a warm evening, and the pot plants were looking rather limp and thirsty, so I filled a can from the water butt and gave them a good drenching. I ignored the parched veggie patch as this was an altogether lengthier job now we had a hose ban, and it was Not My Turn. I was wondering whether I could be bothered to brave the mutant monster spiders in the shed and bring out the patio furniture when a shrill bleeping reminded me that I'd left the grill on. I raced back into the kitchen, beating my way through billows of greasy smoke, to switch off the cooker before attempting to disable the alarm, which was still emitting an unbearable noise. There seemed to be no off-switch, so I finally resorted to prising off the lid and removing the battery, which was no easy task with my fingers in my ears.

On inspection, it turned out that the culprit was not the bacon – which was surprisingly still edible, if somewhat brittle – but the centimetre of molten fat in the unwashed grill pan.

I retreated to the living room with my plate of food and shut the door, leaving the fan whirring wheezily in the fog-bound kitchen. With no one else at home, I was Queen of the TV Remote, so I made the most of my reign, watching five channels in strict rotation. By switching over every minute and skipping past adverts, it was possible to get a fairly good grasp of five different programmes at once. I wondered if this time-saving method could be applied to other areas of my life, schoolwork for example. If I read every fifth page of *Macbeth*, *Pride and Prejudice*, my GCSE Science Study Guide, Luke's Gospel and *Lernpunkt Deutsch*, would my brain automatically fill in the gaps the way it just had, so effortlessly, with prime-time TV? I made a mental note to try it some time.

Later, when the smoke had dispersed, I returned to the kitchen to tackle the washing up. As usual, someone, probably Rachel, had been taking liberties with the duty roster: as well as the devastated grill pan, there was a pile of crockery on the side left over from breakfast – coffee mugs and cereal bowls pebbledashed with dried muesli – and last night's crusty lasagne dish soaking in the sink. I set to work, turning the radio up high, and plunging my hands into the cold, oily water to dig out the flabby pasta that was blocking the plughole.

"I predict a riot!" I sang defiantly at my reflection in the darkened window above the sink, as hot water thundered into the bowl, spraying me and the surrounding worktops with foam. Something moved just the other side of the window, a black shape in the blackness of the garden, looking in. For a fraction of a second we were face to face, but it was like no face I had ever seen. Then I let out a sound that was somewhere between a gasp and a scream, and the figure took a step back and ducked out of sight. The soapy bowl slipped from my hands and I turned and ran, across the hallway, up the stairs and into the bathroom – the only room with a lock – a strange, animal instinct making me burrow deeper rather than escape. I slid the bolt home and sat on the edge of the bath, my heart clubbing wildly as I listened for any sounds of breaking glass or forced entry.

Then my heart almost stopped altogether as I remembered the kitchen door: I hadn't bothered to lock it when I came in from the garden; in fact, I couldn't now be sure I had even *shut* it. Surely I had left it open to let the smoke out? I felt dizzy with fear. Perhaps the prowler was even now moving through the house, creeping from room to room to find me? I cowered in the corner of the room, wedged between the washbasin and the wall, hardly daring to breathe, straining to pick out approaching footsteps over the crashing of blood in my ears.

Why had I trapped myself up here with no protection but a feeble brass bolt, instead of running next door for help, or calling the police? I thought of my mobile phone, lying uselessly on the coffee table downstairs, and almost cried with frustration. The window above the basin, a small frosted porthole not much bigger than a dinner plate, faced on to the blank brick side of our elderly neighbour's house. She was deaf and unlikely to hear a call for help, and still less likely to be able to act on it.

I waited, tense with anxiety for what seemed like hours – perhaps it was, I didn't have a watch – but around me the house was silent. By degrees, the sense of immediate and urgent panic began to wear off and I was able to emerge from my corner and make myself more comfortable on a pile of folded towels. But I was still too scared to open the door. He might have been Out There, just the other side, waiting and watching through the strange distorted eyeholes of his balaclava. That was what disturbed me more than anything – his masked face, and the thought that he must have seen my every movement in the brightly lit kitchen, while I had no idea I was being watched.

At the age of fifteen I had discovered something new about myself: I was a coward. Until this moment I had never experienced anything remotely threatening. I had never been abused at home or mugged on the bus, hassled in the street or bullied at school. My life so far had been absolutely peril-free and yet, for some reason, I had just naturally assumed that I was brave. The discovery that I was in fact spineless was a bitter disappointment.

Eventually I must have dozed off where I sat because I was woken by the familiar sounds of Dad coming home – the car engine and the scrape of his key in the lock, and then the various exclamations of annoyance: "What's that smell?" "Look at the state of this place!" and "Every bloody light on as usual!" and I knew I was safe.

At first he was bewildered to find me holed up in the bathroom at past midnight, still in my apron and Marigold gloves, but when I told him about the prowler, he soon stopped smiling.

"Oh, Robyn," he said, gathering me into a fierce hug. "You poor thing. Were you really frightened?"

I nodded, sniffing, from within the hug. He smelled of the office – synthetic carpet and computers and the ozone pumped out by the photocopiers. He hadn't bothered to change after work then.

"I'm so sorry I wasn't here," he said, releasing me at last. "Where's Rachel?"

"I don't know. Out with Frankie somewhere."

"Phone her and tell her to get the cab to bring her right to the door. Don't let it drop her off at the end of the close." Dad had taken his shoes off when he came in; now he started to put them back on again.

"Where are you going?" I asked.

"To check the garden." He fetched the big torch, heavy as an iron bar, from the cupboard under the stairs and strode out through the kitchen, where everything was just as I'd left it: the washing up half done, the cereal bowl in pieces on the floor. A moment later I could see the torch beam – solid and substantial in the darkness –

sweeping along the fence and probing into the bushes. Still keeping one eye on Dad, I called Rachel and delivered his message as best I could over the background racket of music and shouted conversation. "Where are you?" I asked, out of habit.

There was a pause and then, "Where are we?" I could hear her asking someone. Back came the reported answer: "Wadham College bar." Sometimes I wondered about her state of mind.

"No one there now," Dad said, coming in and locking the back door behind him.

"It was hours ago."

"All the same. Got to call the police. These nutters. God, they don't waste any time, I'll say that for them." He disappeared into the study and returned holding the local directory, flipping through the pages with one hand while trying to put his glasses on with the other.

"What nutters?" I said uneasily.

"Oh, you know, Animal Rights," said Dad.

"Why do you think it's got anything to do with them? It could just be some random weirdo."

Dad shrugged. "Maybe. Funny coincidence if so."

"What..." He was thumbing in the number as he spoke and held up a hand to shush me as the phone was picked up at the other end. I wandered into the living room to look out for Rachel, chewing over what Dad had just said about Animal Rights. Of course, I knew that he worked at the Institute, a new high-tech complex just inside the ring road, dedicated to research and development of drugs for everything from baldness to beriberi. And I suppose I must have known that a lot of the experiments and trials involved animals – laboratory rats, specially bred for the purpose. But Dad worked in the office – he wasn't a *vivisectionist*; he was an accountant. He'd probably never even set foot in a lab. Plus, he was if anything an animal *lover*: witness his treatment only last year of the runaway springer spaniel that got clipped by a car on Banbury Road and left for dead. He took it to the vet to get it patched up and paid the bill himself. Then he took out an ad in the local paper and stuck dozens of leaflets on trees to trace the owner. A proper good Samaritan, she had called him, weeping tears of gratitude and relief over the heartbreaking doggy plastercast.

While this anxious internal monologue was going on I could hear Dad impatiently spelling out his details. "Richard Stenning. S-T-E-N-N-I-N-G … OX2 6FZ… No, F. F for Flatulence. Z for Zoroastrian." He always got ratty with telephonists, receptionists, all those poor women in the front line, just trying to do their jobs. "Do you really need my date of birth?" he spluttered. "If I was ringing to report a murder-in-progress, I'd be dead by now."

He joined me at the living-room window, peering out into the darkness. Always resentful at wearing his suit outside work, he'd undone his top button and pulled his tie down to half mast like a scruffy schoolboy. "Sorry you were frightened," he said again, putting an arm round my shoulders and giving me a squeeze. "They're going to send someone round. I didn't think they would."

"What did you mean about Animal Rights nutters?" I asked.

"Oh, there are loads of anti-vivisection groups in Oxford. They picket the Institute now and then, when they can get themselves up and out of bed. Peaceful demonstrations are fair enough. But there's a hard core who are into direct action. Terrorists basically. They've even got kids as young as twelve involved in sabotage and stuff. You must have read all that in the papers last year about the place that breeds the rats for us. The guy who runs it has had so much intimidation, death threats, a bomb under his car, family graves desecrated, it's all but closed down. He can't afford the security."

"But you don't get involved in any of those animal experiments. You're not a scientist."

"I know, but the Institute pays my wages. Everyone who has anything to do with the place is a target. The cleaners, the caterers, everybody. Even the binmen. We got a memo about it only last week: the company that gets rid of our toxic waste has had its premises torched."

"What do they want?"

"Ultimately they want the place closed down, and the easiest way to do that is to intimidate people into not working there."

"How do they know where you live?"

"You can find anything off the internet."

"But it could just have been a prowler. I mean, they do exist."

"Maybe," Dad said, without much conviction. "Would that make you feel better?"

"I don't know." In truth it wasn't his motivation so much as his intentions that worried me. "Do you wish you still worked at the John Radcliffe?"

"No fear." Dad had only been at the Institute six months. He'd been so glad to get out of the National Health Service into somewhere free from political interference. He loved the job.

Within fifteen minutes a patrol car arrived, lit up like a slot machine, and in spite of the late hour, curtains began to twitch up and down the close, pale faces appearing in the darkened windows. People love a show. Two uniformed police officers, one of them a WPC, did another sweep of the garden with a flashlight, and then made a note of my rather unhelpful description of the prowler. Medium height: this much we'd established from the fact that his eyes were on a level with mine, but the kitchen was slightly elevated above patio level, though this conclusion didn't strike me as foolproof. He could have been a giant kneeling down, or a dwarf standing on a plant pot. Disguised as he was, I couldn't tell them whether he was black or white and in all honesty, I had no evidence – apart from a conviction that women don't do that sort of thing – that he was even a he.

Their departure was interrupted by the arrival of Rachel, needing change for the cab. She looked slightly squiffy, but sobered up at the sight of the police.

"What time do you call this? Haven't you got an exam tomorrow?" Dad said, handing over a tenner. Education, education, education, even in extremity.

"Not till the afternoon," she replied, not bothering to stifle a yawn. She went back out to pay the driver, but at the sight of the police car he had executed a smart three-point turn and driven off. Another man with something to hide evidently.

"He's probably got no tax disc and no insurance," Dad muttered, shaking his head over this fresh example of the general lawlessness of society.

Once they'd taken my statement and looked the place over, there wasn't much more the police could do, so they departed, advising us to be vigilant and report anything suspicious. Dad did another check of all the locks on the downstairs windows, and set the burglar alarm for the first time in living memory before we all went up to bed. Rachel and I sat up talking in her room till after one. She seemed a bit put out to have missed the evening's drama, which was all it was to her, safely out of it. Even my own experience seemed slightly unreal, now that the threat had passed. I wondered if my sense of terror, so authentic at the time, hadn't been exaggerated, unnecessary.

Rachel was quick to pour cold water on Dad's theory. "Oh, he would say that. He's got a total bee in his bonnet about Animal Rights protesters since he's been in this new job. Before that it was Pro-Lifers. Next week it'll be, I don't know, Buddhists. It was probably just some regular perv trying to see if he can get a glimpse of a woman undressing."

"Well, I don't know," I said, not wanting to be disloyal to Dad, and not especially comforted by the idea of having been spied on by a "regular" perv, whatever that was.

"It'll be all right anyway," said Rachel, her eyes shiny with drunken confidence. "You probably scared him off with your singing. He won't be back."

I was quite comfortable there on Rachel's beanbag and didn't particularly want to go off to my own room, but I was too proud to ask, and besides, she had an exam the next day and needed to sleep, so I said goodnight and left her. But I couldn't seem to settle in bed: I felt too hyper-alert, and all the usual sighs and creaks and taps from the sleeping house sounded strangely loud and menacing.

# Ten

# The Handyman

As I soon discovered, there was more to Auntie Jackie's business than mending seams and removing tyre tracks from taffeta. It wasn't like a normal shop, where customers could stroll in off the street and browse. From the outside, 29 Cliff Street looked like any other house in the terrace, except perhaps slightly shabbier. There was no signage, apart from a business card pinned above the (non-working) doorbell, and no shop window to tempt passers-by. In fact, the front room blinds were kept closed at all times to prevent the hard southern sunlight bleaching the outermost edges of the dresses as they hung on their rails. If you didn't already know what was inside, you would never guess.

Ballgown hire, Auntie Jackie explained when I remarked on this, was not something done on impulse. One did not go out to buy a loaf of bread and suddenly think, *Oh, to hell with it, I'll get a strapless Valentino gown with a three-metre train for the weekend instead.* People generally had plenty of advance warning, by way of printed invitations, that they were going to be requiring formal evening wear, in which case their first resort would be the *Yellow Pages.* Viewings and fittings were by appointment only, one client at a time, except in the case of a mother and daughter, or pair of friends attending the same event, who wanted to ensure there was no duplication.

This system meant that Auntie Jackie didn't need to man the shop all day, every day, but could fit her off-site business into those blocks of time when no clients were due. Odd hours in between bookings were spent doing repairs, alterations and paperwork, but a "free" day might involve a visit to an auction or trade fair to buy fresh stock. She was always on the lookout for new additions to her collection, and was not above scouring the small ads in *Exchange & Mart* or picking a dress up from a charity shop if it was in perfect condition, though she was careful to trawl much further afield than Brighton for bargains. It would be worse than embarrassing to be caught trying to flog a customer her own cast-offs.

Auntie Jackie soon had me trained up in the business of taking phone messages while she was out, and booking appointments in her diary. This item, an A4-sized leather volume, was now broken-spined with dislocated boards front and back. Held together with elastic bands, it was crammed with loose scraps of paper – apparently containing information vital to the smooth running of her business – which would all come slithering out on to the floor every time it was opened. It was her Bible, she told me, and the one possession she would re-enter a burning building to retrieve. "Everything else is insured," she said, with a surprising lack of sentiment.

Other duties that could be safely delegated to me were making tea for clients and taking in the dry-cleaning when the laundry van made its weekly delivery. In the areas requiring practical skill I was no help whatsoever. Auntie Jackie herself was an accomplished seamstress and was appalled at my ignorance of this basic household art.

"Didn't you do needlework at school?" she demanded on one occasion when she came across me trying to mend the fallen hem of my skirt with double-sided Sellotape.

"No. We did textiles. There wasn't much actual sewing."

"Well, what did you do in textiles?"

"We made a slipper out of felt."

"Just the one?"

"Yes." This omission had bothered me at the time and I had always intended to make its partner, but by the time I'd finished the first one, my feet had gone up a size and it hardly seemed worth it. The lone slipper had ended up as a cosy bed for my mobile phone so it wasn't totally wasted.

"Good grief. So you don't know how to read a dress pattern?"

"No." As of last week, I could only think of dress patterns as potential bedding material for mice.

"Or put in a zip? Or set in sleeves?"

I shook my head sorrowfully. It really is no fun when grown-ups do this sort of thing.

"God. And I went to a rotten school too. I wasn't one of the bright girls like you. But at least they did teach me to sew. I made all the curtains in this house myself," she said complacently. "Fully lined."

"But do you know how to set up a website?" I asked. That shut her up. "Or do spreadsheets? Or set up a database using Access?" I was bluffing a bit here, as I'd actually missed most of the Access module because of my clarinet lessons, and never bothered to catch up with the work.

"Point taken," she said. And then I could almost hear her businesswoman's brain whirring into action. "Tell you what. If you're an IT whiz, Robyn, maybe you could teach me how to use Access, and get all my accounts and stuff on to the computer."

"Er... well... I wouldn't call myself a *whiz*," I said, outmanoeuvred.

"And in return I could teach you to use a sewing machine." She burst out laughing at my expression, which must have been one of deepest horror, and I started to laugh too. Somehow Auntie Jackie's nagging, unlike Dad's, had no power to annoy. Maybe it was because it was all for show: she was too easy-going to lose any sleep over my failings and, in any case, lacked a parent's proper anxiety. The conversation ended with her promising to take me along on her next day trip to acquire new stock. These jaunts around the south east – which apparently involved regular stops for refreshment at pubs and coffee shops – had been impossible lately as the car was still at the panel beaters, following her collision outside Asda, but as soon as it was repaired she was keen to get back out on the road.

Rachel would have to miss out as for the last week she

had been gainfully employed by the tattoo and piercings parlour. The receptionist who had taken her number during that dispiriting day of job-hunting had been the only person to ring back with an offer of work. Rachel's gratitude was short-lived when she realised it entailed walking around the precincts all day foisting ten per cent off vouchers on to reluctant shoppers. Commission only, so she couldn't even cheat and dump a pile in the bin, but had to make a conscious effort to approach, smiling, those people most likely to indulge in self-mutilation. "It's only one step up from begging," she moaned at the end of her first day. "I might as well be selling *The Big Issue*."

"You didn't think you'd be doing the actual tattoos, did you?" Auntie Jackie asked.

"Well, no. But I thought I'd be indoors at least." Since Rachel's notions of the world of work were, like mine, taken mostly from *Ugly Betty*, reality was bound to be a little disappointing. I was surprised she'd stuck it for five whole days, but then Frankie's unmissable party was looming and she needed money for her fare to Oxford. To cheer her up I offered to come and meet her for lunch – my treat – but she grew evasive and finally admitted that she was in the habit of having lunch with Adam during his break from work at the leisure centre. "But you can come too if you want," she said, without much enthusiasm.

"No, it's all right," I said, deflated. "I just thought if you were on your own and bored."

"Meet me for coffee in the morning instead," she suggested, now that I was the one who needed cheering up. "I usually have a cappuccino and a muffin about half ten."

"I thought you didn't like Adam much anyway."

"I don't like him *much*. He's OK to talk to as long as he doesn't get started on computers. Plus, who else is there at the moment?"

Despite their unfortunate start, I knew Adam was keen on her because he often dropped in to Auntie Jackie's on some minor errand for his granny, and ended up staying all evening, sitting at the kitchen table watching TV with the rest of us, or dropping hints about a return tennis match, which Rachel would deliberately fail to pick up. The thing is, I actually quite like tennis and I much prefer playing against someone better, even if it means losing, but he never asked me.

Adam wasn't the only dropper-in at number 29. One morning, when Rachel was at work, I shuffled sleepily into the kitchen in my Mad Cow pyjamas to get a glass of water and nearly tripped over the protruding legs of a man who appeared to be trying to crawl into the cupboard under the sink. Before I could react, he had backed out, and I realised that it was the policeman who had brought Auntie Jackie home on the day we had first arrived. He was holding a shovel on the end of which was a very stiff rat.

"Here we are," he said, slightly red-faced from his exertions in the cupboard, and then started when he saw me. "Oh. Hello."

"Hello," I said, thinking, *Wow! Is there nothing the police round here won't do?*

Auntie Jackie appeared at the back door, carrying a garden refuse sack. "Oh, well done, you've got him," she said, averting her face as she held the bag open to receive the dead rat – its mouth frozen open in a pinched snarl to reveal tiny curved teeth, its front claws held up as if in shock.

"You've got a gap around the waste pipe," the policeman said, as the corpse was unceremoniously bagged and dumped in the wheelie bin outside the back door. "That's where he got in. I'll come back and fill that in for you some time."

"Oh, would you?" said Auntie Jackie rapturously. "You are wonderful."

She turned to me, blushing faintly. "This is Dave, by the way. He's my special friend and handyman and general saviour."

"Ah," I said. That explained a lot. I can be very dim sometimes.

"This is my niece, Robyn," she said to Dave. And then, in an unforgivable attempt to pass the burden of embarrassment on to someone else, added, "Isn't she gorgeous?"

Dave cleared his throat. "Well, gorgeousness is obviously in the genes," he replied carefully. Considering that I was standing there fresh out of bed, unwashed and unbrushed, furry of tongue and greasy of face, I thought he'd fielded this pretty well.

As I retreated to my room, I overheard Auntie Jackie saying, "And I'm not even going to introduce you to her older sister, Heidi on Heat," and Dave replying, "Spoilsport." I shut my door on the sounds of a passionate farewell.

When Rachel got home that evening, I told her about the incident with the rat, and Dave-the-policeman being Auntie Jackie's boyfriend (omitting the reference to Heidi on Heat which I didn't really understand, but sensed was not a compliment) and she looked at me as if I was a bit simple.

"Yeah, well I'd clocked that on day one," she said. "What planet are you on?"

I began to wonder whether I was in fact as bright as I'd always supposed, and what other obvious things I was failing to notice.

# Eleven

# Total Peace of Mind

One of the immediate effects of the prowler incident was that Dad made sure he was around in the evenings so that Rachel and I never had to be alone in the house after dark. He was also suddenly more available to chauffeur us to and from our various social engagements, and less fanatical about switching lights off.

He didn't admit that he was in a state of raised alert, but we both knew what was behind his new attentiveness. I certainly didn't complain because I no longer enjoyed having the house to myself. It was all right in daylight: when the sun was shining, our cul-de-sac seemed the safest place on earth, but as soon as darkness fell, I began to feel the old anxiety and to see shapes in every shadow.

When I'd related my True Life Drama at school of course, half the class felt obliged to come out with bigger, better stories of their own. This always happens. You go in with a good story to tell, and immediately a dozen prima donnas are lining up to elbow you out of the limelight. Jade Coyle said her stepmother had been mugged at the cashpoint in George Street and had the rings *ripped off her fingers*, and pretty soon everyone was chipping in. You'd think we were living in a ghetto, not North Oxford. Anyway, I came away with the impression that if I'd got this far without being happy-slapped, gang-raped or hung, drawn and quartered, I'd got nothing to complain about.

A week later I came home to find a white van outside the house and a workman on a ladder fixing a bracket to the front of the house, just below the eaves. My spirits soared. Satellite TV as last! Our years of whingeing had finally melted Dad's stubborn, telephobic heart, and MTV, the Movie Channel and round-the-clock reruns of *Friends*, *Lost* and *Sex and the City* would soon be ours.

Then, as I got closer, I noticed that it wasn't a Sky van after all, but something called JDH Home Security. *For Total Peace of Mind* read the ten-centimetre-high lettering. We already had a burglar alarm, which until this week we had never bothered to set in case it went off and disturbed the neighbours, so I wondered what new precaution was in the offing.

Indoors, Dad was in the study, helplessly watching as another JDH operative tinkered with the computer. There were plugs and lengths of cable all over the desk. I've learnt from experience to keep a low profile when there's any kind of computer trouble. It's one of those things which sends Dad into orbit, so I withdrew to the kitchen where Rachel was cutting herself a large piece of Wensleydale-with-apricots.

"Do you think this counts as one portion of fruit-or-veg?" she asked.

"No. What's going on out there? I thought for a moment we were getting Sky."

"Some hope," she replied through a mouthful of cheese. "No, it's CCTV cameras."

"Oh. Cool."

"Not cool. I don't want my comings and goings under twenty-four-hour surveillance, thank you very much."

"I think it's a good idea," I said. "Maybe we could work on Dad to get a guard dog next." I'd always fancied having something really big and fluffy like a collie or an Old English sheepdog.

"I wouldn't mind a Yorkshire terrier," Rachel admitted. "You can get them these really cute little coats." I don't think she was taking the issue of security very seriously.

Anyway, when the workmen had gone, Dad called us into the study and showed us the set-up. On the computer monitor was an image of the driveway, the car and most of the front garden, in the foggy grey and white particular to CCTV footage. With a click of the mouse, the picture changed: the patio, the back lawn, the bushes, the fence, all in the same monochrome. We stared at these murky realms, transfixed, as if waiting for criminals to materialise.

"Is it going to be on all the time?" Rachel asked. "How am I supposed to use the computer?"

"It's recording all the time, but you don't have to have the picture up. Just use the computer as normal," Dad replied. To demonstrate, he hit a key and the screen reverted to our home page. "We don't need to sit here monitoring the premises twenty-four hours a day," he added. (The funny thing was, from now until the time we had to clear out, every time I came into the study I found him at the computer doing just that.)

To reassure himself that all approaches to the house were covered, he sent Rachel outside to see if she could storm the building unobserved. Of course, she had to ham it up, skulking in the bushes with her collar up, mincing along on tiptoe, and then grinning and waving at the camera when she knew she'd been seen. But her efforts proved that, short of parachuting down the chimney, there was no way up to the house, front or back, that didn't pass beneath the unblinking eye of the cameras and, for a while at least, we felt safer.

........................................Twelve

# Brass

The weekend of Frankie's party arrived and Rachel set off on Saturday morning, frothing with excitement at the prospect of twenty-four hours of undiluted pleasure. Somehow or other she had earned enough to pay for her fare and buy Frankie a silver bangle and a bottle of perfume. At the dismal level of commission she was being paid, I reckoned this worked out at about two tattoos for every man, woman and dog in Brighton, but never mind. She had been in a strange mood for a couple of days: when I asked if I could meet her for lunch on the Friday, she put me off with the lamest of excuses, which made me immediately suspicious that she was up to something. I knew it couldn't be Adam she was

95

meeting as he was up a ladder next door at the time, painting the front of the house a blinding shade of white that made our side look even dirtier.

Auntie Jackie had lent Rachel a gold cocktail dress for the party – a proper Charleston number, with layers of fringes from top to bottom which flew out to ninety degrees when she spun round, like one of the roller-brushes in a car wash. Rachel gave us a demonstration in the kitchen on the Friday night and Dave, who had come to block up the rat-hole as promised, said she could wash his convertible any time. Aunty Jackie slapped him with a wooden spoon and left a big floury print on the back of his jeans.

She was making macaroni cheese for tea, though this had to be taken on trust as it was like no macaroni cheese I'd ever experienced. The sauce was similar in consistency to the sludge Dave was trowelling into the rat-hole – it was stiff and lumpy and had to be smeared flat on top of the pasta with the back of a spoon. When the dish came out of the oven, Auntie Jackie served it up in slices as if it was a pie. I'd had a couple of claggy mouthfuls and was marvelling to myself at its strange lack of flavour, when Auntie Jackie suddenly said, "Oh bum! I forgot to put in the cheese." She corrected this minor omission by whacking the block of cheddar into four and giving us a slab each as a side order. In my top ten worst-ever meals, it ranked right up there with Adam's granny's fish-flavoured ham.

After Rachel's departure on the Saturday morning, I slobbed about the house, feeling abandoned. I sent a text to two of my Oxford friends, Suzie and Jo, remembering just too late that Jo was in Florida. Back came the reply: **It is 3 am here! Duh!** Suzie didn't even answer.

Auntie Jackie was crashing around upstairs doing housework – I could hear her slamming the hoover into the skirting boards, and then dragging it *bump, bump, bump* down the stairs like Winnie the Pooh. No wonder the paintwork was all chipped. After a while it went quiet and I emerged, guiltily, to see if I could help. She was walking along the hallway twirling a long feather duster along the picture rails, gathering up cobwebs as though making candyfloss. Her face was red and shiny from her labours and she was wearing a pair of baggy grey tracksuit bottoms and a T-shirt with white sweat rings under the arms. Normally she would be smartly dressed, in full make-up and big jewellery by the time I surfaced, and was almost unrecognisable in her natural state. I began to see that a lot of what is called beauty is just plain *cheating*.

I offered to finish up the hoovering, and she escaped gratefully to have a shower in Rachel's en suite while it was free. She reappeared half an hour later, dressed and painted, looking her old (younger) self, and tutting over the state of Rachel's bedroom. "She's not exactly tidy, your sister," she muttered, pulling a face over several festering coffee mugs, and the wizened remains of an elderly peach, which she had rescued from the chaos. I thought this was a bit unfair from someone who until very recently had had her own resident rat.

"Clothes all over the floor, bin overflowing, wet towels on the bed, tissues, knickers, half-eaten chocolate bars…" For a second, she sounded exactly like Dad. It had always been a source of despair and wonder to him that Rachel could emerge every day from the compost heap of her room looking so fresh and pretty. "Plus, she's gone off leaving her hair-straighteners switched on. There's a dirty great scorch mark on the dressing table. It's a miracle we haven't been burnt alive in our beds. Anyway, my lovely, what are you going to do with yourself today? Would you like me to ask Adam to take you to the cinema or something? I bet he'd be glad to get down off that ladder for a while."

I shook my head in horror at this suggestion. What

sort of tragic figure needed her Auntie to drum up dates for her?

She laughed at my outraged expression. "OK, maybe not. I always thought he was rather sweet myself. Don't you like him?"

I smiled non-committally. I wasn't going to walk into her trap. "It's Rachel he's after anyway," I couldn't help saying.

"Well, I suppose she's closer to his age," Auntie Jackie conceded. "And men are such shallow creatures." She left this last remark hanging, unexplained.

"You don't have to stay in and entertain me," I said, in case she was looking for a get-out. "If you want to go out with Dave…"

"Oh, I'm not going anywhere. Dave's not really available at weekends," she said wistfully.

"I suppose policemen have to work all sorts of funny hours," I replied. I knew this from experience.

"Luckily for me or I'd never see him," Auntie Jackie replied. She seemed not to want to pursue this conversation, but said brightly, "There's a new Italian restaurant called Violetta's near the marina. They put a flier through the door with a two-for-one offer. I wonder what I did with it. We could go there if you like. Or I could cook something. Whatever you prefer."

"Let's go out," I said quickly.

I overdid it at Violetta's. I'm not sure whether my greed was a result of the two-for-one offer, or a determination to make the most of decent cooking while I had the chance, but I stuffed myself with fettuccine alla gorgonzola and tiramisu and went to bed racked with stomach ache.

Some time in the early hours I was woken from cheesy dreams by a loud scraping noise. It was accompanied by a rush of cool night air and, as I opened my eyes, I saw in the bluish light of a full moon the figure of a man, all in black, climbing in through my bedroom window.

What happened next took only a matter of seconds – much longer to describe than to experience. I tried to sit up and scream, but I was still in that half-paralysed state on the edge of sleep, and couldn't move a muscle. Instead of a scream, all that emerged was a whimper of fear – the sort of sound a dog makes when it's having a nightmare. It was loud enough to startle the intruder, who twitched violently, lost his balance and toppled into the room, putting his foot through the papier-mâché pig with a sickening crunch. He was clutching a solid black case, which landed on top of him as he fell, immobilising him for a moment and prompting a groan of pain.

I was fully awake now, and sitting up, but for reasons to do with his bag – which was unmistakably a trumpet case – no longer totally afraid. Or rather my brain was no longer afraid because it had already worked out who he was, but my heart hadn't quite caught up and was still pounding mercilessly.

"Sorry, sorry," said the man from the floor. "I'm not a burglar. I live here."

I switched on my reading lamp and we squinted at each other. He looked so funny on his back, with Gunter impaled on one boot, that I couldn't help laughing.

"I know," I said. "You're Charlie."

He seemed surprised, but relieved to have been correctly identified. "Sorry if I frightened you," he said. "I didn't know there'd be anyone sleeping here. I couldn't find my key and I didn't want to get Jackie out of bed." He eased himself into a sitting position and extricated his foot from the crushed papier-mâché shell. "Whoops," he said, giving it a guilty look. "I seem to have demolished Gunter." Then he looked at me in a funny way and said, "What were you going to do with that – bash me on the head?"

I followed the direction of his gaze and realised I had

at some point picked up the Swiss cowbell from beside my bed, and was clutching it like a weapon. "I don't know," I said, and suddenly the absurdity of the whole situation, and the shock and relief, all hit me at once and I started to giggle helplessly. Once I'd started, I couldn't seem to stop – it was the sort of borderline hysteria that could easily turn weepy, and it took all my self-control to keep things jolly.

Charlie began to laugh too, showing very even, American-style teeth. He clambered stiffly to his feet, and I could see that he was quite small for a man, and chunky, though that may have been the effect of his motorbike leathers. I remembered now that Auntie Jackie had said he had a bike: he had unplugged the freezer to recharge the battery.

"Who are you anyway?" he asked, pulling off his padded gloves and snapping open the clasps on his trumpet case to check that the instrument hadn't been damaged in his tumble through the window.

"I'm Jackie's niece, Robyn. I'm here for the summer."

"Are you? She never said. Hello, Robyn." Having satisfied himself that his trumpet was intact, he advanced with outstretched arm and we shook hands solemnly across my duvet cover. "Well, it's very nice to have met you and I'm sorry I woke you up. Next time I'll use the front door like a normal person."

He clumped across the room in his biker boots, and then paused as he caught sight of my clarinet resting on its stand by the fireplace. "Is that yours?" he asked.

I nodded.

"I mean, can you play it? Are you any good?"

"I'm on grade seven," I said primly, and then felt hot with embarrassment as he bit back a smile.

"Can you play sax?" he wanted to know next.

"I have lessons, but I don't practise much because I haven't got my own sax," I admitted. "I have to borrow the school one."

Charlie nodded to himself, as though filing this information away. "Interesting. Can you sing?"

"No. Do you always do this?" I said.

"What?"

"Start interrogating people about their musical ability when you've just climbed in the window at three in the morning."

Charlie reflected for a moment or two. "No, this is a first for me. The interrogation, I mean, not the climbing in windows – I do that quite often. And I have been known to climb *out* of bedroom windows in a hurry on occasions," he added, giving me a meaningful look. It was only later, thinking over our conversation, that I realised what he meant by this. As I've said before, for a bright girl I can be exceptionally slow on the uptake.

"Well, goodnight, Robyn. What's left of it. See you in the morning." He checked his watch. "Or afternoon, if I'm being realistic."

He pulled the door closed behind him and I could hear him whistling cheerfully to himself as he climbed the stairs.

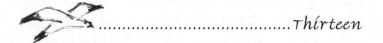 

# Dark Chocolate

As well as saddling me with a boy's name, as though they had always expected a son and hadn't bothered with plan B, my parents had also had the bright idea of giving us matching initials. Richard, Ruth, Rachel and Robyn. Perhaps they thought it sounded cute. Whatever their reasons, they evidently didn't foresee the tussles that would follow in later years when letters arrived addressed simply to R Stenning.

The problem didn't arise when Rachel and I were little, as we never got any post. But now we occasionally did, and were both inclined to defend our privacy. Rachel, for example, didn't particularly want Dad opening up her boxes of mail-order shoes from VivaLaDiva or her

Figleaves bra and thong sets, and I didn't want her snooping through my bank statement to see how much I had stashed away. Dad himself wasn't bothered: he had nothing to hide, he said.

Over time, Rachel and I had devised the following system. If a letter or parcel arrived for R Stenning, with no other clue as to the intended recipient, the protocol was that one of us should wait to ask the others if they were expecting anything before ripping into it, even if this meant a certain amount of delay.

So it was that I came home from an after-school rehearsal for jazz band to find Rachel inspecting a sealed Jiffy bag addressed to R Stenning, postmarked Oxford but with no other identifying marks. "Feels like chocolates," she said, giving it a shake. "Ring any bells with you?"

"No. Let's open it. Or do you think Dad's got a secret admirer?" We hooted with laughter at the notion as Rachel tore into the packaging. Her prediction was correct: the contents were revealed to be a two-decker box of supermarket Belgian chocolates tied with red ribbon. It was unaccompanied by any card or note so we were still none the wiser.

Rachel and I looked at each other, frustrated, and then at the Jiffy bag again. There was no return address, and the handwriting – nondescript biro capitals – gave nothing away. I could tell Rachel was disappointed. She had hoped the gift was for her, and no doubt had someone in mind she wanted it to be from too. "How annoying," she said. "We could just eat them anyway."

Although I generally had no restraint when it came to chocolate, something about this anonymous freebie made me slightly uneasy. "I dunno. Better wait for Dad."

Dad was slightly later than usual because it was his turn to cook, so he'd stopped to get a Chinese takeaway on the way home. The unmistakable smell of sweet-and-sour that heralded his arrival, and the emergency presented by the tub of hoisin sauce bursting open over the prawn crackers, drove all thoughts of chocolate from our minds. It wasn't until after we'd feasted on special fried rice, sweet and sour pork, crispy Peking duck and not-so-crispy prawn crackers, and Dad was obsessively washing and sorting the foil trays for recycling, that I thought to mention the mystery package.

Dad was immediately on full alert. "Where? What chocolates? You haven't eaten any, have you?" he said in horror.

"No, no. We haven't even opened them," said Rachel, slightly taken aback by his reaction.

He pounced on the box and studied it closely for a few seconds. "Well, someone has," he said at last. "You can see the seal has been peeled back and stuck down again."

Rachel and I almost clashed heads as we bent to inspect this evidence of tampering. It was clear that Dad was right.

"When did they arrive?" he wanted to know.

"I just found them on the doorstep tucked behind the boot-scraper when I came home," said Rachel. "The postman always leaves stuff that's too fat for the letter box there, so it doesn't get rained on."

A slow trawl through that morning's CCTV footage showed that the postman had been the only visitor to the house. It also showed that he had spat his chewing gum into the water feature as he left, but this act of vandalism was eclipsed by the matter at hand.

"I don't like this at all," Dad was saying, taking it upon himself to tear off the suspect seal and examine the contents of the box at close quarters. They looked innocent enough – a couple of the chocolates had flipped over in their little capsules, but that could easily have happened in transit, and there were no obvious signs of interference. "I'm going to take them into work tomorrow," he went on, resealing the lid. "Get someone in the lab to test them to see if they're contaminated. I'd better have the envelope as well." He retrieved the Jiffy bag from the floor. I couldn't help thinking that any fingerprint evidence would have been seriously compromised by the mauling it had taken from Rachel.

"In the mean time," Dad added, "if any more parcels arrive like this, don't open them. Leave them for me."

"Do you really think they might be poisoned?" said Rachel, beginning to sound anxious. Perhaps she was thinking how very close she had come to tucking in. "It's a pretty random way of targeting someone. How are they to know it's going to be you who eats them? You might be diabetic and pass them on to your secretary or the old biddy next door or someone."

"I don't know. These fanatics don't think like normal people."

"Look at this," I said, reading the ingredients label. "Diglycerides of fatty acids – ugh – *beef gelatine*! They haven't even bought vegetarian chocolates. How hypocritical is that?"

Dad seemed to find this quite funny, and for a moment the tense atmosphere lifted and I felt slightly better. I didn't like it when Dad was the worried one. I wanted him to be strong and fearless, and sweep aside all our insecurities on a great wave of parental infallibility the way he did when we were young. Monsters in the wardrobe? No problem: I'll go and chase them away. Nightmare? Come and sleep in my bed and yes of course you can bring Tinky Winky, Piglet and your seven teddy bears with you. Thunderstorm? Excellent: we'll watch it from the window together. Even when he used to rescue a spider from the bath while Rachel and I quaked on the landing, he wouldn't just chuck it out of the window; he would carry it right to the end of the road in a glass so it couldn't find its way straight back.

Lately it seemed increasingly that the tide had turned, and the job of reassurance was passing more and more from Dad to us. "No, of course I won't give my personal details in internet chat rooms… Yes, of course I'll make sure no one spikes my drink… No, of course I'm not getting any funny dieting ideas… Yes, thank you, I know all about chlamydia and the many horrific side-effects of unprotected sex, but I don't especially want to hear about them from you."

Dad returned from the Institute the next day with the news that the chocolates had definitely been contaminated, though it was unclear with what. It would have taken days for the lab to perform exhaustive tests, and the matter was in any case now in the hands of the police. "Well, we know it wasn't poison," he said. "Not rat poison anyway."

"How?" I asked, a little slow to catch on.

"We fed a champagne truffle to one of the lab rats and he's still very much alive."

"Oh, that's so mean," said Rachel.

Dad rolled his eyes. "Remind me: whose side are you on?"

"I don't take sides," said Rachel. "I'm like Switzerland."

Later, Rachel and I were in the living room playing crib while watching a DVD of *Casino Royale*. Everyone at school said Daniel Craig was so hot, but to my mind he looked like a PE teacher. I could just see him in trackies, with a whistle round his neck. I couldn't follow the plot anyway because I was half eavesdropping on Dad, who was in the study making phone calls. He had turfed me off the computer earlier so he could look through the day's CCTV footage to see if anyone had been loitering. As far as I could gather, he was phoning his boss to discuss the possibility of taking some unpaid leave in August. From his deflated tone, I gathered that the answer was no. For the next call he dropped the ultra-polite voice, but before I could work out who was on the other end, the noise of gunfire, squealing tyres and an exploding fuel tanker erupted from the TV, drowning him out, and he shut the study door.

He wandered back into the living room just as James Bond was having fully-clothed sex with the evil guy's wife. After watching them distractedly for a few seconds, he hit the pause button, leaving them frozen mid-hump.

"How do you girls feel about going on holiday to Brighton?" he asked, with no apology for the interruption.

"Why Brighton?" I asked. We hadn't been expecting to go anywhere this summer: we'd had two weeks' skiing in Austria over Christmas and that was supposed to last us all year.

"I've been talking to your Auntie Jackie. Remember her?"

I did, not entirely favourably.

"She'd be happy to put you up if you want to go. I can't get any time off till September, and I don't like the thought of you hanging around here on your own all day every day."

"But all our friends are here," Rachel protested. "What is there in Brighton?"

"Sun, sea, sand," said Dad, gesturing expansively. "Ok, not sand, more like pebbles. But it's a big lively town. Plenty to do. Anyway, I thought your friends were going away in August."

This was true and remained a sore point. While she was going out with Todd, infamous defiler of bathroom washbasins, Rachel had turned down the chance to go to Corfu with a bunch of mates so that she'd be free to go backpacking with him. There had been ambitious talk of Thailand and Bali, but nothing had materialised, and then they had split up, by which time it was too late for her to join the Corfu trip.

"*Hmph.*"

"I wouldn't mind going for a week," I said. "But only if Rachel goes. I'm not going by myself."

"But what would we *do*?" Rachel persisted.

"Do?" Dad's tone was impatient. "Do whatever you like. Amuse yourselves in some appropriate manner. Auntie Jackie is offering to put you up, that's all. She's not running a holiday camp."

"I suppose a week would be bearable," Rachel said grudgingly.

"Oh, forget it," Dad snapped. "Auntie Jackie's doing you the favour, not the other way round. She's a busy woman. The last thing she needs is two bored teenagers mooching around complaining that there's nothing to do. If you don't want to go, fine."

"Fine. Can we watch the rest of the film now?"

Dad slammed out of the room and a few minutes later the lawnmower roared into life. Whenever Rachel wound Dad up by being more than usually princessy, he took out his frustration on the garden, digging up some underperforming shrub, or viciously pruning the laurels, depending on the season. This time he was stomping up and down the lawn, forcing the grass into parallel stripes. I think the energetic activity calmed him down. Plus, it was a way of saying, *Look at me, working my butt off while you laze around.*

But one thing I'll say for Rachel: she can't keep up a sulk. If there's an atmosphere indoors, she just can't dig in and settle for being unpopular. So even before the film ended she was regretting her ungrateful words and went out to try and repair the damage. She stopped short of offering to take over the mower, but she did bring Dad a bottle of cold beer from the fridge, and this small gesture was enough to restore friendly relations, without either side having to climb down and say sorry. And for the time being at least there was no more talk of Brighton.

# An Invitation

When I woke up on Sunday morning, I wondered if I'd dreamt the whole Charlie episode, but there was Gunter, lying on the floor with one cheek dented and a boot-shaped hole in his back to prove it had happened.

I'd intended to go to the beach today, maybe even swim if it was hot enough, but I could tell without getting out of bed, just from the quality of the light leaking down from pavement level, that the weather wasn't going to be great.

All around me the house was quiet. Generally, on Sundays, Auntie Jackie came down and made herself a pot of tea and went back to bed with the *Mail on Sunday*. "There's nothing in this paper; it's just a load of old rubbish about celebrities," she would grumble, reading on avidly.

Rachel wasn't expected back from Oxford until early evening so I took advantage of her absence to use her bathroom. It was newer and cleaner than the one downstairs, which smelled of drains and had a clammy shower curtain with a way of sucking up against you as you leant over to shave your legs. While I was there, I borrowed some of her Blonde Goddess shampoo, but it didn't work; I still came out looking like me. Rachel's snowy-white jeans hung, freshly washed and ironed, over the wardrobe door. I wrestled with an impulse to try them on, but finally resisted.

Apparently, there are some people in remote parts of China who won't have their photo taken because they think they'll lose part of their soul. Rachel's a bit like that about lending her clothes. Certainly, borrowing them without permission would entail a degree of personal risk, and it would be just my luck to spill ketchup or Coke all over them on a first outing.

As I crept out again, I could hear the murmur of the radio coming from Auntie Jackie's bedroom, but there was no sound from the landing above, and Charlie's door remained closed.

I decided to go out for a run, perhaps rewarding myself on the way back with a chocolate doughnut from the baker's. So I pulled on my grey trackies and a T-shirt and retrieved my trainers from the trunk by the front door where Auntie Jackie hid unsightly items from visiting clients.

Outside a gusty wind was whipping up eddies of dust and litter, and driving the clouds in a busy, energetic sky. I sat on the step tying up my laces, plugged myself into my iPod and then straightened up, glancing furtively around to check that no one was looking, and jogged off feeling hugely self-conscious. My embarrassment was justified: after only a few paces I was overtaken by a dustbin lid, bowled along by the wind. What hope was there if I could be so easily outperformed by inanimate objects?

About halfway around the block, I became aware of a presence at my heels, as though someone was trying to pass. I moved aside humbly at this suggestion that I was causing an obstruction to other, fitter pedestrians.

"Hello," said Adam, falling in beside me and laughing at my startled expression. He was carrying a baguette and a newspaper in one hand and a coffee in the other. "I thought it was you. Are you going somewhere or are you just doing this for fun?"

"I thought I'd go for a run," I said, unplugging my earpiece. "A jog, I mean," I corrected myself, picking up the pace fractionally.

"Where to?" He loped beside me on long legs with no apparent effort, barely breaking out of a walk and without spilling a drop of coffee, while I puffed away. Really, I was disgustingly unfit. It was a miracle I could find enough lung power to get a note out of my clarinet.

"I don't know. I hadn't really thought further than the cake shop," I confessed.

"Is it all right if I come with you? I was going to go out for a bike ride, but I might as well jog instead."

"No, I don't mind," I said. "But I'm only going at my pace," I added, remembering Rachel's complaints about his competitive tendencies on the tennis court.

"That's fine," he said innocently. "Just say when you're ready to start."

"Oh, ha ha," I retorted, unable to stop myself lengthening my stride.

We jogged down to the promenade in companionable silence, Adam taking the occasional swig from his coffee and tearing off chunks of baguette to eat on the way. *Any second now he'll get the newspaper out and start doing the crossword*, I thought.

The wind was even stronger here, ruffling the canopies of the ice-cream stalls and tugging at the row of potbellied deckchairs that lined the front. Above our heads, seagulls surfed the breeze. Adam broke off some chunks of bread and we lobbed them into the sky, watching the birds swoop and dive faultlessly. There's no such thing as a seagull that can't catch.

"I was going to come round later," he said at last, dividing the end of the baguette between us. I ate mine rather hastily and it lodged in an indigestible clump about halfway down my gullet.

"Rachel won't be in till six," I said.

"I know. She's in Oxford at 'the best party ever'."

"Oh. She told you."

"Yes. She asked me to lend her the money to get there."

"She never!"

"Well, she didn't actually *ask*. She said she was going to hitch a lift so I told her that was totally crazy and gave her the train fare instead."

"Oh my God! I can't believe she's done that. She's so devious. She's got no..." I spluttered, brought to a standstill by a combination of indignation and violent stitch.

"What's the problem?" asked Adam.

"The problem," I said, doubled over with pain, "is I'll

have to pay you back, because she almost certainly won't. And she'll never pay me back because she never does, because she's always, always broke."

"You don't have to pay me back? It's not your responsibility."

"Yes, it is. She's my sister."

"How old are you?" Adam demanded.

"Fifteen," I said, a trifle defensively.

"And how old is Rachel?"

"Eighteen."

"There you are then. She's an adult. Let her sort out her own finances."

All this while I had been fumbling my purse out of my pocket and trying to extract and hand over a twenty pound note without the wind snatching it. Adam kept his hands firmly wrapped round his coffee and bread, refusing to accept.

"You let that go and it'll blow out to sea," he warned. "You'd better put it away."

With a sigh, I gave in. "I suppose you've been paying for all those lunches too," I muttered.

He didn't deny it. "I don't get what's bugging you," he said.

"How's she ever going to learn if people like you are

always stepping in to bail her out," I said, my voice rising in frustration. "If I want something I can't afford, I have to save up and save up and do without other stuff, but if she wants something, she just somehow seems to get it straightaway and someone else pays. It's so unfair."

"Sorry," said Adam, bewildered by this outpouring of resentment. "I didn't realise there were issues."

With a huge effort, I pulled myself back from the brink of a deeply unattractive sulk. "No, I'm sorry," I mumbled. "But," – I can never issue an apology without immediately qualifying it – "sometimes I get so fed up always being the Sensible One."

My stitch had unknotted itself, so we set off running again, separated briefly by a woman on rollerblades, swaying gracefully from side to side on long polished legs.

"So stop being sensible," Adam suggested, lobbing his empty coffee cup into a bin as we passed. "Do something really irresponsible and selfish."

"Maybe I will one day... When the time is right," I added, realising just too late that this was a typically Sensible remark.

"I was going to ask you something actually," Adam said, as we turned back inland towards Cliff Street. He sounded slightly embarrassed.

"Oh?"

"Thing is, I've got to go to a ball at the Grand Hotel in a few weeks' time. Black-tie job. I did some voluntary work for this children's charity over Christmas, designing their website and doing some IT stuff, and they've now given me a £200 double ticket as a sort of thank you. So I feel I've got to show up even though it's not my sort of thing really: champagne and dressing up..."

"Oh."

"And I was wondering..."

"Mmm." Somewhere inside me a tiny spark of hope flickered into life.

"Do you think Rachel would go with me if I invited her?" he asked, extinguishing the spark with a bucket of icy water.

Luckily my face was already red from all the fresh air and exercise, so my blush of humiliation passed unnoticed.

"I don't want to ask her if it's not her sort of thing, or she's just going to turn me down flat," he went on, oblivious to my efforts to recover some inner dignity.

"Oh, champagne and dressing up is totally her sort of thing," I reassured him.

"So you think she'd come?"

"I dunno. You'd have to ask her." Let him do his own dirty work, I thought.

He nodded, apparently encouraged, though I hadn't intended to be particularly encouraging. The truth was Rachel didn't fancy him, but unless a better offer came along would probably say yes to a £200 ball ticket.

"OK, I'll ask her. She's a difficult person to pin down though," Adam said. I had a sudden image of brightly coloured butterflies under glass, their bodies stapled to a board.

"Come on, let's speed up for this last bit," he said, prodding me with his rolled newspaper. He took off up the road without waiting and I only caught him up at the baker's where he had stopped to buy a baguette to replace the one we'd demolished. For some reason I'd lost my appetite, but I bought two chocolate doughnuts – one for me and one for Rachel – and then ate them both for lunch anyway.

In the afternoon Auntie Jackie said I could use the computer, which was in the back room with her sewing machine and workbench, so I sent Dad an email giving him all the details of life at Cliff Street. Pointless really, as he was at that moment no doubt hearing it all first hand from Rachel. I left some messages for Jo and Suzie on Facebook, for when they came back from their holidays, and then I lay on my bed for a while reading *The Lovely Bones* nice and slowly to make it last.

It was warm and rather airless in the basement, with a stripe of sunlight across my page, making me pleasantly drowsy. From the top of the house came the sound of a trumpet – smooth, round notes, tripping lightly up and down the scale, each one perfect as a bubble. In spite of three flights of stairs and the closed doors between us, it was surprisingly loud. I couldn't imagine having the confidence to practise at that volume in someone else's house. When I was first learning the clarinet at home, I used to play it in the wardrobe. But then Charlie was a professional, used to people paying to hear him play, so a sense of entitlement was understandable.

After a few minutes of warming up he began to run through some pieces, a couple of which I recognised from jazz band – 'Birdland' and 'How High the Moon' – and several which sounded familiar, but I wasn't sure why. Then the music stopped and I heard pounding footsteps on the stairs. I wondered if he might be coming down to the kitchen, and whether or not to go out and say hello, but before I had decided one way or another, the front door banged and a moment later I heard his motorbike start up with a roar and take off down the road. One thing I'd discovered about Charlie: he didn't bother to keep the volume down.

Rachel arrived back in the evening, looking a bit off-colour after her weekend of fun. She had only had three hours' sleep, which is worse than no sleep at all, and now had a vicious headache to show for it. This she told us as she rifled through the kitchen drawer in search of paracetamol, while Auntie Jackie and I sat at the table playing crib.

"Good party then?" Auntie Jackie inquired, dealing the cards briskly.

"Great party," said Rachel, having disposed of two tablets and half a pint of water. "There was a band and a big marquee in the garden, and masses of pink champagne, which is brilliant stuff because it doesn't give you a hangover at all hardly. And there was a hot air balloon on the lawn, and you could go up about thirty metres and look down on the party, but I didn't go in it because I couldn't be bothered to queue up. And they let off a load of huge fireworks at midnight – not those piddly ones you buy at the newsagent – real whoppers, and then some guy decided to dive in the pool in his DJ, and so everybody started jumping in fully clothed. Not me of course," she added hastily, catching Auntie Jackie's expression. "I didn't want to ruin your dress so I went in in my bra and knickers. But everybody else did."

"*Hmph*," said Auntie Jackie. It was perhaps a mistake to expect the owner of a ballgown-hire business to be impressed by this aspect of the festivities.

"Oh and guess who I saw at Paddington on the way back?"

I decided to try. "Er... Prince Harry? Ozzy Osbourne? Nicole Richie?"

"Don't be silly, I mean a real person. No, I saw Todd."

"Oh. What was he doing in London?"

"I don't know. I didn't ask. I noticed that he'd had a tattoo – some Chinesey letters."

"Did you tell him you could have got him a ten per cent discount?"

"I did actually. He's quite sweet really."

"You're not going to start seeing him again, are you?" I said, suddenly suspicious.

"No. You can't go back to someone you've dumped. It's never the same."

For a moment I considered telling her about my final encounter with Todd and then decided against it.

It really did him no favours. About two weeks after she had dumped him, I had come home from school and found him sitting on the garden wall smoking a skinny roll-up. He seemed to have lost weight – his clothes looked as though they'd been borrowed from a much bigger man – and there were bruise-coloured shadows under his eyes.

"Rachel's not here," I'd said, as kindly as possible, since he was looking a bit dejected.

"It was you I wanted to see anyway," he said, picking shreds of tobacco off his lip. "I wanted your advice."

This was a relief – for a horrible half-second I had thought he might be going to ask me out. "Oh. OK." I didn't invite him in, but stood ready to dispense advice on the pavement.

"I just wondered if Rachel had ever mentioned why she's gone off me. You know – if there's any major thing about me that she doesn't like, that I could change so that she would. I just wondered."

"Er no," I said, embarrassed. "She never said anything." He hadn't pursued this any further, just shrugged and nodded, and gone on his lonely way.

"Did your Dad know you were going to be in Oxford?" asked Auntie Jackie, who was tearing around the crib board with a hand of fives and jacks.

"Not exactly. I didn't want to tell him in advance in case he tried to stop me, so I rang him this morning from Frankie's and we went to Browns for lunch." From her bag Rachel produced a cheque and handed it over. "He told me to give you this."

Auntie Jackie made half-hearted protestations about not wanting his money, before putting it in her purse. It occurred to me for the first time that she was probably quite poor, but you can never really tell.

"You never said you were going to meet Dad," I protested. I would have quite liked to go to Browns. "When's he going to come and see us anyway?"

"He could come down one weekend," Auntie Jackie suggested.

Rachel looked slightly uncomfortable. "He said he'd like to see us, but he doesn't want to impose on Auntie Jackie. He said he'd stay at a hotel."

Auntie Jackie looked offended. "Did he tell you to say that?" she spluttered. "What does he want to stay in a hotel for? There's plenty of room here. You girls could share and he can go in Robyn's room."

"That's what I said," Rachel agreed. "He has some funny ideas sometimes."

Auntie Jackie shook her head. For some reason Dad's overpoliteness had annoyed her, and I wondered whether they really had got over their ancient quarrel after all.

"I'm going to lie down," said Rachel, dumping her empty glass in the sink. "See if this headache will go. Don't wake me up – If I drop off, I'll try and sleep right through."

"But you haven't finished telling us about the party and stuff," I protested. If she'd been off having fun all weekend, the least she could do when she got back was entertain me with some gossip.

"I have. There's nothing more to tell."

Considering she'd been looking forward to Frankie's eighteenth since, well, Frankie's seventeenth, she wasn't sounding very enthusiastic.

Before she could leave, the front door slammed with a force that made the whole house quake, and a moment later Charlie bounced into the kitchen. He was carrying what looked like a gas canister with a bicycle pump attached to it. "Jackie, have you got a net curtain…?" He tailed off as he took in the fact that she had company.

"Certainly not," said Auntie Jackie. "What a vulgar idea." She turned to us. "This is my lodger, Charlie

Gamble. He's responsible for that horrible bugling noise you heard earlier."

"We've already met," I said.

Charlie looked at me with belated recognition. "Oh yes, hello again. You look different out of bed."

Rachel's jaw dropped.

"He climbed in through my window last night," I explained, to clear up any misunderstanding.

"You didn't!" said Auntie Jackie.

"Well, I wouldn't have if I'd known there was someone sleeping in there," Charlie protested. "You didn't tell me you had visitors."

"How could I? You're never here." It would soon become clear that this low level bickering was their normal style of conversation, and was not necessarily the prelude to a major argument. "What do you want a net curtain for anyway?"

"There's a wasps' nest under the eaves just outside my window. I've got some of this poison stuff to zap them, but I thought I'd be safer if I wore some sort of net thing over my face in case they go for me."

"I don't have any net curtains," said Auntie Jackie crisply. "You're not in Orpington now, you know." I assumed this must be a joke about Charlie's humble background.

"What about some of that gauzy stuff you keep in your dressing-up box?" He gestured upstairs towards the shop. "You've got loads of old netting up there."

"I'm not lending you one of my chiffon evening stoles to go killing wasps in," Auntie Jackie retorted. "Unless, of course, you'd like to hire one…"

"How much?" asked Charlie.

"Twenty-five quid a day."

*"Twenty-five quid!* No wonder you never get any customers. Anyway, I only need it for about five minutes. What's that *pro rata*?" He screwed up his face with the effort of performing this mathematical feat. "About a pound an hour… so for five minutes we're talking… 8p. Done!" He solemnly counted out the change on to the kitchen table.

Rachel and I began to giggle.

"Oh. While you've got your wallet out," said Auntie Jackie, "you owe me two months' rent."

Charlie looked wounded. "Do I really?"

"No hurry," she said, beaming. "Any time in the next two minutes will be fine."

From his back pocket Charlie produced a brown envelope containing more cash than I'd ever seen outside a bank. Rachel's eyes bulged. From this bundle he peeled off twelve fifty pound notes. At this point I began to harbour a secret suspicion that Charlie was a train robber in his spare time. It seemed the only possible explanation.

"Thank you, darling," said Auntie Jackie. "You can go and sort out your wasps now."

"*My* wasps?" Charlie grumbled. "Pest control is actually the landlady's responsibility, I think you'll find." A few minutes later he clumped upstairs to do battle in his motorbike leathers topped off prettily with a pink silk veil.

Rachel went to her room to lie down and didn't reappear. Even the smell of frying bacon for supper didn't rouse her. I saved her a couple of rashers and made a BLT which I took up on a tray with a glass of Coke. There was no reply when I tapped on the door, so I went in anyway. She was lying on her bed with her back to me, but she rolled over as I approached and I could see watery tracks of mascara on her cheeks.

"What's the matter?" I said. "Have you been crying?"

She shook her head, but wiped her wet cheeks all the same. "I'm all right." This was clearly rubbish. She looked as worried and unhappy as I'd ever seen her. I put the tray down on her bedside table and sat next to her on the bed, waiting. "Robbie," she said at last. "Don't have a go at me. I've done something really, really stupid."

# A Quick Exit

There is no better feeling than the realisation, at the fuzzy boundary between sleep and waking, that it is the first day of the summer holidays and there is no reason to get up, not just today and tomorrow, but for weeks and weeks to come. This year I even kept my alarm set for 7.00 a.m. just for the pleasure of silencing it and burrowing back down. At about 7.45 I was disturbed again by the familiar sequence of noises which proclaimed Dad's inflexible morning routine: bathroom door bang. Loo flush. Thundering of power shower. Airing cupboard door bang. Stairs. Kettle. Fridge door *whump*. Front door bang. Car door *crump*. Silence.

When I resurfaced, it was midday and the house was

quiet. Rachel was off somewhere. The remains of her breakfast were still on the kitchen table: a cereal bowl with a lone Cheerio floating in a centimetre of milk like a tiny lifebelt, and a scatter of chocolate powder describing the exact position of her cappuccino. An open bottle of milk stood in full sunlight, already lukewarm and beginning to separate. The espresso machine had been left on and nearly boiled dry: a treacly pool of coffee bubbled fiercely at the bottom of the glass jug, giving off a smell like scorched rubber. I seized the jug and ran it under the cold tap. There was a loud crack as the glass split cleanly in half and fell into the sink, leaving me holding the plastic handle. Damn.

By the time I had cleared away this and everyone else's mess, it was lunchtime, so I made a cream cheese, banana and honey sandwich and went back up to my room. It was a modest ambition of mine at that point to go through a whole day, right up to bedtime, without getting dressed. This was harder to achieve than it might sound unless Dad was out for the evening, as he seemed to have a peculiar aversion to dressing gowns, and would freak out if he caught me or Rachel mooching around in ours during the day. "Can't you get some clothes on, for God's sake?" he would rant. "It's like living on a hospital ward. Why don't I rig up a drip and a bedpan, then you wouldn't need to get up at all?" As Dad had stopped going out in the evenings lately, it would take considerable cunning to achieve this twenty-four-hour pyjamathon.

There was a pile of old magazines on the bottom shelf of my bookcase which I'd put aside for recycling. I couldn't resist having a last flick through before they were consigned to the black box. Some of the beauty tips were hilarious. *For a natural summer glow, crumble some gold eyeshadow into your regular moisturiser. Apply to shoulders, cheekbones or wherever you need a little sparkle, but go easy on the face unless you want to look like a Christmas tree bauble.*

Amber, fourteen, from Gwynedd was given some advice on how to disguise her huge nose with different shades of foundation and highlighter. There was even a diagram showing where to paint the stripes, like a relief map of a rocky peninsula. It seemed to me there was a good chance that Amber's nose might be more conspicuous than ever after this treatment, a suspicion underlined by the defeatist tone of the closing sentence: *Remember, nothing diverts attention from your least favourite feature like a bright smile!*

I was still smirking over this and similar inanities when I was drawn to the window by the sound of an idling diesel engine. A red Parcelforce van had pulled up opposite, the driver glancing briefly up at the house before emerging with a large box, which he carried across the road and left on the doorstep of number 6. Shaken from my idle reveries about nose-painting, I scooped up the pile of magazines and took them downstairs to the recycling box. As I opened the front door, I nearly fell over the van driver who was crouching beside the doorstep in the act of tucking a large Jiffy bag behind the boot-scraper. We both started in surprise.

"Sorry, I didn't think there was anyone home," he said, straightening up and handing me the parcel, which as I was already burdened with a pile of slippery magazines, I managed to fumble and drop. "Whoops," said the man, retrieving it and putting it safely inside the doorway. "Nothing breakable I hope." We had both heard the faint tinkling sound on impact and exchanged grimaces.

I could see straightaway that it was from Them. It was the same sort of envelope as before – padded not with bubble wrap but with grey wadding like hoover fluff. And the writing was the same too: R STENNING in carefully anonymous blue biro. Sensible as always, I left it unopened on the kitchen table for Dad, and went into the sitting room to see if I could track down an old episode of *Lost* which I'd taped but never had time to see. After a frustrating hour of fast forwarding through piles of unmarked videos of half-erased episodes of *Doctor Who* and *Ugly Betty* and Dad's endless documentaries on climate change, it began to seem that *Lost* was living up to its name. *One day*, I thought, *I will go through every single tape and label them all, and take out the ones that can be reused and put them on a separate shelf. But not today because it is the first day of my holiday and I want to enjoy it.*

I never did get any further with *Lost* because at that point there was the scrape of a key in the lock. It was Dad. "Can't stop. Forgot my glasses," he explained, casting an unfriendly look at my dressing gown before bounding upstairs. He reappeared a moment later, tucking the object of his quest into his jacket pocket. "I managed to get through a budget meeting without them, but I've got a forty-page document to proofread this afternoon," he said, heading for the front door. He paused on the threshold. "Hey. Do you want to hear a funny thing?"

"Yes."

"I got the lab report on those chocolates this morning. Do you know what was in them?"

I shook my head. "What?"

"Laxatives."

I burst out laughing. "Is that all? How weird."

"I thought so too. What next from these terrorist masterminds? Itching powder?"

"That reminds me," I said, gesturing towards the kitchen. "We've got another one."

"Oh? You haven't opened it?"

"No. I left it for you. As instructed."

Having been in such a tearing hurry to get back to work, Dad now couldn't resist investigating.

The phone rang in the study. I left Dad eyeing the parcel suspiciously and went to answer it. "Consolidate your debts with one easy monthly payment," purred a woman's voice, without any preamble.

"Hello? Who's this?" I asked, and then felt hot with embarrassment as I realised I was talking to a recorded message. "Take advantage of our new low rates," the voice flowed on, "But hurry—" here the tone grew more urgent, "this exciting offer only lasts until the end of the month." As I hung up, I became aware of the even more urgent tones of Dad, calling my name.

"ROBYN!" he was shouting. "GET OUT OF THE HOUSE!"

A simple enough instruction you might think, but in certain matters, such as the wearing of pyjamas in the street, it's in my nature to seek a little extra clarification.

"But I'm not dressed," I said idiotically, dithering in the hallway by the open door.

And then Dad, who was the most hands-off parent alive and had never smacked or shaken me, even at my most obnoxious, burst out of the kitchen, roaring something which I later translated as "NOW!" and, slamming into my back with the force of a truck, half-knocked and half-bundled me out into the street.

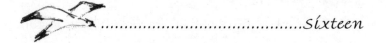

# Evacuation

Dad and I sat in an interview room at the police station in Oxford, waiting for somebody to tell us what to do next. It was four o'clock in the afternoon and I was still in my dressing gown and monster feet slippers. I was now completely cured of my ambition to go through an entire day dressed like this. We had been questioned by two police officers who took down a statement. Then another woman – not in uniform – came in and made me repeat the whole thing again, right from the beginning, including the prowler and the chocolates, with many interruptions and corrections from Dad. The woman seemed to be very interested in his references to the Institute, and the threats to its various contractors, especially the arson attack on the offices of the waste disposal company.

"The people who did that are on remand at the moment," she told him. "I was on that investigation."

"They're probably just one tiny cell in a much larger organisation," Dad insisted.

She shook her head. "It was an insurance fraud. There was no terrorist agenda in that particular case." All the time we had been talking her mobile phone kept bleeping and she would glance down at it to check that the caller could be safely ignored. Now it was obviously someone important, as she excused herself and left the room.

Dad sat hunched over, elbows on knees, his hands gripping the back of his head. The air in the room was warm and overdry and I now had a desperate thirst. Soon after our arrival, a woman had popped her head around the door and offered to bring us a cup of tea, and then disappeared, never to return. There was a vending machine at the end of the corridor, but I couldn't venture out to use it in case somebody saw me in my PJs. My unspoken dread was that we were soon going to be told we could go and I would have to walk through the streets of Oxford dressed like an escaped lunatic.

But of course, we wouldn't be going home, not properly home, for a long time.

People complain about the police and say that they're racist, and beat confessions out of people and don't catch enough burglars, but if you've just got a letter bomb, they are absolutely the best people to call.

Within minutes – almost seconds, it seemed – of Dad pushing me out of the house and telling me to run to the end of the road, two squad cars had come screaming into the Close, sealed it off and evacuated the neighbouring houses. The woman directly opposite with the new baby brought him out wrapped in a blanket and continued to breastfeed him, sitting on the grass verge on the other side of the police tape. Mrs Finch next door had to be helped out on her zimmer. She was wearing slippers too, I noticed, though they weren't quite as big and furry as mine. "Will it take long? I've left a Victoria sponge in the oven," she kept saying to anyone who would listen.

The other houses were empty, the occupants all out at work during office hours, but even so, the sound of sirens and the spectacle of flashing blue lights and police cars blocking the turning had brought out a few nosy parkers from the street beyond. Soon a gaggle of onlookers had collected, eagerly awaiting some drama, the sort of people who would no doubt turn out to watch public executions if they were available, I thought bitterly. I hoped the police would shoo them away, but they didn't.

Then a van arrived, and three men in protective suits and helmets got out and, after conferring with one of the officers, came across and spoke to Dad. Having established what they were looking for, two of them went into the house, carrying cases of equipment as if they were gasmen just popping in to fix the boiler. A third swept the underneath of the car with what looked like a giant dentist's mirror.

Dad was pacing up and down, one hand over his ear, making phone calls: one to his boss at the Institute so that he could issue an alert to all staff; one to Rachel, who was at Frankie's, telling her to stay there and leave her phone on so he could keep in contact, and one to his best friends, Mark and Kathy, to ask if they could put us up for the night.

I stood waiting, just the other side of the tape, keeping my distance from the spectators, looking anxiously towards the blank face of the house and tensing myself against the possibility of an explosion. Mrs Finch was still fretting about her cake, and how long it would take before the oven caught alight. It seemed a real possibility that the onlookers might get to enjoy two emergencies for the price of one. Even in extremity I could see a sort of sick comedy in the situation. How it all unfolded I never had the chance to see because a moment later, one of the uniformed officers came over and asked me to come with Dad to the station so that we could make a statement.

All heads turned to watch as we climbed into the back of the car. I wasn't sure whether I felt more like a celebrity or a criminal. "Will it be all right?" I asked Dad, casting anxious glances back at the house. "The front door's wide open. Do you think they'll remember to shut it when they've finished?"

"There may not be a front door when they've finished," Dad said grimly. "There may not even be a front…"

This wasn't at all the reassurance I was hoping for. "What are we going to do?" I asked, my voice rising to a wail. "Where are we going to stay?"

"We're staying at Kathy and Mark's tonight," Dad said, putting his hand over mine. "Longer, if necessary. It's all arranged." Mark was an ex-colleague of Dad's from the John Radcliffe. He now worked for Oxfam and lived in a two bedroom terrace in Summertown with his wife, three children under the age of five and several rescue dogs. I remembered the house from previous visits as being chaotically untidy from never-ending renovations and smelling strongly of damp laundry; the sort of place you have to stand up to eat because every chair has a pile of clutter on the seat and a wet shirt draped over the back. It was inconceivable that they could accommodate three more strays, but typical of their generosity and optimism that they should offer.

"It'll probably just be one night," Dad said, as if reading my mind. "I'll sort something else out tomorrow. One thing's for certain: you're not coming back home until these nutters are caught."

"What do you mean 'you're not'?" I demanded. "What about you?"

"All right. We're not," he conceded.

"I could stay with Jo," I said. "Her mum likes me. Only," I remembered, "they're going to Florida for the summer."

Suddenly the hand that covered mine began to tremble violently. Even when he tried to subdue it by folding his arms tightly, the vibrations made his whole body quake. "Sorry," he said, teeth chattering. "It's shock. I was just thinking, thank God I came home when I did. I never come home in the day, do I? All morning I was cursing myself because I'd left my glasses behind. But thank God I did. Someone's watching over us."

We relapsed into silence for the rest of the journey, gazing out of the window, and enduring the high level of visibility that comes from travelling in the back of a police car.

It was six o'clock before someone could be found who was able to tell us that the parcel had been dismantled without incident and taken away, and the house was still intact. Mark came and picked us up in his ancient, clunky estate car and I sat in the back on the dog blanket, squeezed uncomfortably between two baby seats, but thankful to have been spared a dressing-gowned hike across town.

Back at their house – as a mark of the gravity of the situation – Kathy had cleared the table and excavated a couple of chairs from beneath the clutter so that we could sit down. She fed us cauliflower cheese and pecan pie, and Dad had several glasses of Mark's murky homebrew and we tried to talk over the background racket of dogs barking and interruptions from the twins until they were finally put to bed. There was something about the uproar and overcrowding that felt strangely comforting and safe.

When it came to our turn, Dad slept on the couch downstairs and I was given a zed bed and a Thomas the Tank Engine duvet on the landing. I was woken at 6 a.m. by hot, cereal-scented breath on my face and excited three-year-old voices trilling, "She's awake! She's awake!"

Dad had been busy while I slept. He had contacted his friend Roger, who had rooms in New College that would be empty over the summer, and was moving in that afternoon. Frankie's parents had offered to drop Rachel off at Mark and Kathy's straight after breakfast and Mark would then drive us back home to pick up the car. We would have five minutes, maximum, in the house to pack a bag and then Dad would take us to the railway station. He had spoken to Auntie Jackie who would meet us at the other end.

It was non-negotiable: we were going to Brighton.

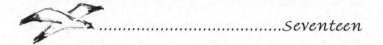

# A Little Favour

When Rachel was nine or ten, she filled in a coupon on the back of one of the Sunday magazines and sent it off without telling anyone. She didn't need a stamp, or even an envelope – the coupon had a cunning way of folding so that the reply-paid address label ended up on the front. The advertisement had promised a FREE GIFT of three exquisite, bone-china farm animals to those who replied within fourteen days.

When the parcel arrived it contained, to her great excitement, not three but six exquisite, bone-china animals: "the start of a collection to treasure" the accompanying leaflet explained, adding that to receive further monthly deliveries she need do nothing!

Over the next few months, more of these thumb-sized figures arrived and were displayed on her windowsill in pens made of Duplo. Taken individually, the animals were quite realistic, but it was a weird looking farm: the chicken was the same size as the shire horse. The piglet stood shoulder to shoulder with the bull. Inside the packages were various pieces of paper which were of no interest and went straight in the bin. Rachel must have sensed something was not quite right about this arrangement because when I became unable to contain my envy and said I was going to ask Daddy if I could send off for some free china animals of my own, she made me promise not to, and bought my silence with the duck and the bull (her least favourites, and mine too, but better than nothing).

I don't know how long this situation would have carried on because one evening, over dinner, I said, "Daddy, what does *invoice* mean?" and with that innocent inquiry, the whole thing unravelled.

Rachel was inconsolable: she hadn't meant to do anything wrong. The word FREE had been in such large print, and the stuff about monthly payments so small, and she hadn't really understood what all the bits of paper meant, but they kept sending more and more china animals so she had assumed it must be all right. The most recent *invoice* was exhumed from her waste paper basket, and Dad reeled at the size of the debt. It would all have to go back. He wasn't paying them a penny, he declared. It was extortion. In fact, if they wanted their rubbishy bits of made-in-China back, they could jolly well come and collect them. He'd rather go to prison than pay.

Rachel and I began to sob. We only had one parent and now he was going to prison. Who would look after us? Dad calmed us down and promised to sort it all out in the morning without getting himself locked up. We weren't to worry: it was all perfectly straightforward.

"Can I just keep the sheepdog?" Rachel wanted to know as soon as the spectre of jail had been chased away. "And the little piggy?"

For some reason, this long forgotten incident came back to me with perfect clarity as Rachel sat on her bed in tears on the night of her return from Frankie's party, and confessed to an altogether more serious lapse of judgement.

The previous week, Rachel had been having a particularly bad time at the tattoo parlour. Her pay packet had contained far less than she had expected, and when she'd queried it, the boss had become quite shirty. Rachel had been tempted to tell him to shove his crappy job, but she still hadn't saved anything like enough money to fund her trip to Frankie's so she had been forced to bite her lip.

As well as contending with issues over pay, she was also developing a deep hatred for the general public. People were so rude! She would never have believed anyone could be so resistant to the idea of accepting a free leaflet. It was one thing to weave away from her as if she was a beggar, but quite another to follow it up with an earful of abuse. Even worse were the people who would willingly take a leaflet, then give it a cursory glance and chuck it on the floor. Old-age pensioners, she hated to admit it, were the only ones with any manners, but since she was being paid by results, she could hardly afford to target this unprofitable sector of the market.

It was as she was contemplating the unsatisfactory nature of the job in particular, and Life in general, that a small boy came wobbling towards her on a scooter. His ability to steer was somewhat compromised by the fact that he was holding a can of Coke, which slipped from his grasp as he fought with the handlebars to avoid a collision. Before Rachel could leap aside, the can had landed at her feet and pumped its foaming contents over her white canvas shoes. The boy, eyes watering with disappointment, seemed about to try and retrieve the last dregs of his Coke, and then catching sight of Rachel's face, thought better of it and scooted away very fast.

Rachel herself moved away quickly, hot with embarrassment at being on the receiving end of so many amused and pitying glances. Her favourite shoes were ruined – Coke stains were impossible to shift – but what was really intolerable was being made into a public spectacle. She felt quite capable of killing anyone who laughed or stared. When she was far enough off, and quite satisfied that she was unobserved, she put her hand in her pocket for a tissue to begin the futile rescue work on the shoes, but found instead a business card with a phone number on the back. For a moment or two she looked at it, mystified, and then recognised it as the one given to her by the woman on the pier from the modelling agency. Mags, she had called herself. Rachel had thought she remembered chucking it in the bin, but here it was, intending to be found. *There's someone in Brighton who'll do your pictures for nothing if you tell him Mags sent you.*

Rachel's phone was in her other pocket. She hesitated. There was something slightly demeaning about ringing up a stranger and asking to be photographed. You had to be a little bit vain even to consider it. On the other hand, the idea of modelling and all that it implied in the way of easy money, beautiful clothes and idle luxury had never seemed so remote from her present circumstances and so desperately appealing. Dad, she reminded herself, always used to say: "Never let an opportunity pass you by." (This was invariably in the context of education – for example, the "opportunity" to go to science summer school, or take an extra A Level – but Rachel conveniently overlooked that. She also forgot one of his other favourite sayings: "There is no such thing as a free ANYTHING.")

Having convinced herself she had the full backing of Dad, Rachel decided there was no harm in ringing up and making enquiries. Otherwise she'd always wonder what she might have missed. If she didn't like the sound of it, she would simply not turn up; she could give a false name and no one would ever know. These comforting thoughts carried her through the process of dialling, and the phone was picked up on the first ring. The male voice on the other end sounded wheezy and a little gruff, but soon warmed up at the mention of Mags. He told her the address of the studio and an appointment was fixed for Friday.

"What's your name again, love?" the man croaked. Rachel could hear the phlegm rattling in his lungs as he spoke. She looked around her at the shops for inspiration. "Millie," she said, thinking, *Why have I chosen to call myself after a cookie?*

Finally she gathered herself to say what was worrying her: "You're just going to take some normal pictures, aren't you? For my portfolio. I'm not doing topless or anything like that. I'm not interested in that sort of modelling."

The man laughed indulgently. "That's fine. Just bring four or five different outfits that show you at your best. And a swimsuit or a leotard or something like that so the agency can get an idea of your figure."

"OK." Rachel felt slightly reassured by this mention of "the agency". "See you Friday then."

"Lovely."

Rachel did keep the appointment of course, even though she told herself right up to the last minute that she might not. I remembered, as she related her story, that I had offered to meet her for lunch on the Friday, but she had refused. "Why didn't you just tell me where you were going?" I couldn't help interrupting. "I'd have come along to make sure you were OK."

"Because I felt a bit embarrassed about the whole thing," Rachel said in a watery voice. "I thought if I get somewhere with this, I'll tell people, but if nothing comes of it, and the agency doesn't like me or my photos, nobody needs to know. I suppose, deep down, I must have known it was too good to be true."

There had been nothing untoward about the photo session itself: the proprietor/photographer was a middle-aged man with a heavy summer cold. When Rachel entered the shop, he was sitting behind the reception desk stirring a hot lemon drink with a lead pencil. The bin was brimming with balled-up tissues.

"Don't come too close," he said, unnecessarily in the circumstances. Rachel was only just inside the door and ready to bolt at a moment's notice. "This cold's a nightmare." When he spoke his chest crackled like burning twigs.

He showed Rachel into the studio – a bare white room with a curved screen from floor to ceiling and various lighting rigs with reflectors like toy umbrellas. A number of soft vinyl cubes and a bar stool were the only items of furniture.

"Where shall I...?" Rachel asked, holding up her carrier bag of clothes. He surely didn't expect her to change right there.

The man opened a concealed door in the back wall, with handles that flipped over to lie completely flush, like the entrance to a squash court. Beyond was a small changing room with a long mirror and a chair over which was draped a pair of discarded tights which still retained, in slightly withered form, the shape of a woman's legs. For some reason, this detail struck Rachel as revolting, but she couldn't bring herself to touch someone's old tights, even to twitch them aside, so there they stayed.

The photographer had been reassuringly matter-of-fact as he clicked away. *Angle your body, chin up, head to the left, eyes towards me, that's the one,* and, after initial embarrassment, Rachel had relaxed and found it, not enjoyable exactly, but easy. She had made four costume changes, including the gold flapper dress that had been such a success at Frankie's party, and – the bit she'd been dreading - her red tankini-with-boy-briefs, none of which raised any eyebrows.

Towards the end, she had sensed the man's concentration beginning to flag, so she had made an excuse about needing to get back to work and he had left her to get changed, while he returned to the reception area. He offered to put a selection of the best pictures on a disc and send it to her, but she remembered just in time not to give her address, and instead said she would call in some time next week and pick it up. Just as she was leaving, Rachel realised she didn't have her iPod. The man was already talking on the telephone behind the desk, and waved her back in the direction of the studio in answer to her anxious, pocket-searching gestures.

Dumping her bags, she entered the studio and opened what she thought was the concealed door to the changing room, finding herself instead in a small office containing a computer, a desk and various metal filing cabinets. Flustered, she backed out, selecting another door which turned out to be a store cupboard. On the third attempt she successfully located the changing room, immediately spotting her iPod lying in the dust and fluff on the unswept floor.

She could hear the murmured telephone conversation coming to an end so she hurried out, suddenly desperate to get away without having to exchange any more conversation. She had seen something on the computer screen in that tiny office room which made her scalp prickle, but it was only later, as she was walking home to

Auntie Jackie's thinking back over the whole experience, that she realised its significance. It was a webcam image of an empty, white-walled room. Empty apart from a mirror, a chair and a pair of ghostly tights.

At the end of Rachel's account – here retold without her digressions or my astonished interruptions – she looked at me with the most abject expression, as if she was the one who was somehow guilty.

"Why would he bother spying on you?" I asked her. "I mean, you'd already been prancing around in your bikini quite willingly."

"Yeah, but to get in and out of it I had to strip right off."

"Maybe it was just a security camera, like our one at home."

"Security for what? There was nothing in the changing room to nick. No. He was obviously filming me getting undressed."

"Oh, Rachel."

"And now he's probably put it on the internet for all his pervy mates."

"We should tell Auntie Jackie."

"No!"

"Why not?"

"Because it's so *humiliating*, people knowing. It was bad enough telling you." She wiped her eyes on the corner of the duvet cover, leaving inky smears on the white cotton.

"But that's why people like him get away with it. You should go to the police."

"No way. Then there'll be a load of pervy policemen looking at pictures of me on his laptop. I'd have to go to court and it'd get in the papers." Her voice rose as each fresh implication dawned on her.

"Not all policemen are pervy," I said, feeling bound to defend Dave-the-ratcatcher, as well as the nice people from the anti-terrorist squad who were now watching our house in Oxford.

"Promise you won't talk about this to anyone ever."

"OK. But perhaps you should at least report him to the woman from the modelling agency. So she doesn't use him any more."

Rachel shook her head with impatience at my naivety. "There is no modelling agency. It's a scam. I went to the address in London on that business card she gave me to check it out."

"When?"

"On the way back from Frankie's party. That's why I was so late home. It was a grotty little side street off

Tottenham Court Road. There was no modelling agency there – just a flat above a kebab shop. When I rang the bell, this Chinese woman came to the door. She didn't speak very good English, but she said she'd been there for six months and didn't know who lived there before that." Rachel sighed noisily. "We should have known that Mags woman was a phoney just from her trousers," she added spitefully.

"So if you won't go to the police, what are you going to do?"

"There must be a way of hacking into his computer and destroying any images stored on it. Infecting it with a virus or something so it stuffs up the hard drive. Why didn't I pay more attention during IT lessons?" She turned a blotchy face towards me. "If only we knew someone who could do that sort of thing."

I got there a fraction of a second before her. "We do," I replied.

# A Promise is (usually) a Promise

"He should be here by now," said Rachel, using her longest nail to score a noughts and crosses board in the foam on her cappuccino. Like most people who are always late she hated being kept waiting by others.

"It's only one minute past," I said, though I was equally impatient to get the thing over with. It was midday and we were sitting in an Italian deli, not quite opposite the smeared and dusty shopfront of a photography studio called A Thousand Words. Behind this murky glass were a few framed prints which showed off the photographer's art. A bride in a frothy off-the-shoulder dress peeped coyly between some overhanging branches of cherry blossom; a barefoot family group lounged on a pile of beanbags; a girl in a pink prom dress posed stiffly with her date, who looked about as comfortable as if he still had the coat hanger inside his dinner jacket. I couldn't help thinking that it was an unlikely setting for criminal operations. But then again, it seemed equally unlikely as a launch pad for a modelling career, so perhaps Rachel's suspicions were well-founded. For the thousandth time since she had told me her sorry tale, the same ungenerous thought crossed my mind: *How can someone so bright be so stupid?*

Presently, the bell above the door jangled and Adam walked in. He must have cycled over as he was still wearing his helmet: tufts of his curly hair poked between the plastic slats. He bought a bottle of Lucozade Sport from the chiller cabinet before joining us at the table.

"Hello," said Rachel sheepishly. "Thanks for doing this."

"Don't thank me yet. I might not get anywhere. Have you done me a floor plan?"

Rachel handed over a sketch she had made of the interior of the building, showing the layout of the various rooms: the reception area, studio, changing room and the crucial doorway.

"What's that blob?" he asked, screwing up his face.

"That's the desk where the laptop was," Rachel explained.

"OK. You ready?" he said to me. "Know what you've got to do?"

"Yes, but I warn you, I'm a rubbish actress. I didn't even get in the chorus for *South Pacific* at school."

"Oh, there won't be any singing involved," Adam reassured me.

"Good luck," said Rachel.

"If we're not out in half an hour, call the police," he instructed her. "Only joking," he added as she looked anxiously at her watch. "We don't want the police involved. We're the criminals now."

Adam's immediate response, when I had told him a much-condensed version of the scam, was that it was a police matter and not something for amateurs. Privately I agreed with him, but Rachel must have superior powers of persuasion because as soon as she got hold of him, he allowed himself to be convinced in no time.

"What are you expecting me to do exactly?" Adam wanted to know.

"Well, can't you somehow hack into the computer and delete all the files?" asked Rachel.

"Just like that? You've been watching too many movies," he said.

"Can't you send him an email with a virus attachment which would stuff up the hard drive?"

"He's hardly likely to give us his private email address, is he? Or to open a strange email for that matter."

"You could steal the laptop and then if it turns out not to have anything dodgy on it, just return it anonymously."

"Oh, thanks. I'd really rather avoid a criminal record if you don't mind. My CV is shaky enough as it is."

"I thought you were supposed to be a computer whiz. Didn't you tell us you had hacked into the university exam system and changed your grades?"

"I might have exaggerated," Adam conceded. "Leave it with me. I'll think of something. I can't do anything from here though. I'd have to get access to the actual laptop." He turned to me. "I don't suppose you fancy pretending to be another would-be supermodel?"

I gave him a look that would have turned butter rancid at fifty paces.

"I thought not," he said. "You're way too sensible."

It wasn't exactly a belter of a compliment, but it could have been so much worse.


As Adam and I crossed the road from the café to the photography studio, I felt a surge of anxiety and I wondered whether other criminals suffered from this form of stage fright before a job. It wasn't so much a twinge of conscience as fear of being caught out, an outcome which seemed all too likely given our inexperience in the field of cyber-vandalism. For some reason, I didn't have much confidence in Adam's acting ability. Charlie, I felt, would have been a much more competent liar.

The reception area was empty when we entered, but a buzzer sounded somewhere deep in the building to warn of our arrival and a moment later the proprietor appeared, just as Rachel had described him, minus the streaming cold.

Adam and I immediately produced matching fake smiles, which must have screamed insincerity to all but the most trusting. Fortunately the beneficiary of our lousy acting was preoccupied with trying to silence the buzzer, which continued to sound because Adam had left the door slightly ajar, in readiness for a quick exit.

"Yes? Can I help?" he asked, when he had shut us in and retreated behind his counter.

"Well, yes, I hope so..." I had barely begun my well-rehearsed speech when a door to our right opened – leading to the studio, if Rachel's diagram was accurate – and a girl came out, carrying an overstuffed canvas holdall from which various items of clothing bulged. She had striking red hair and the bluish-white skin that often accompanies it, and she looked familiar, but it was a moment or two before I remembered where I had seen her before: on the wall outside Auntie Jackie's house, the day I had gone out jogging.

"All done?" said the man. "Lovely. I'll be in touch."

The girl nodded and then, as she caught sight of me, her face seemed to tighten and blush slightly with the effort of disguising the fact that *she* had recognised *me*. Then she gathered her features back into neutral and hurried out of the shop. It was all very odd.

This encounter had interrupted me mid-sentence so when the photographer said, "Sorry, you were saying?" I was momentarily at a loss, and it was left to Adam to butt in and finish my speech.

"It's our parents' twenty-fifth wedding anniversary next month and we were thinking of getting a big family portrait done. But we wanted some idea of costs and the sort of thing you do," he said, and took a swig of Lucozade from his bottle to hide his embarrassment. It reminded me of the way contestants on TV quiz shows always take a little sip of water after they've answered a question right.

The man ducked behind the counter and pulled out an album of laminated prints to show us, while Adam shot me an urgent look which I interpreted as "Get a grip".

We turned the pages of the album, nodding judiciously over the examples of rigidly posed family groups, occasionally pointing at one or other setting that we felt our fictitious parents would particularly like and trying not to look shocked at the prices.

"Is there any chance we could see the studio?" I asked. "Just to get an idea of the space." This was meant to be Adam's line, but we seemed to have swapped roles.

"There are quite a few of us," Adam explained. "Cousins and stuff."

"Sure." The man opened the door through which he had recently emerged and showed us into a bright, white room with a curved screen from floor to ceiling, and lighting apparatus. My eyes immediately sought out the concealed doorways in the far wall.

"A lot of people are going for the less formal portrait nowadays," he said, picking up a piece of artboard on which was mounted a poster-sized print of a family having a pillow fight.

"I don't think my granny would be up for that," Adam remarked off script, and I couldn't help laughing, even as

I realised that the word "my" was a mistake. Fortunately the man failed to notice this lapse, distracted as he was by the telephone shrilling in reception. Even though I was expecting it, I flinched violently at the sound. This phone call was no happy coincidence: it was Rachel's job, from her vantage point in the café, to call the man up on her mobile as soon as she saw us all disappear into the studio.

"Excuse me while I get that," he said, returning the way we had come and leaving us alone in the studio. Wasting no time, Adam crossed the floor in two strides and located the tiny back office which was our target, at the same time shooing me in the direction of reception so that I could waylay the man with some questions about prices in case Rachel failed to keep him talking.

"Yes... I can do that... mmm... .yes.... mmm..." he was saying, in the falling tones of someone whose attention is flagging, as I rejoined him, closing the door carefully behind me. He covered the receiver with his hand and mouthed the word "Sorry" while rolling his eyes.

I tittered politely, wondering what on earth Rachel was finding to talk about. I risked a glance across the street. Through the misted glass of the café window I could just distinguish her outline at one of the tables.

The photographer's contributions to the conversation

had dwindled to an occasional grunt. He held the receiver at arm's length for a moment, before replacing it to his ear, so that I could hear the caller's breathless chirruping.

"OK, do that, that's the best thing," he said when the torrent of words had slowed to a trickle. "Goodbye." He hung up, exhaling breezily. "Women do go on sometimes," he said to me, as if I wasn't one. And then Adam was there behind me, the faintest pressure from his fingers on the top of my arm letting me know it was done and we should go.

"Well, that all sounds great, Mr... er..." I said, waving the promotional leaflet and price list which I had picked up from the counter and moving towards the exit.

"Gundry."

"Mr Gundry. I think this looks like just what we're after."

"As soon as we can get the whole clan together, we'll be in touch to arrange a session," said Adam, steering me out through the door ahead of him.

"Right. Bye then," said Mr Gundry, looking slightly puzzled at the sudden evaporation of our curiosity.

Aware that he was probably still watching, we strolled along the street, as casually as our shredded nerves would let us, and it was only when we were safely around the corner and out of sight that we broke into a run.

"Did you do it?" I gasped, racked with stitch, when we finally stopped for breath in the safety of Asda car park.

He nodded. "System well and truly disabled."

"How?" I asked, marvelling at the unfathomable talent of geeks. "Did you manage to hack into it?"

"God, no. There wasn't time for that." He held up his empty drink container. "I just poured half a bottle of Lucozade Sport into the hard drive. It's well and truly knackered now."

Rachel joined us five minutes later, wheeling Adam's bike, which was too tall to be comfortably ridden. We had agreed not to head straight home in case we were followed, but this precaution turned out to be unnecessary: we had given Mr Gundry no reason to be suspicious and it might be hours before he discovered the damage. Rachel could tell from our smug expressions that we had succeeded before we had even said a word, and rewarded us with hugs and high fives, and then we were all laughing with relief and talking over each other, to make sure nobody's part in the drama went unacknowledged.

"Lucozade?" Rachel echoed, astounded at this particular

revelation. "I thought you were supposed to be Brighton's answer to Bill Gates."

"Sometimes simple solutions are the best," Adam insisted.

"What did you find to talk about on the phone for so long?" I asked Rachel. "You seemed to be babbling on for ages."

"Oh, I gave him this great story about wanting a portrait of my dog, and how flash photography made it go hyper and bite people. And I did it all in a Scottish accent so he wouldn't recognise me," she added proudly. "I think it was Scottish anyway."

Beneath all the excitement, I still felt a tiny twinge of uneasiness. Suppose Mr Gundry was after all quite innocent and we had caused untold damage and destruction to his business? Would he perhaps even now be calling the police and giving them a detailed description of me and Adam? I summoned up the courage to mention these doubts and risk poisoning the atmosphere, but Adam was quick to reassure me.

"There's no innocent reason for having a webcam in a changing cubicle," he said. "When I went into the little office it was still filming and that girl had just come out – the one who passed us in reception. He must have been spying on her. I don't think Mr Gundry is going to be contacting the police any time soon. They're the last people he'd want crawling all over his sleazy little business. I think it's more likely that our stunt on the computer is going to make him panic and head for the hills."

"Good," said Rachel. "The further the better."

I couldn't help feeling that although we might have solved *her* problem, we hadn't really solved *the* problem.

Later, when Rachel and I were back at Cliff Street and skulking in my basement room, while Auntie Jackie saw a client upstairs for a fitting, Rachel said, "I don't think I really wanted to be a model anyway. It's all so shallow."

"It's probably not as much fun as people think," I agreed.

"All that pouting and posing. You feel like a right prat." She sashayed up to my dusty mirror and peered at herself critically. "Do my teeth look a bit yellow to you?"

"No. Why?"

"Oh, no reason. It's just something that Gundry bloke said. I was asking him about digital photos and if he could airbrush out the mole on my neck, and he said, yes, he could do that and he could even make my teeth look whiter."

"He probably just meant it as an example of what they can do. He didn't mean it personally."

"Mmm," Rachel said, non-committally, continuing to inspect her smile from different angles.

"Adam's got nice teeth," she said a moment later. "I couldn't kiss a guy with horrible teeth, could you?"

*Who said anything about kissing Adam?* I wondered.

"You know he's asked me to go to a ball with him in a couple of weeks? Some posh do at the Grand Hotel."

"I knew he was going to," I admitted. "What did you say?"

"I couldn't very well refuse, could I, after what he did this morning. I owe him a favour."

*That's the difference that beauty makes*, I thought. If someone offered to take me to a £200 ball, I would naturally assume that *he* was doing *me* the favour, but Rachel's sense of entitlement was made of far sterner stuff.

# Confusing Behaviour

Rachel wasted no time in choosing herself a ball dress from the shop, managing by some unerring instinct for luxury to settle on the most expensive in the entire collection – a champagne-coloured, backless column of slipperiest silk, held up by strings of seed pearls and sheer willpower it seemed to me. Auntie Jackie didn't mind – a ball at the Grand was good for business, which had been rather slack recently, and it wasn't long before the phone was ringing and her disintegrating diary was once more filling up with appointments.

I was back on reception and tea-making duties, for which Auntie Jackie would slip me the odd fiver. It was also my responsibility to keep the entrance hall tidy: as at home, Rachel was in the habit of coming in, kicking off her shoes and dumping whatever she was carrying at the bottom of the stairs before proceeding on her way. Charlie, too, was not above leaving his crash helmet and gloves on the trunk, next to Auntie Jackie's vase of carefully arranged flowers.

One afternoon, while Auntie Jackie was helping a client to choose between safe black and the more daring emerald green, I came into the kitchen to prepare the tea tray – china cups, teapot, Earl Grey, lump sugar with little silver tongs – to find Charlie balancing a packet of frozen peas on his head. It was the first time I had seen him since the wasp episode: Auntie Jackie had not exaggerated when she said he was seldom around.

He had the contents of the medicine drawer spread out on the worktop in front of him. "What is all this stuff?" he asked me, discarding box after box of pills. "Xyzal, Zimovaine, Diclofenac, St John's wort, glucosamine. Christ, she must be a raging hypochondriac. All I want is a paracetamol."

"Have you got a headache?" I asked brightly, fetching down the posh cups and saucers and checking the sugar bowl for mouse droppings.

"Yes. I always seem to get one at this time of day. Why would that be, do you think?"

"I don't know. Look it up on the internet. There are these sites where you type in all your symptoms and they tell you what you've got."

"Oh, they're useless," said Charlie, discarding the peas and ripping into a box of ibuprofen which he had discovered buried under the pile of packets. "I tried one of those and it told me there was an eighty per cent chance I was pregnant."

I burst out laughing.

"One of the questions was, 'Are you currently having periods? Yes or No.' So I ticked No."

Auntie Jackie came whisking in. "Client wants a glass of water," she said, and then caught sight of the upturned medicine drawer and raised her eyebrows.

"Charlie's got a headache." I explained. "He gets one at the same time every day."

"That's funny," said Auntie Jackie. "So do I. Usually about five minutes after he starts playing his trumpet." Having scored this unexpected hit she departed in triumph.

"She fancies me is what it is," Charlie said to me, projecting his voice up the stairs after her.

In the shop, the client – an auburn haired woman of about forty – had been persuaded to take the emerald-green dress which was now hanging on a rail by itself awaiting minor adjustments. It was a proper red-carpet affair, with a stiff, beaded top and a full skirt billowing miles of taffeta.

"Long gloves are such a faff," the woman was saying, as Auntie Jackie brought out pair after pair for her inspection. "And they leave the worst bit of your arms showing anyway."

"A little lace shrug is great for hiding bingo wings," Auntie Jackie replied, slapping her own chumpy upper arm to demonstrate. "Although you're nice and slim - you probably don't need one as much as I do," she conceded.

I put the tea tray down on the coffee table, well out of range of the precious dresses. In the background Auntie Jackie's CD of fifty great waltzes was playing faintly. *A nice touch that*, I thought. Soothing.

"I'm not being very decisive, am I?" the client said, looking more interested in the tea than the gloves. "I don't really do dressing up. I'm happier in jeans and a T shirt."

"Oh, so am I," lied Auntie Jackie, who wouldn't even leave the house unless her handbag matched her shoes. "Some people love clothes and others just want to be comfortable. My eldest niece, she'd wear a new designer outfit every day if she had the chance, but this one," – she indicated me, beaming as if she was about to bestow a huge compliment – "prefers slobbing around in a pair of old trackies."

I slunk out of the room, blushing. I hadn't really considered myself as someone who was guilty of "slobbing around". It was such a revolting expression: it made me think of one of those grey rope-headed mops, sloshing dirty water back and forth across a floor. It was true that I'd never made much effort with my appearance: there was no point trying to compete with Rachel in the looks department so it had always seemed more dignified not to bother. No one wants to bust a gut to come second out of two.

It was the same with music. Rachel started playing the piano when she was seven, and although I was really envious because it was Mum's piano, when it came to my turn, I didn't want to play an instrument at which Rachel already had a head start, so I chose the clarinet. Then, of course, Rachel quit a year later because she didn't like the teacher's haircut or something, so now we've got a huge, silent piano at home which none of us can play.

I made my way back downstairs, drawn by the unmistakable smell of frying. The atmosphere was decidedly foggy and, as I opened the kitchen door, I was almost beaten back by billows of greasy smoke. Charlie stood at the stove, tending a pan of spitting sausages, oblivious to the pollution he was causing. Any moment Auntie Jackie would have to show her client out, from the sanctuary of Johann Strauss and Earl Grey and silver sugar tongs, into a hallway which stank like a chip shop. I started to feel nervous on Charlie's behalf. My ears strained to pick out the sound of the front door, which would give us about ten seconds before Auntie Jackie came storming down the stairs to give him a mouthful.

"Is your headache any better?" I asked Charlie, who was now applying a thick layer of butter and a smear of mustard to four slices of white bread.

He blinked at me through the smoke. "Not really. But I think these sausages will see it off." He fished them out of the bubbling fat with a slotted spoon and dumped them on the bread, constructing two unwieldy sandwiches. "Would you like one?" he said, passing me the plate.

I shook my head in amusement.

"This is just a snack," he explained, "but one day I'll cook you my world famous battered squid."

"Please don't," I laughed, pushing open the back door to let out the smoke and finding it blocked by an obstacle, which turned out on further investigation to be Dave-the-policeman, crouching on the patio like a burglar.

"Oh, hello," I said, nonplussed by this discovery.

"Hi," Dave whispered, straightening up slightly, but still keeping close to the back wall of the house.

"Er… are you coming in?" I gave the door a few wafts to ventilate the kitchen.

"Is she finished up there yet?"

"Not quite," I found myself whispering back.

He hesitated and looked at his watch. "I'll give it a few more minutes," he said, giving me a wink before squatting back down.

This was bizarre in the extreme. Admittedly we were supposed to keep a low profile when a client was visiting, and Auntie Jackie had been known to chuck Charlie's biker boots out of the back window when he'd left them in the middle of the hallway, but it seemed quite a leap from this to making Dave wait out in the garden. I began to wonder if I was the only person in the house who was entirely sane.

A clatter of shoes on the stairs and a burst of

cheerful singing proclaimed the arrival of Rachel back from work. She had left the tattoo parlour and had found a job in a pub kitchen through a friend of Auntie Jackie, two lunchtimes and two evenings a week. She wrinkled her nose at the fatty smell then brightened at the sight of Charlie, who was now well into his second sandwich.

"Oh, that looks nice," she said wistfully. "I've been serving up food all lunchtime and I never had time to eat."

Charlie obligingly offered her his sandwich, now missing a large bite. I wondered whether she would accept and was surprised to see Rachel, who was usually so fastidious and would freak out over sub-atomic specks of "dirt" on cutlery, take a mouthful from the crescent-shaped indentation in the bread where Charlie's teeth had so recently been.

"Too much mustard," she said indistinctly as she handed back what was left.

Charlie clicked his tongue at this display of ingratitude, but it didn't stop him offering her a second bite, or her accepting, and they continued to share the remainder of the sandwich in this way until it was gone.

Auntie Jackie came into the kitchen, but instead of laying into Charlie, stood in the doorway looking preoccupied, as though trying to remember what she was doing there.

"Another satisfied customer?" asked Charlie brightly.

"What?" asked Auntie Jackie vaguely. "Oh… yes… yes."

"Dave's here," I said. "In the garden."

That seemed to wake her up. "*Dave?*" she echoed. She couldn't have been more shocked if I'd told her Elvis was lurking in the shrubbery. She strode across the room and flung the door open. No Dave.

"Perhaps he got bored with waiting," I said, trying to be helpful.

"Why was he out in the garden?" Rachel asked. "Was he having a fag?"

"No," I admitted, happy to share my bafflement with the company. "He was just sort of crouching."

"He was probably trying to get some fresh air," said Auntie Jackie, catching up with the Charlie issue at last. "Do you have to start frying sausages at three o'clock in the afternoon when I've got a customer in? I'm trying to create a bit of ambience up there, you know. A bit of class. It's like trying to run a dress shop out of a kebab van."

"I have to eat early," Charlie protested. "I've got to get up to the Haymarket and be in the orchestra pit by seven. The show must go on."

Auntie Jackie shook her head, still looking out into the garden. She wasn't really giving the matter her full attention – to Charlie's relief. "Oh, and speaking of ambience and class," he went on, attack being the best form of defence, "I found another dead mouse in my room – underneath the boiler."

"Well, if it's dead, what's the problem? You don't expect me to set a trap for a dead mouse?" Auntie Jackie retorted.

"Why do they have to keep coming into my room to die?" said Charlie gloomily.

"When are you going to get me a ticket to your show, Charlie?" Rachel asked to head off a potential argument. "Didn't you say you could get free tickets sometimes."

"Sometimes," he conceded. "Or if you like jazz, my swing band does a set at the Indigo Club up the road here on Sunday nights."

"I work at the pub on Sunday night," Rachel said in a disappointed voice.

"Well, the West End run ends in a couple of weeks. I might be able to wangle something on the last night if you're interested."

"Definitely."

"I could take you up on the bike if we could borrow some leathers."

"That'd be cool," said Rachel.

"Absolutely not," said Auntie Jackie in horror. Then, without thinking, added, "The whole point of your coming here in the first place was to get out of danger not into it."

"Oh?" said Charlie, looking from Rachel to me with fresh interest. "What danger were you in then?"

"Oh, nothing," said Auntie Jackie, flustered by this slip-up. "I just meant that I'm supposed to be looking after them. How am I going to tell her father that I let her go off on the back of a motorbike with some disreputable character?"

"I am eighteen," Rachel protested.

"Am I really a disreputable character?" asked Charlie, greatly flattered.

"I bet you weren't such a good girl yourself," Rachel went on. This wasn't intuition: Dad had told us as much. "I bet you'd have gone off with a disreputable biker like a shot."

"Yes, but not with *permission!*" the former delinquent retorted. She was spared from having to defend this curious statement by her phone which suddenly burst into a tinny version of 'Walking in Memphis'.

She checked the caller's identity in the display before answering. "Hello, Dave," she said in a frosty voice, leaving the kitchen and closing the door on the rest of the conversation.

"Sounds like Dave's in the poo," said Rachel. "I wonder what he's done."

We shook our heads in a moment of silent sympathy. "Hope he's got his flak jacket handy," said Charlie.

"He's probably calling for back-up as we speak," said Rachel, and we all laughed disloyally.

Charlie stood up, dumping his plate and frying pan in the sink and looking guiltily at his watch. "I'd better be off," he said. "Don't want to miss the overture. Sorry about the washing up. I'll do it tomorrow if I'm here. Or the next day or something. Promise."

"Don't worry. I'll do it," Rachel offered, jumping to her feet. Another baffling example of someone acting wholly out of character! I pretended to topple back off my stool in astonishment, earning myself a glare from Rachel.

"Farewell then, my lovelies," said Charlie, and he departed in the buoyant mood of someone escaping the domestic arena for better, higher things.

As soon as he had gone, of course, Rachel had second thoughts about the washing up. "This pan is gross," she declared, peering at it through the fatty water. "Better leave it to soak." She went off upstairs and changed into her red tankini and spent the rest of the afternoon on a sunlounger in the back garden, drinking Auntie Jackie's Pimm's.

It was only much later that evening when I was lying in the bath, partially submerged so that the water in my ears blocked out all external noise, and thinking over the events of the day, that I experienced a greatly overdue glimmer of intuition. It wasn't a blinding flash so much as a gradual lifting of fog, so that a picture began to emerge and the various odd things that had bothered me began to make sense. Dave was no ordinary policeman and no ordinary "boyfriend". He was here, I was now convinced, by arrangement with Dad and the anti-terrorist police, who had been watching the house in Oxford, to keep an eye on me and Rachel. This explained his peculiar behaviour this afternoon: skulking around the back of the house like a spy. It also accounted for his frequent comings and goings during the day, when he should otherwise have been at work. Perhaps we were his work!

If he really was Auntie Jackie's boyfriend, he didn't take her out much. In fact, now I came to think of it, they had never actually been *out* anywhere together in all the time Rachel and I had been staying at Cliff Street. Auntie Jackie had never even introduced him as her boyfriend –

she'd called him her handyman and saviour or something daft. It was Rachel who had drawn that conclusion, and implied that I was the airhead for not having worked it out myself. There was no reason, of course, why Dave couldn't be involved in covert surveillance as well as being Auntie Jackie's boyfriend. The one might very well have led to the other – quite rapidly given that Auntie Jackie was not exactly the shy and retiring sort where men were concerned.

I was so pleased with my theory that I cut short my bath, and wrapped in a dressing gown and turban, padded damply into Rachel's room to share it with her.

She was sitting on her bed, forcing a set of foam separators between her toes so she could paint her nails. She heard me out and when I'd finished, she said the strangest thing. She came hobbling over on her heels, varnished toes splayed, and gave me a hug which made my towel turban collapse. "Oh, Robyn," she said into my shoulder. "You're so innocent. Don't ever change."

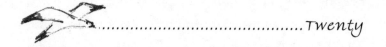 

# Twenty

# LBDs and All that Jazz

One Sunday morning I was replying to a text from Dad and was just thumbing in **Miss you loads** when I realised with some shock that it wasn't true. I hardly missed him at all. In fact, unless something happened to jog my memory that he actually existed, he barely figured in my thoughts from one day to another.

The truth was I had been enjoying the parentless freedom of Auntie Jackie's rather lax establishment, and since I had recovered from that initial bout of illness, hadn't had much time to be homesick. Having admitted these feelings to myself, I felt so pierced with guilt, imagining Dad in various kinds of peril, all of which would now be my fault, that I immediately rang him to check that he was all right and tell him how much I was missing him!

The sound of his voice, and his evident pleasure that I had bothered to ring, was another jab to my conscience, and in a complete reversal of my original position, I found myself welling up with tears and begging him to come and visit us soon.

He promised to try and organise a Monday or Friday off work so that he could come for a long weekend, and I repeated Auntie Jackie's offer to put him up here at Cliff Street. He wanted to know all the news, but as I wasn't allowed to mention the most interesting event – Rachel's photo-shoot and its aftermath – I confined myself to details of her new job and the invitation to the ball at the Grand Hotel. "What about you?" he wanted to know.

"Nothing much happens to me," I said.

"You haven't been getting up to anything you shouldn't?"

The question was sufficiently vague to deserve only the vaguest sort of denial. "Nothing major."

The most significant news from his end concerned the letter bomb. According to the police, it wasn't a proper bomb at all. Although the parcel had contained various *ingredients* for a bomb – a timing device, liquid explosive, wires, broken glass and nails – the timer hadn't been connected and there was no detonator. In other words, there was no possibility that it could have exploded. This information – which sounded like good news to me – seemed to have caused Dad more disgust than relief, as though the amateurishness and general incompetence of modern terrorists was just another example of falling standards. I couldn't see it that way myself.

It turned out, too, that Dad had been sitting on this news for some time. "I didn't want you thinking it was safe to come home. You're better off where you are."

"Have you been back home at all?"

"Only to pick up the post. The garden's looking a bit neglected. I might go and cut the grass this afternoon."

"Don't!" I exclaimed. "You just said yourself it wasn't safe. Who cares about the grass?"

"There hasn't been any activity at the house since we left. They've put cameras in the Jerrolds' place opposite, and there's been nothing. But, OK, you're right. Stuff the gardening. I'll go and play golf instead."

He finished by asking how the money was lasting and I must have said, "Oh, OK, I think," with just the right amount of hesitation and wistfulness as he promised to put a cheque in the post on Monday.

By the end of the night I had every reason to feel relieved that Dad hadn't chosen this particular weekend to come and stay.

I'd spent the evening helping Auntie Jackie to undo the hundreds of spindly braids in her hair, a process which involved unwinding lengths of cotton and rows of wooden beads, with scissors being called upon as a last resort, before carefully unplaiting every strand. She had decided that (overnight) she had become too old for this particular look and needed something sleeker and more groomed as befitted a mature woman. There was nothing sleek and groomed about the result however. After two hours of painstaking work, Auntie Jackie's neat braids had been transformed into a clump of dull purple frizz like a thatched roof, which moved as one piece when she shook her head. I was mildly surprised to learn that the previous style had been all her own hair – I had assumed that it was made up of extensions and bits and pieces clipped on afterwards, and that once it was dismantled, she would be left with a scalp like a clipped poodle.

"I feel so light I could float away," she said, trying and failing to run a hand through the thatch. "Shame I look like a Gonk. I hope to God no one calls round." She was also dismayed to discover that without the facelift effect of the tightly pulled braids, her face now looked slacker and more tired. "I've aged five years in five minutes!" she wailed at her reflection in the dressing-table mirror.

"Well, you wanted to look more mature," I reminded her.

She gave me a slap on the bum with the flat back of a wooden hairbrush, catching me at the perfect angle so that it rang with pain. I could just imagine what a "hands-on" parent she would have made and I had a sudden memory of one of those wildlife documentaries where a lion playfully cuffs one of its cubs with a giant paw, sending it bowling away in the dust. Possibly it was her shaggy mane that prompted this train of thought.

For supper she had roasted a chicken, and we ate half of it cold with bread and coleslaw, and then picked at the carcase on the carving dish until we'd stripped it clean. It was an unusually successful meal by Auntie Jackie's standards.

When I had praised her cooking and done the washing up, I thought I had amassed enough credit to ask if I could use the computer, but she looked so crestfallen at the suggestion that I immediately backtracked. It was my company she wanted: the others were out – Rachel working at the pub and Charlie off somewhere on his motorbike – and there was nothing on TV.

"I thought we could play Scrabble," Auntie Jackie wheedled. According to the evidence on the whiteboard on the kitchen wall, she and Charlie were engaged in a long-running Scrabble tournament in which both parties shared a positively gladiatorial will to win. The score in games stood at 21–19 to Charlie – a source of much gloating and exchanges of scrawled insults on the whiteboard. I suppose Auntie Jackie saw me as a sort of training partner.

Although I was itching to get online, I naturally caved in to her request and in the course of the game that followed, learnt something about my aunt that I didn't know before: she can't spell. Again and again I'd catch her taking liberties with even quite ordinary words like "adress" and "suprise", and when I challenged her, she would start blustering and insist that she was used to American spellings. I could see that winning was important to her, so I did my best to lose without making it look too obvious, which wasn't easy as she had a run of lousy letters. It was such a relief when she finally put down a seven-letter word and stormed into the lead that I didn't have the heart to point out that "paultry" didn't actually exist.

The only way to avoid a rematch was to go to bed, so I gave Auntie Jackie a hug and left her flicking through *Hair & Beauty* magazine in search of a new look.

I sat up reading for a while, until my eyelids felt droopy, and had just put down my book when I heard heavy footsteps descending to the basement. A moment later, there was an urgent knocking on my door and Charlie barged in without waiting for an answer.

"Ronnie, thank God you're awake. I need you," he said briskly.

"Wh... what for?" I said, taken aback by this sudden visitation. He had the air of a man on a mission and I envisaged another battle with wasps, mice or worse.

"My sax player has come off his bike and bust his arm. You'll have to stand in. Quick. Get dressed. We're on in..." he checked his watch "...forty minutes." He strode across to the wardrobe and began rifling through my clothes.

"Who's we? On where?" This was far, far worse than mice.

"My band. We do a set at the Indigo Club at midnight.

No good, no good," he was muttering, skimming metal coat hangers along the rail, as he dismissed one after another of my clothes. "Haven't you got an LBD?"

"What's an LBD?"

"A little black dress. All girls are supposed to have one."

"Well, I haven't. Anyway, I can't play the saxophone."

"You told me you could," he said accusingly.

"Not in front of people!" I wailed.

"Don't be daft. Anyway, I'll bung you at the back and you won't even be seen."

"But I don't know the music! I can't just get out of bed and start playing at the drop of a hat. I'd have to practise for weeks." As I said the words "out of bed", I realised that I was actually out of bed and looking over Charlie's shoulder into the wardrobe, with no recollection of how I had got there.

"Oh, it's all easy-peasy jazz classics," he said, dismissing my whimperings of denial with a wave. "'Take the A Train.' 'How High the Moon.' You probably know most of them, and if you don't, just vamp along or mime or something. No one will hear you over the rest of us anyway. You won't be doing a solo."

"Well, if I won't be seen or heard, it won't really matter that I'm not there, will it?"

"Look. I've promised the management a five-piece swing band. I can't turn up with just four. The only problem is, what are you going to wear?"

"That isn't the problem!" I squeaked indignantly. "The problem is that I'm not doing it."

For a moment Charlie looked flabbergasted, as though he had never before experienced refusal in any form and had no idea how to proceed. He drew himself up, gathering fresh reserves of charm.

"You want me to grovel? All right, I'll grovel," he declared, throwing himself on to the floor at full stretch and grabbing hold of my ankles – easily the most ticklish part of me, and doubly untouchable because of their proximity to my bristly legs and hideous feet, which it seemed terrifyingly possible that Charlie was about to kiss.

My screams brought Auntie Jackie running from the kitchen. She stopped short as she took in the scene, which to the casual observer must have displayed all the elements of ritual abuse. "What the…?"

Charlie sprang up. "Jackie – darling – you've got to help us. Ronnie's got to play in the band tonight. She's being difficult about it, and *if I had world enough and time*, I know I'd be able to persuade her, but there isn't

197

time, dammit. I've got a cab waiting outside. And she needs a little black dress from your collection, right now. I wouldn't ask if it wasn't urgent."

The assault on my ankles had left me too traumatised to speak.

"Her name's Robyn, and you can't take her into the Indigo Club," Auntie Jackie was saying. "It's over-21s."

This detail had clearly not occurred to Charlie. "This is different," he improvised. "She's not a client – she's an *artiste*. Anyway, I'll smuggle her in the stage door with the band. I promise I'll look after her and bring her home in a cab afterwards."

"You'd better hope her father doesn't find out."

"He'd be proud of her. It's not every young musician who gets a chance to play with Charlie and the Gamblers."

Auntie Jackie rolled her eyes and departed in search of a little black dress. My own objections to the scheme had been left far behind.

Five minutes later I was sitting in the back of a cab trying to apply black eyeliner as we careered towards the town centre, and yelping every time we hit a pothole. I wondered if Charlie would still make me play if I put out both my eyes, and decided he probably would.

"Ray Charles was blind," he remarked as he watched my struggles, as if reading my mind.

I was wearing a black velvet cocktail dress, which was slightly too big, and a pair of gold pumps, which were slightly too small. "You look very pretty," he said, and even though I knew it was just a piece of typical Charlie charm, the pleasure I felt in the compliment was real and lasting.

The Indigo Club, despite its enticing name, looked like any large city pub, except that its lower windows were blacked out and decorated with peeling posters, advertising forthcoming attractions. One of the headline acts was a percussionist called Gunter Korner, which made me think of Auntie Jackie's pig, still unrepaired on my window seat. The "stage door" was down an unlit alley, past a row of overflowing wheelie bins, and led directly into the kitchens.

Carrying our instruments, Charlie led the way along an uncarpeted corridor, which felt sticky underfoot, into what he referred to as "the Green Room" – another colourful sounding place which didn't quite deliver on its name. The carpet was a dull red colour, scarred with blackened chewing gum, and the walls were papered in gold and brown stripes, faded in places and darkened by greasy headmarks in others. Although no one was now smoking, the whole room reeked of decades-old cigarette smoke.

Two blokes, dressed in dinner suits and black bow ties, were lounging on a scuffed leather sofa. One was idly warming up by making duck noises through his mouthpiece, while a third stood tuning his double bass. The band.

"Hey," said Charlie. "I got us a sax player to stand in for Ollie. This is Robyn."

"Hey, Robyn," said the band, as one. They didn't seem the least bit perturbed by this last-minute substitution. "This is Jack on drums, Al on bass and Sam on trombone," Charlie finished the introductions for my benefit and I smiled apologetically, for being an impostor and the wrong sex and six years too young to walk in through the front door.

"Where do you usually play, Robyn?" asked Sam when he had finished his duck impressions and reattached the mouthpiece to his trombone.

I glanced at Charlie for guidance, sensing that "St Cecilia's High School Senior Band" was not the answer that was required.

"This is her first gig," Charlie explained. "And she's only doing this as a favour, so be nice to her."

There were fifteen minutes left to rehearse: as soon as I picked up the absent Ollie's saxophone, I could tell it was a superior instrument to the tin can I was used to borrowing from school. The keys were so responsive, with just the right amount of spring, and when I gave an experimental run up and down the scale, the sound produced was smooth and chocolaty, without a trace of woolliness on the low notes, while the top notes were bright and true. It was a beauty. I couldn't even imagine how much it was worth.

Charlie ran through the programme, from which I identified four numbers that I knew reasonably well from band practice. For the rest, I was to ad-lib, mime, or just go offstage and get a glass of water.

"This is just a suggestion," said Jack, five minutes before the off. "But wouldn't it make more sense for Robyn to play what *she* knows, and we go along with that."

"Yeah, fine, whatever," said Charlie. "What else do you know, Robyn?"

"Er… 'St Louis Blues', er… 'Birdland'…" I said. A trawl through my memory of recent concerts brought our joint repertoire to seven. That still left me with a lot of miming, and the prospect of more glasses of water than even a case of acute dehydration would warrant in one evening. A final running order was agreed and I tucked the list, written on a scrap of poster torn from the Green Room wall, into the carrying strap of Ollie's sax.

"Let's go," said Charlie, giving the back of my neck a reassuring squeeze, before leading the way out on to the stage.

I have to admit that my miming skills were tested to the limit during the next forty-five minutes, and there were certainly moments when I wished I had gone to bed early and locked the door. The whole experience had similarities to an anxiety dream where you are in a public place and suddenly realise you're naked from the waist down. All those things, and more, were true. But it is also true that after the first two numbers, to which I managed to make a reasonable contribution, the cold sweat of fear began to evaporate, and I realised that no one in the audience was going to start pelting me with rotten fruit or demand my removal. Later still, once I had started to listen to the music properly, and appreciate what a great sound four professional jazz musicians and one floundering amateur can make, I actually began to relax.

Midway through the set, when Charlie took the microphone and introduced each of us to the audience – Al on bass, Ronnie on sax – and I got my own separate round of applause, which didn't seem to be fake or prompted by pity, I realised I was actually happy, enjoying myself and finally unafraid.

When the set was over, and we had taken some more applause, we retreated to the Green Room, where I was congratulated by the rest of the band. Now that I had apparently passed this initiation test, Charlie felt able to admit to the others that I was in fact only fifteen, to which they responded with polite expressions of disbelief and amazement.

"If we'd known you were so young, we wouldn't have thrown you in the deep end like that," said Jack, who had large turned-down eyes, which gave him a permanently mournful expression even when he was smiling, as he now was.

"Yes, we would," said Al.

"OK," Jack conceded. "But we'd have had the decency to feel bad about it."

"So same time next week then, Ronnie," said Sam, snapping home the catches on his trombone case.

I laughed non-committally, assuming this was a joke,

but a glance at Charlie told me that he was serious. "Ollie's not going to be playing again for ages," he confirmed. "You're hired."

Once again my own preferences seemed to be irrelevant. But that was the thing about Charlie: he was so charming and so persuasive, and it would have taken such a colossal effort of will to oppose anything he had decided on, that you found yourself roped into things that you would never have chosen in a million years, and then, bizarrely, enjoying them.

It was normal practice after a gig for the band to unwind with a few beers, but Charlie remembered his promise to Auntie Jackie and brought me back to Cliff Street in a cab. As it drew up outside the house, he produced a dog-eared envelope of cash from the pocket of his DJ and separated a new, unblemished fifty pound note from the pack.

I assumed this was to pay the driver, and was trying not to look outraged at the price when Charlie handed the money across to me with the words, "That's for you."

"Are you sure?" I hadn't considered *payment* as a factor. If only he had mentioned it earlier, the pleading and ankle-grabbing might not have been necessary.

"Of course. We don't play for nothing, you know.

Musicians are very particular about that sort of thing. Get a bunch of us together and all we talk about is money."

He jumped out to open the car door for me and see me safely inside, but said he wasn't coming in himself; the cab was taking him back to the club to rejoin the others.

"Were you serious about me playing next week?" I asked.

"Absolutely. I can't leave Ollie's sax with you till then because he's a bit attached to it, but I might be able to get my hands on another one for you to practise on before then. If you like."

"Yes please."

Someone had left the light on above the front door. As I fished in my bag for the key, Charlie's lips brushed my cheek.

"See you," he said as I let myself in, but when I turned back to wave, he'd been swallowed up by the darkness of the cab.

"Where the hell have you been?" said Rachel, glaring over the banister in the manner of a grouchy parent kept from sleep by anxiety. In truth, she had not long been home from her shift at the pub and had just come out of the shower.

"I've been playing sax at the Indigo Club," I said, as casually as possible. "In Charlie's band."

She did her best to conceal it, but I could see the news had rocked her. It was a reversal of the natural order that I should be out having fun while she was indoors, waiting. "Well, look at you," she said.

"It's one of Auntie Jackie's," I explained, plucking at the excess fabric. "It's too big."

"So how did you talk Charlie into letting you play in his band?"

"I didn't *talk him into it*," I replied loftily. "He asked me. In fact, he begged me. I didn't want to go at all, but he and Auntie Jackie sort of overpowered me. I'm playing next week too," I added, just to make a point.

Rachel's expression darkened again and she shook her hair back as though envious feelings could be dislodged by force. "I must come and watch," she said. "I'd quite like to go to that Indigo Club myself. I'll leave work early or go sick or something."

*Must you?* I thought, feeling suddenly territorial about the Indigo Club and the band, and even Charlie himself, who I considered chiefly my friend and my discovery since he had climbed in through my window.

"That would be nice," I said, adding with an air of

helpless apology, "but unfortunately it's over-21s…"

When you're the Little Sister, and the Plain One, you have to take your triumphs where you can.

# Twenty-one

# Mr Elkington

To celebrate the return of her Renault Clio from the garage, Auntie Jackie offered to take me out for a day trip deep into the Sussex countryside. The plan was to set off early and drive to Arundel, browse around the castle and the shops, have a pub lunch and then go to an antiques fair or a junk shop to look for bargains. Every so often, Auntie Jackie said, she had an overwhelming urge to spend money on something completely useless and impractical, and she felt one coming on now. Previous urges had led to the purchase of the one-stringed double bass and the archery target among other things. Unfortunately these funny turns always seemed to coincide with periods of direst poverty. This was no exception, so she hoped that my natural good sense would act as a restraining influence if she threatened to get carried away.

"If I start waving my credit card around too much, just say 'Ruth! Ruth!'" she said mysteriously.

We were slightly delayed in setting off by an unexpected delivery. I had opened the front door to discover a vast bouquet of lilies, carnations and long-stemmed roses advancing up the steps towards me. Behind it, her upper body completely obscured by the mass of cellophane and foliage, was the florist. "Flowers," she panted helpfully, bracing herself like a weightlifter to deposit them on the doorstep.

A small card, gripped by a plastic pitchfork among the blooms, revealed Auntie Jackie to be the recipient.

"How exciting!" she exclaimed, tearing into the tiny envelope. "It must be from Dave... It is from Dave. Silly old fool," she said fondly, tucking the card into her purse for safekeeping. "Now where the hell am I going to put all these? I haven't got a vase big enough."

It seemed a shame to break up the bouquet, so artfully arranged, so Auntie Jackie filled a bucket with water and propped the whole thing in a shady corner of the kitchen.

As we set off, I couldn't help sending up a private thank you to Dave myself – his gift had put Auntie Jackie in a tremendously good mood.

She had been to the hairdresser the day before to repair the aftermath of the braids and emerged, transformed, with a smart, flicked-up crop. The frizz was gone, and so was the curious shade of purple-with-grey-streaks – replaced by a more convincing chestnut brown. It made her look more intelligent, somehow, and calmer.

It was the first really hot day since we had arrived, with a brilliant blue sky and only a few modest clouds at the horizon, too far out to sea to present a threat. The sort of day that might have been better spent on the beach than inside a stuffy car or a chilly castle, but Auntie Jackie wasn't someone to be deflected from a mission. She admitted, when questioned, that she had never put so much as a toe in the sea in all the time she had lived in Brighton. "It's not the sort of thing you do on your own, is it? Unless you're a mad fitness fanatic. I suppose you can swim brilliantly. All the kids can nowadays."

I said I'd had lessons when I was young. "Dad wanted us to learn because we lived near the canal and he was worried we'd fall in."

"He was always a worrier, your dad. I suppose all

parents are. Anyway, I'm not criticising him: he's done a brilliant job of bringing up you two. Without any help from me," she added wistfully.

"You did help," I reminded her. "You came and lived with us in Oxford when I was a baby. Dad said you gave up your job in London and everything, just to look after us, and you were really great."

"He really said that?" Auntie Jackie sounded pleased.

Just outside Hove we hit a traffic jam – a column of cars crawling along the coast road in search of a parking spot, with more and more joining the queue. "Ah, the open road," sighed Auntie Jackie, as we sat, gridlocked, with the stench of hot exhaust and the indignant hooting of horns blowing in through the open windows. At the first opportunity she took a right turn off the promenade and into the town. Soon we were on the dual carriageway and chewing up the miles.

Arundel was a pretty town built on the skirts of a hill, and crowned by a medieval castle, with views right across the Sussex Downs. A short walk from the car park there was a café with a terrace overlooking the river, to which we headed for Auntie Jackie's first cappuccino of the day. She had an insatiable coffee habit, as evidenced by the wad of well-stamped loyalty cards in her purse. I'd tried many times to acquire a taste for the stuff because it always smelled so promising, and I liked the dinky espresso cups it was served in, but no amount of sugar could disguise its essentially dirty flavour. I had a similar relationship with champagne: I loved its reputation; I just wished it tasted a little more like Diet Coke.

Once Auntie Jackie had been successfully re-caffeinated, we made our way to the castle, which was a tasteful mixture of ancient and modern, and while part of it was open to the public, a large section was still used as a family home. Certain windows and parts of the battlements were discreetly boarded to preserve the privacy of the inhabitants. An occasional chink in the wood allowed a tantalising glimpse of the hidden life beyond: a wheelbarrow of gardening tools standing on an immaculate lawn; a sleek silver car on the gravel drive, its doors left wide open; one corner of a tennis court.

I could imagine myself tripping across the velvety grass with my pet peacock, my racquet under my arm ready for a quick knock-up with the gardener's gorgeous son, just to kill time before all my friends arrived for a weekend of partying in the fountains. I could picture it so clearly, and it seemed so absolutely right and proper that I should live in a moated castle rather than a Brighton basement with mice and the occasional rat, that for a moment I felt a great upsurge of indignation at the unfairness of things.

Then I thought of Auntie Jackie, who'd surrendered her living room for me, looked after me when I was sick, let me go to a nightclub with a Disreputable Character and was now trying her best to treat me to her idea of a fun day out, and was overcome with guilt at my ingratitude. There she was, brandishing her ancient Olympus camera at a Japanese tourist so that he could take a photo of the two of us looking windswept on the battlements. Of all the visitors milling around she had managed to pick the one non-English speaker. With much miming and hand-signalling, she instructed him in the art of pre-digital photography, and then scuttled over and stood beside me, smoothing her skirt and tugging her top down to display a bit more cleavage.

Remembering her previous comment about me "slobbing around in trackies" I had made a special effort to look presentable today in pink cropped jeans and a black vest with white spots. At least they had looked like spots in the subdued lighting of the shop – on closer inspection in daylight they had turned out to be tiny skulls.

Unlike Dad, who could easily spend all day looking round a stately home or museum, and insisted on reading every word on every display board, Auntie Jackie had a limited appetite for culture and whisked from room to room, hardly breaking her stride. In fact, she spent far longer in the gift shop looking at the souvenir mugs and tea towels than she did admiring the portraits or the furnishings in the castle. She was determined not to leave the place without a selection of merchandise – apron, paperweight, coasters, bookmark, guest soaps, notepad, keyring, thimble. It reminded me of Rachel, this mania for spending, and I suddenly understood why there was often the faintest atmosphere of antagonism between them; they were so similar, in lots of ways, and it bothered them to see their own least favourite qualities reflected back so faithfully.

"Ruth, Ruth!" I hissed obligingly, as a calligraphy set and a solid silver paper knife went into the shopping basket.

"Who's Ruth?" Auntie Jackie asked, picking up a bone-handled walking stick and hobbling a few paces as if trying it for size.

"I don't know. You told me to say Ruth if you start spending too much."

"Did I? What would I say that for…? Oh, *roof*," she said,

hooting with laughter. "God, yes, don't remind me."

"What about the roof?"

"It's falling in. Sagging like a hammock, according to the bloke who came to fix the guttering last year. The whole thing needs replacing, but unfortunately I don't happen to have twenty thousand pounds to hand."

"Oh dear," I said, thinking of Charlie up in the attic room. "Do you think it will actually fall down?"

"No, I shouldn't imagine it would just collapse in one go like that," Auntie Jackie said, without much conviction. "It might start leaking," she conceded. All the same, back went the calligraphy set and the paper knife and the coasters and, with a regretful glance, the walking stick.

"You'd better keep the paperweight," I advised. "You might need something to stop your papers blowing away when there's no roof."

We had lunch in a pub which came recommended by Dave as having particularly hearty food. We both chose steak and chips, served on red-hot iron skillets which arrived at the table still sizzling and spitting fat. When Auntie Jackie shook a sachet of vinegar out over her chips, it vaporised instantly, billowing up into her face in an acrid cloud, to the great amusement of the nearby diners. When you were out with Auntie Jackie, there was no hope of making yourself inconspicuous.

Her show of restraint in the gift shop had left her with an unsatisfied craving to spend, so having settled the bill, we made our way through the town in search of further temptation. The early afternoon sun was hot on my shoulders as we walked up towards the cathedral, the heat pressing down from a windless sky.

Outside the village hall a banner hanging limply from the fence announced: ANTIQUES, BRIC-A-BRAC, ADMISSION FREE. Auntie Jackie needed no further invitation and was in through the door and foraging before I could say "roof". I followed her in, my eyes struggling to adjust to the gloom of the interior, after the glare of sunlight on pavement. I found her examining the price tag on a large copper coal scuttle.

"You can't have a coal fire at home," I reminded her. "It'd make the dresses all sooty."

"I wasn't thinking of keeping coal in it. I could use it as an umbrella stand or a bread bin or something." She moved on, discouraged by my lack of imagination. I could tell she wasn't going to leave the place empty-handed. It was just the sort of Aladdin's cave of old junk that was guaranteed to tempt her. Trestle tables creaked and bowed under the weight of assorted dusty relics of glass and china, tarnished silverware, paintings, ornaments, jewellery and bits of horses' tack. Stallholders sat penned in by cliffs of clutter. Auntie Jackie was drooling over a wind-up gramophone player with a huge horn-shaped speaker. It came accompanied by a positively encyclopaedic collection of six records.

"Isn't this fabulous?" she said, practically swooning with pleasure. "So romant—" she broke off, her eye caught by something across the other side of the room and began to move towards it, entranced, as if pulled by an invisible force. "Mr Elkington!" I heard her say, as though greeting a long-lost friend, and was slightly taken aback to see that the subject of this rapturous reunion was in fact a full-sized human skeleton on a stand.

"We used to have one of these in the biology lab at school," she told me as I approached warily, repelled by the grinning skull's long, gumless teeth. "We called it Mr Elkington, after the head of science. People were always trying to kidnap him – the skeleton, not the head of science – and put him in silly places. The captain of the football team once got him as far as an away match. I think they put him in goal for the first half." She cackled to herself at these reminiscences, picking up the skeleton's long skinny hand and stroking it. "I wouldn't be surprised if it wasn't *the* Mr Elkington," she said, peering into his eye sockets. "It certainly looks like him."

Now that I was closer I could see that it wasn't an actual dead person, but a model made of some sort of hard plastic or resin, the bones held together in their properly articulated formation by metal hooks.

"I've got to get him," Auntie Jackie declared, rummaging in her purse. "He'd make a great hatstand."

"Or you could use him in the shop to model your size zero dresses," I suggested, and we both folded up, giggling.

The £75 price tag wiped the smile off Auntie Jackie's face, but after a period of haggling/flirting with the stallholder, she managed to beat him down to £60.

"Are you all done here?" she asked me, hoisting the stand up in the air so that Mr Elkington dangled and twitched alarmingly. "Let's go."

To say that I felt a little self-conscious walking through the middle of Arundel with a skeleton doesn't give quite the full flavour of the experience. Our progress certainly didn't go unremarked, and long before the bottom of the hill we had amassed quite a following of small children and dogs. By the time we had gained the sanctuary of the car park, I was sweating with embarrassment.

The Renault Clio was too small to accommodate Mr Elkington at full stretch, and Auntie Jackie was worried about having him protruding through the sunroof in case a gust of wind took his head off, so we finally dismantled the stand and sat him in the back, pinning him more or less upright with the seatbelt.

"Where are you going to keep him?" I asked.

"I'm not sure," Auntie Jackie replied, glancing in the mirror as if to check that he wasn't eavesdropping. "But I know where I'm going to put him tonight," she added, beaming at an elderly couple in a white Toyota, who had pulled up alongside us at the lights and were gazing at our passenger in some alarm.

"Where?"

"Charlie's bed. Can you imagine him coming back from the West End at three o'clock in the morning and finding that under his duvet?" She went into convulsions at the thought of it.

"He'll get you back," I warned her. "You know he will."

"Mmm, that's true." Auntie Jackie considered the possibility for a moment. "But it's too good an opportunity to miss. I'll just have to be on my guard."

Although I had to admit it was a good prank, I couldn't help feeling sorry for Charlie, and sorry in advance for Auntie Jackie for whatever revenge he took. I could see a certain inevitability in the pranks escalating. What would be the next surprise under the duvet? A crocodile? A python?

But Auntie Jackie wasn't going to be deflected. Every so often on the journey home, in the middle of an unrelated conversation, she would suddenly start tittering to herself all over again and I knew she was imagining the moment when Charlie innocently pulled back the bedclothes.

We arrived home at 4.30, in the heat of Brighton's day-long rush hour. Mr Elkington had collapsed against the back seat as though trying to keep out of the sun. The motorbike wasn't parked outside, which suggested Charlie had already left for London, but Auntie Jackie suggested I check indoors to make sure before she smuggled Mr Elkington in. She didn't want to ruin the joke by bumping into Charlie in the hallway.

Inside the house all was silent, the air warm and soupy as if long undisturbed. Minute particles of glittering dust moved sluggishly, stirred by the opening of the front door. Slowly, I climbed the stairs to Charlie's room, the floorboards setting up their familiar rhythm of creaks. *He's not here*, I thought. *He's never this quiet.* But for some reason

I kept going, all the way to the top of the house. The door to his bedroom was ajar: I could feel a thin breeze filtering on to the landing from his open window. I gave the handle a gentle push and stepped into the room, stopping just over the threshold in surprise. Lying on the bed, wearing nothing but a crumpled sheet, was Rachel, sleeping peacefully as though quite at home.

I backed out abruptly, my heart thudding in protest. The movement must have disturbed her because I heard the bed creak as I fled downstairs. By the time I had gained the sanctuary of the hallway, the sound of her footsteps descending was followed by the *click* of her bedroom door. I stood for a moment, paralysed, the blood crashing in my ears, unable to subdue a storm of emotions, until a reproachful hooting from the street reminded me that Auntie Jackie was still in the car awaiting the all-clear.

"You took your time," she said, as I ran down the steps. "Is it safe?"

"Yes," I said. "He's not there."

She looked at me strangely. "Your face is very red. Are you OK?"

"Yes," I insisted, my voice bright with denial. "I'm fine."

Leaving her to bring in Mr Elkington, I went back inside to seek refuge in my room. For some reason I didn't want to face Rachel just yet and have to make normal conversation while I was still seething. I needed a few moments alone to calm down and talk some sense into myself.

It wasn't simple jealousy I was feeling, but something more complicated and poisonous. I didn't want Charlie for myself: he was much too old to consider me as "girlfriend material", and there had never been a trace of romantic interest in his friendliness. I knew that. But it was typical of Rachel that, having already secured Adam's slavish devotion, she should switch her attention to Charlie the minute he singled me out for notice. The truth was she probably didn't much like either of them, but she was used to being the heroine of every story and had to assert herself against me. All these bitter thoughts were bubbling away as I clattered down the steps to the basement.

It was just as well that I hadn't intended to throw myself on the bed in a temper as there was an obstacle in the shape of a saxophone case in the way.

*Ronnie*, said the accompanying note. *I have managed to borrow a sax. It's not quite in the same league as Ollie's, as you will hear, but it might do for practice. Get blowin'. Charlie x*

I couldn't help smiling. This piece of thoughtfulness

was like a lifebelt, thrown out to rescue me from a dark whirlpool of self-pity, just at the point when I was about to go under.

# Twenty-two

# Bad Behaviour

Charlie failed to return that night. In fact, Mr Elkington was still lying in state, undisturbed, at the end of the week. It was hard to tell who was the more agitated by Charlie's non-appearance, Rachel or Auntie Jackie. Rachel was clearly mystified by his absence, and wondering if and why he had suddenly lost interest in her. Auntie Jackie was impatient to see the fulfilment of her prank.

I'd managed to avoid Rachel for most of the evening after finding her in Charlie's bed, but she had finally cornered me in my room, desperate to talk about him. There was a glittery-eyed excitement about her, as if she'd been drinking. But it wasn't drink unfortunately. It was love.

"Ohmygod," she said, throwing herself on to the bed where I was sitting and squashing herself up against me, "I think I'm in love. I think I actually am."

"Who with?" I said, deciding to act dumb just to be annoying. "Adam?"

"No, not *Adam*," she said impatiently. "*Charlie*. We just had the best time today. We totally clicked. It's like we've known each other for years. It's so weird."

*You hardly know him*, I thought. *I know him better than you do and I hardly know him.* I didn't say this of course. Instead I tried telling her about my day, but I could tell she wasn't really listening so we ended up having two separate conversations, taking it in turns to say our piece, while refusing to follow up what the other person was saying. "Auntie Jackie bought this skeleton and we had to carry it along the street," I said.

"I never felt like this about Todd or anyone."

"Everyone was staring at us. It was so embarrassing."

"We kept doing this thing today where Charlie would go to say something and I would say the exact same thing. It's like I could read his mind."

*Oh, please*, I thought. It's lucky she couldn't read mine.


"Charlie hasn't been home lately," Rachel said casually one

lunchtime, when all three of us were in the kitchen, preparing separate snacks. Rachel, who had only just surfaced, was trying to fillet a grapefruit for breakfast, I was cooking a cheese toastie in the sandwich maker and Auntie Jackie was grinding coffee beans for her regular fix. "I wonder where he stays when he's up in London."

"I think there's some woman in Pimlico that he shacks up with when he can't be bothered to come back to Brighton," Auntie Jackie replied breezily, unaware of the dismay this revelation might cause. Rachel hadn't chosen to confide in her about the developments in her relationship with Charlie, and so I hadn't mentioned it either.

"You mean a sort of girlfriend?" Rachel asked in an admirably even voice.

"Oh, I don't know," said Auntie Jackie over the buzzing of the coffee grinder. "It's none of my business what he gets up to in London. As long as he pays his rent and doesn't leave his boots in the hallway, I don't care what he does."

"I suppose he'll be back on Sunday to play in the band," I put in, watching in fascination as a river of melted cheese began to spew out of the back of the sandwich toaster on to the worktop.

"Mmmm," said Rachel, as though she had already considered this possibility. "The thing is," she went on, jabbing more forcefully at the grapefruit to try and detach the pith, "I've got a bit of a dilemma."

I retrieved my – disappointingly hollow – sandwich from the toaster, wondering if Rachel was going to confide at last.

"Oh? What's that?" asked Auntie Jackie, who fancied herself a fount of good advice.

"Well, Charlie's got me a ticket to the last night of his show on Saturday and the cast party afterwards. But the thing is, it's the same night as the ball which I'm supposed to be going to with Adam. So I'm in a bit of a quandary."

"There's no quandary," replied Auntie Jackie, puzzled by Rachel's apparent confusion. "You accepted Adam's invitation ages ago. So you have to turn down the later invitation. It's perfectly simple."

"But the thing is," Rachel persisted, "I didn't really want to go to the ball in the first place. And I did ask Charlie if he could get me tickets to one of his shows *before* Adam asked me to the ball, and he said he'd try, and now he has, so really that arrangement takes precedence over the ball. It's just unlucky that they're on the same day."

"Rubbish," spluttered Auntie Jackie, slopping hot

water into her cafetière with a shaking hand. "The fact is you said you'd go to the ball with Adam and now something better has come up and you want to try and wriggle out of it. Well, that's just not on. You can't let someone down like that."

"But I'll be letting Charlie down otherwise."

"You won't. You'll just be explaining that you've unfortunately already got a prior engagement. That isn't letting him down."

"Oh, forget it, I'll sort something out," said Rachel crossly. She was evidently regretting ever having brought this particular problem to public notice. But Auntie Jackie was clearly not to be deterred from her crusade.

"Basically, Rachel, there are certain codes of behaviour that you have to accept. If you've got a clash of fixtures, you don't just choose the one you prefer; you have to stick with the one you accepted first and swallow your disappointment. Adam's a nice guy and he doesn't deserve to be treated like that. If you pull out, where is he going to find another partner at the last minute?"

In the mutinous silence that followed, Rachel's eyes slid towards me.

"No way!" I protested. "I'm not being your stand-in. If Adam had wanted me to go, he'd have asked me in the first place. Anyway…" I was about to remind her that she owed Adam a big favour, remembering just in time that Auntie Jackie didn't know anything about Rachel's photo shoot and the trashing of Mr Gundry's computer and sensing that this wasn't the moment to enlighten her. "Well, whatever," I finished lamely.

"I'm afraid you'll just have to lump it, pal," said Auntie Jackie. "Some of us would love to be going to a ball at the Grand Hotel."

"You can't tell me what to do. You're not my mother," Rachel retorted in the carelessly brattish tone that she'd fine-tuned over the years. "Anyway, you can't exactly lecture me about 'codes of behaviour'." She gave Auntie Jackie a meaningful glare and for once her perfect features looked almost ugly.

"What do you mean?" Auntie Jackie asked, faltering slightly.

"You *know* what I mean," was Rachel's parting shot as she slammed out of the room.

"Well, I think your attitude stinks!" Auntie Jackie bellowed at the shut door. Then her shoulders sagged and when she looked up, I could see she had the beginnings of tears in her eyes. Patches of red veins flamed beneath her make-up on each cheek.

"That went well..." she said in a dry voice. "Expertly handled by me, as usual."

"Don't be sad," I said, feeling sorry for her. "You can't make Rachel do something she doesn't want to do. In fact, she's probably already told Adam she's not going with him." In the time it took me to say the words, the possibility had solidified into absolute certainty. Rachel wasn't asking for advice; she'd already done it.

Auntie Jackie shook her head. "If she thinks she can trust Charlie to stick to an arrangement, she's an idiot. He's probably given his tickets away by now or lost them, if he ever had any. He's as unreliable as she is." The thought of Rachel's inevitable disillusionment seemed to soothe her and presently she stood up and began clearing away the mess on the kitchen table in a businesslike manner, carefully covering the abandoned grapefruit with clingfilm and putting it in the fridge for later, like any mother would.

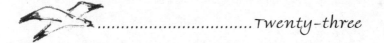

# Confessions of an Understudy

My prediction was proved correct that afternoon. I had decided to go jogging again and was on the doorstep tying my laces when from next door, Adam's granny emerged from the house, pushing a small upright hoover. With some difficulty she dragged it down the steps and then set off up the road, pulling it behind her. It was a warm August day so the fact that she had a rather floaty summer dress on under her cardigan didn't ring alarm bells at first, until I noticed the fluffy slippers on her feet and realised it was a nightie. At this point, the nagging voice of conscience began a sort of internal quarrel with my natural inclination not to get involved.

*It is not illegal to wear nightclothes in the street*, I told myself.

(I had, after all, done just that only a matter of weeks ago.) *Dress sense is highly individual. Likewise, if someone decides to take their hoover for a walk it is no business of mine.*

*She is old and confused*, my conscience replied sternly, *and shouldn't be left to wander off.*

*She isn't my responsibility*, I insisted.

*But if she gets lost or mugged or run over, it'll be your fault for doing nothing*, came back the immediate riposte.

There was another reason, apart from selfishness, that made me hesitate to intervene: I couldn't remember – if I had ever known – Adam's granny's name and I couldn't bring myself to shout, "Oy you!" or its equivalent at an old-age pensioner. Sighing, I climbed over the low wall which divided our two front gardens and rang the bell. Adam would know what to do – if he was in. To my relief, I could see a shadow of movement through the stained glass and a moment later he had opened the door.

"Hello?" he said.

I pointed down the road. "Your granny's doing a runner with the hoover." Her progress had slowed considerably because a long coil of electric cable had unwound itself and was trailing a three-pin plug along the pavement, snagging on every uneven slab.

"Oh God." Adam took off up the street, taking care

not to startle her as he approached. Very gently, he put his arm around her shoulder and stood talking to her for a minute, before reeling in the cable and tucking the hoover under his arm as if it was as light as an umbrella. Very slowly, the old lady turned round and they began to walk back towards the house. "Come on, I'll make you a cup of tea and then it'll be time for *Countdown*," Adam was saying to her, as they passed me at the gate. "Wait for me," he mouthed over his shoulder as they went indoors.

When he rejoined me five minutes later he was in shorts and running shoes. "Sorry I didn't invite you in, but I'd have had to explain who you are all over again and it would have confused her even more. I don't know what she was doing then. Anyway, thanks for warning me. God knows where she'd have ended up."

"That's OK. I don't know what I'd have done if you'd been out though," I admitted. "Is she all right to go out by herself ever?"

"Up until recently. She used to walk round to the shops most days and get a newspaper and stuff, no problems. But lately she's been forgetting to put on proper clothes, or she'll do something else like leave the front door wide open, and I'm a bit worried that she's going to get lost. But short of locking her in, there's not much I can do."

"Can't your parents look after her?" It didn't seem right that Adam should have to shoulder all the responsibility.

"It may come to that. But she'd have to go and live with them in Telford and she'd hate that."

We had started to jog down Cliff Street during this exchange, without having made any decision about the route, and I assumed that we would be heading for the promenade like last time, but at the end of the road Adam turned up the hill instead, away from the sea. "Let's go this way," he said mysteriously. "I want to show you something."

He led me on a zigzag route through the grid of streets at his usual challenging pace, while I grew increasingly puzzled, but as I needed all my breath for running, I didn't question him. After some minutes, just when I thought I had no idea where we were, I recognised a couple of familiar landmarks: the Tasty Kebab shop, and Rascals Pets, with its stack of rabbit hutches and dog baskets out on the pavement. I had noticed them before, on my one previous visit to this neighbourhood.

As we rounded the corner, there was the café which we had used as a base for the infamous raid on the photography studio, and there opposite was the shop itself, dark, derelict and abandoned.

"See," Adam said, as we approached. "I told you he wouldn't hang around." The portraits had disappeared from the window display; the velvet background drapes sagged. The mouth of the letter box was choked with a wad of glossy fliers and an avalanche of unopened post lay on the mat, banked up against the front door. We peered through the glass into the reception area. The furniture – the kidney-shaped counter, two easy chairs and a low coffee table adorned by a withered pot plant – remained, which suggested that the evacuation had been performed in some haste.

"Do you really think it's because of us?"

Adam nodded. "I knew he'd leg it – if he was guilty. The only thing is, he's probably just going to move away and set up in a different part of the country under a new name."

I wrinkled my nose in disgust. "Why do men have to be so pervy?" I said, directing this question, somewhat unfairly, at Adam.

"I don't know," he said, indignantly. "I'm not 'men' – I'm just me."

"We should have gone to the police, shouldn't we?"

I said, as we began to jog home. Our only concern had been for Rachel. We hadn't given a thought to any other past or future victims.

"We still could," said Adam. "But it's up to Rachel of course. And we all know that you can't make Rachel do something she doesn't want to do," he added bitterly, in a perfect echo of my words to Auntie Jackie. I looked up sharply.

His face was flushed, from the running perhaps. "I suppose you know she's blown me out for the ball," he said.

"No... yes... well, she mentioned something about it, but I didn't know, exactly..."

"Apparently she got the dates confused and didn't realise she would be up in London that night." He shrugged.

"Mmmm," I said non-committally. I didn't see why I should help Rachel by propping up this particular fiction, but on the other hand, Adam's feelings had to be considered. Even if he suspected he had been unceremoniously dumped, he wouldn't thank me for pointing it out. Much better to believe himself a victim of careless double-booking. Sympathy is the last thing you want when you are feeling humiliated: it's like sandpaper on sunburn.

"I don't suppose you're free that night?" he said, scuffing a pebble into the kerb as he ran. "I mean, if you've got nothing better to do. I can't think who else to ask. Seems a pity to waste the ticket..."

It would have been difficult to be flattered however he had phrased it, knowing that I was a last-minute stand-in, but the clumsiness of the invitation and his evident lack of enthusiasm made me laugh out loud.

"What's funny?" asked Adam warily.

"You certainly know how to sweep a girl off her feet," I said, unable to stop a sliver of ice creeping into my voice.

"What...? Why? What do you mean?" Adam asked, bewildered by the change of atmosphere and only gradually registering that he might have been the cause.

"I know I wasn't exactly your first choice, but you don't have to make it sound as though you are completely scraping the barrel." I was about to ask him if he wouldn't rather take Mr Elkington, but remembered that he wouldn't have a clue what I was talking about, which would tend to kill the joke.

"I never said anything like that, did I?" Adam replied, aghast. "I was just offering you a ticket if you wanted it. It was no big deal."

"Not for you evidently. You made it sound as though

you couldn't care less one way or another." My chest was heaving with the effort of trying to conduct an argument while running along. "As invitations go, it's just not very tempting. That's all."

"Look, I don't get what's bugging you. If you don't want to go, just say so."

"I don't want to go," I snapped, and then, because it was the only way to bring this disastrous conversation to an end and I knew I couldn't outrun him if we carried on in the same direction, I tacked off down a side road and sprinted away, powered by the energy of still unused indignation.

I hate confrontations of any kind and before I was halfway home I was regretting my outburst. Now he would think I was immature and emotionally unstable and would probably avoid me for the rest of the summer. A polite "No, thank you" would have been so much more dignified; or even a polite "Yes, thank you", since the truth was I did want to go to the ball with him, more than anything, and it was only bruised pride that had made me refuse. If this was the result of the plain-speaking that everyone insisted was so healthy, then frankly they could keep it. Bottling things up had always served me just fine and I resolved to stick to it in future. In the mean time, I had blown my chance to go to the ball and would be home alone on Saturday night while Rachel, Charlie – and even Auntie Jackie – were out enjoying themselves.

I took a deliberately circuitous route back, to give myself a chance to run off my bad mood, and to make sure I didn't arrive at the same time as Adam. I didn't entirely succeed in the first of these objectives, and as I turned into Cliff Street, momentarily dazzled by bright sunlight flaring from the west, I saw an indistinct figure leaning against the wall opposite 29 and my heart lurched. *He's waiting for me*, I thought, but when I put my hand up to shield my eyes from the glare I could see that it wasn't a guy at all. It took my overheated brain another second or two to realise that it was the girl with red hair. Still fired up by my quarrel with Adam, I decided to acknowledge her this time and see if she pretended not to recognise me.

She was talking into her mobile phone and didn't notice my approach until I was about twenty metres away, but the moment she caught sight of me, she spun on her heel and began to walk away at an unnaturally brisk pace. I was convinced now that there could be no innocent explanation for this weird behaviour. If she had merely been waiting for someone in the ordinary way, which was perfectly possible, there would be no good reason for scuttling off as if she had something to hide.

"Hey!" I called after her. I knew she had heard me because she flinched slightly, but she didn't turn around or slow down. Following her at a run, I reached the corner of the road a matter of seconds after her, but there was no sign of her in either direction. She must either have broken into an Olympic sprint as soon as she was out of sight, or have ducked into one of the houses.

In spite of the warmth of the day I felt suddenly chilly – I had experienced just this feeling of unease before, in Oxford. It was a sense of danger, not immediate but somewhere "out there", and all the more alarming for being vague and undeclared. I tried to tell myself that this was pure paranoia, and that this girl couldn't possibly have any connection to the events back home, but then I remembered something Dad had said about "even kids as young as twelve" being involved – and once the idea had taken root, it wasn't so easy to dismiss.

I was wondering if I should mention my worries to anyone indoors, but Auntie Jackie was busy with a client, and Rachel had shut herself in her bedroom and hung a DO NOT DISTURB sign on the handle, so she was clearly still fuming from the row earlier. I tapped gently and tried the door, but it was locked and a very muffled voice from inside said something like "Hump Pork", so I gave up and went downstairs.

Forgetting Auntie Jackie's injunctions about background noise when clients were in, I took out Charlie's borrowed saxophone and was about to tackle the trickier numbers from The Gamblers' repertoire, when a paper dart flew in my open window and swooped elegantly on to the rug at my feet.

I could see the impression of handwriting through the paper so I unfolded it, to find the following note.

*Sorry, sorry, sorry.*

*You were right: that was the crappest invitation ever and I don't blame you for refusing. I'm rubbish at putting things into words, but I didn't mean to offend you. Please, please change your mind and come with me to the ball. It might be good – and if it isn't, we can still have fun laughing about how bad it is!*

*PS Sorry for this primitive method of communication. I haven't got your mobile number.*

I strode to the window and peered out. Adam was loitering in the narrow trench between my basement room and what passed for a front garden. He did his best to look humble.

"Hello," I said, with just enough of a smile to let him know he was forgiven, but no more.

"Is it all right if I come in?" he asked. "I feel a bit like a burglar skulking around out here."

I nodded, standing back as he hoisted himself up over the spongy wood of the sill, bringing with him a shower of flaking paint. I couldn't help wondering at some people's strange reluctance to use front doors. (It didn't occur to me until later when he chose to leave by the same route that he might be trying to avoid bumping into Rachel.)

"Oh," he said, noticing the piece of paper in my hand. "You got my dart then."

"Yes." I waved it at him. "I was just about to reply actually." Selecting a pen from a homemade clay pot on the mantelpiece, I turned the page over and wrote, *OK then*, before folding the whole thing up again and launching it towards the open window.

It wasn't quite so aerodynamic on its return flight after all that manhandling, and was easily intercepted by Adam as it arced up to the ceiling.

He put on a great show of trepidation as he opened it out, and then beamed with relief.

"Oh, good. Great. That's settled then."

"Yes. Good." I knew I ought to offer some sort of equivalent apology for stropping off, but I couldn't do that without rehashing the whole episode and reminding him how precious I'd been, so instead I said, "You didn't happen to see a girl with red hair sitting on the wall over the road when you came back just now?"

"Er... there was someone there. Didn't really look at her. Why?"

"Have you seen her in the street before?"

"Not sure. Wasn't paying that much attention."

"Before the beginning of the summer, I meant. Before we came here?"

"I can't really remember. Why?"

"No reason. I just keep seeing her. I wondered if maybe she lives in this road."

"It's possible. People come and go all the time around here. There are a couple of student houses up the top end. They have new tenants every year."

"She's not a student. She looks about thirteen. Oh well." I realised that if I pursued this conversation any further, without providing the full background explanation for my paranoia, my interest in this complete stranger might start to look weird and unhealthy, so I changed the subject by offering Adam a beer. I knew Auntie Jackie kept a crate of Grolsch in the fridge for Dave and wouldn't miss the odd one.

Adam couldn't be persuaded; he wanted to get out of his sweaty running gear and showered before his muscles seized up. "I just wanted to get this ball-invite-fiasco sorted out. I'm really glad you're going to come," he added hastily, in case I objected to his phrasing all over again. "Shall I knock for you at eight? I'll order a cab – I don't suppose you want to walk there all poshed up."

I confirmed that I didn't. The matter of getting myself "poshed up" still remained to be faced.

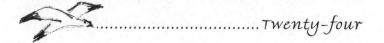 

# Cinders

The day of the ball started – at 3.07 a.m. according to the backlit face of my alarm clock – with a yell and a crash that shook the house. Charlie was home at last.

As a sadistic refinement to her prank, Auntie Jackie had unscrewed the lightbulb in his room, predicting correctly that he wouldn't bother to go all the way back down to the kitchen to fetch a new one in the middle of the night, but would instead climb into bed beside Mr Elkington in the darkness. Over the next few days, and at the most inappropriate moments, my mind kept returning to the image of Charlie slipping innocently between the sheets, realising he had company, and reaching across... The fact that he might have been half expecting it to be Rachel lying there added an extra – if slightly sinister – dimension to the joke.

He made no mention of the incident when he came down to breakfast mid-morning, and seemed determined not to meet Auntie Jackie's eye as he cracked four eggs into a bowl and began whisking them vigorously.

"Sleep well, Charlie?" she enquired.

"Like a log, thank you," he replied with great dignity.

"Did you? Lucky you," she said, tearing one end off a croissant and dipping it in her coffee, leaving a layer of flakes floating on the surface like fish food. "I was woken by the most incredible racket. I thought the roof had fallen in."

"I didn't hear anything," Charlie replied, standing in front of the open fridge and frowning at the contents of his designated shelf which, as he had been away for nearly a week, looked less than appetising. He produced an open carton of milk and sniffed it, recoiling at the smell, before tipping it down the sink in disgust. It emerged as a watery green trickle followed by a jellified lump.

"Have some of mine," said Auntie Jackie kindly, pushing a bottle of semi-skimmed towards him. "Where have you been lately, anyway?"

"Staying up in London," Charlie replied, splashing milk

into his egg mixture and pouring the whole lot into a saucepan on the hob, before grinding pepper over it with a vengeful, throttling action. "Flat-hunting," he added with emphasis.

"Oh?" Auntie Jackie said, unable to disguise her dismay. "Really? Oh." Distracted, she left her croissant too long in the coffee, retrieving it just too late to stop the soggy lower half collapsing under the surface. "What sort of place are you looking for?"

"I don't know," said Charlie, stirring his pan of eggs thoughtfully. "Just somewhere of my own. Somewhere without wasps' nests, or a roof that's about to fall in and kill me in my sleep. Somewhere generally rodent-free, if possible. Apart from that, I'm not really fussy."

I left Auntie Jackie to digest this news and went upstairs in search of Rachel. It wasn't like her to prolong a sulk and I was beginning to wonder about her anti-social behaviour the night before. I tapped on her door and after a pause it opened a chink. "Who is it?" she hissed.

"Me. Robyn. Are you all right?"

"Are you on your own?"

"Yes." The door opened for the briefest interval and she dragged me inside. She was still in her pyjamas and had her hair pulled back into a ponytail and held off her forehead with grips. The lower half of her face looked strangely puffy. "I've had a right disaster," she moaned. The effort of speaking made her wince, and she put her hand up to her mouth.

"What's the matter?"

"I used one of those tooth-whitening kits," she said woefully, pointing to the bedside cabinet on which stood various tubes and a Shrek-green rubber mouthguard. "It said you have to wear it overnight – at least I thought that's what it said: all the instructions were in French – but when I woke up this morning, my gums were all totally blistered. Look." She pulled up her top lip to reveal a row of pink welts, flinching with pain at this manoeuvre. Her teeth looked much as they always had – longer perhaps, as though her gums had attempted to retreat from the advancing tide of bleach.

"Yuk," I said, with all the sympathy I could muster. "That looks really painful."

"It is. It's agony. It even hurts to smile. I must have put too much bleach in the tray."

"What on earth made you do it?" I said, picking up the empty box from the bedside cabinet. The illustrations were so phoney it was a joke. The "before" picture showed a set of teeth stained like the inside of a teapot, restored in the "after" shot to blinding whiteness, complete with computer-generated dazzle on the front incisor. "Your teeth were white already."

"Not white enough. Owwww."

"Where did you get this stuff from anyway? It looks well dodgy."

"I got it in this Chinese chemist in Tottenham Court Road, when I was in London after Frankie's party."

I rolled my eyes.

"I thought it would be OK because it was really expensive, not like that cheapo stuff in Boots that doesn't work."

"How expensive exactly?"

"Eighty quid."

"*Eighty quid!*" And this was the weekend she'd had to cadge her train fare off Adam. "Where did you get that much money from?"

"Dad gave me fifty when we had lunch. I was meant to give you half. Sorry. I'll pay you back," she wheedled tearfully. "I borrowed the rest from Todd."

"*Todd?*"

"Yeah. I told you I bumped into him at Paddington. We got the tube together and looked round the shops for a bit until it was time for me to get my train. He lent me the extra."

For a moment I was speechless. She was practically a professional beggar.

"Why are the instructions all in French?" I demanded, turning my attention to the more pressing matter of the bleaching kit.

"Because it *is* French. You can't normally get this stuff over here."

"Probably for good reasons."

"Oh, why do these things always happen to me?" she wailed. "I just wanted to look nice tonight and now I won't even be able to smile. Owww."

*And kissing's not going to be very pleasant either*, I thought, but didn't say.

"I've got to get to an emergency dentist," Rachel said, grimacing into the mirror again. "Can you sneak down and get me the *Yellow Pages*."

"Why don't you just ask Auntie Jackie. She must have the number of a dentist."

"No, no, I don't want anyone else to know. Promise not to tell anyone. I just need to get something to put on these blisters to stop them hurting and check that I haven't wrecked my teeth forever. *Please*."

"OK."

When I returned with the phone directory under my arm, Rachel was counting money out of her purse. "There," she said, handing over two limp tenners and a handful of mixed change. "That's the £25 I owe you."

Resisting a strong temptation to count it in front of her, I had almost got it as far as my pocket when she said, without any embarrassment, "Actually, that's not going to leave me enough to pay the dentist. Can I borrow it back? Just for today?"

After a few phone calls Rachel managed to locate a surgery in Woodingdean that was open on Saturday mornings, and having made me check that no one was in the hallway, she crept out of the house, hidden behind an enormous pair of sunglasses as though ashamed to look the day in the eye.

In her absence I took the opportunity to tell Auntie Jackie that I would be taking Rachel's place at the ball. I wasn't trying to be a supergrass; it was just the small matter of needing to borrow a dress. I located her in the back garden, trying to revive a moribund hanging basket of brown, shrivelled plants with the aptly named Miracle-Gro.

"Do you think these will perk up?" she asked, stirring a scoop of blue crystals into the watering can and drenching the container until it overflowed. I burst out laughing. Mr Elkington himself stood as much chance of "perking up".

"Auntie Jackie. I'm going to the ball tonight. With Adam. Instead of Rachel. Can I borrow one of your dresses?"

Auntie Jackie straightened up, frothing with indignation. "Oh, she's never… Oh, she is a bad girl. I can't believe she's done that. After everything I said. Poor Adam…Well, he should have asked you in the first place. Men are so stupid… Oh, you are a good sister. Yes, of course you can have any dress you like, my lovely."

She rehung the dripping basket of dead stuff from its bracket on the wall and stood back to admire her efforts. "Oh well," she conceded, "we can't all have green fingers."

I followed her inside and up the stairs. Every time she went through a door she glanced warily upwards, as though expecting a bucket of water or a flour bomb to land on her head. "I've got half a dozen clients coming in to pick up their outfits this afternoon. I hope Charlie doesn't choose today to launch his revenge attack. God, that was funny," she sighed.

It was agreed that I would wait until the last of the

clients had departed before having the run of the shop. Auntie Jackie herself wouldn't be on hand to advise as she was driving up to Gatwick to meet a friend down from Scotland who had an evening to kill before catching an onward flight. "What a pity I won't be able to help you get ready," she lamented. "I could have done your make-up for you. What a shame!"

I assumed a sorrowful expression, while inwardly rejoicing at this narrow escape. From where I stood I could see an orange drip of pooled-up fake tan just below Auntie Jackie's ear, blobs of stray mascara on her upper eyelids and red flecks of lipstick on her teeth. The last thing I needed on my Big Night Out was to play blank canvas to her Jackson Pollock.

"Are there any dresses you'd rather I didn't choose? The expensive ones, I mean. You could put them on a separate rail," I suggested.

"No, you just help yourself to anything. I must remember to leave the door unlocked for you before I go out. There are all sorts of strappy shoes in the trunk, or in my wardrobe. I want you to have a lovely evening. Oh, and make sure Adam brings you home in a taxi. To the door. Knowing him he'll probably take his bicycle. If you need any cash, you can raid the jar on the kitchen shelf."

I knew that it was partly irritation with Rachel that was prompting Auntie Jackie's Fairy Godmother act. As far as she was concerned, the best way to register her disapproval of Rachel was to spoil me. But I wasn't about to complain; for once in my life I was The Fave and it felt great.

Rachel came back from the clinic with a prescription for some strong painkillers and a tube of lignocaine gel for her sore gums. She had had to wait hours, behind more urgent cases – two people with raging abscesses and a kid who had knocked his front teeth out on a bouncy castle – and was another fifty quid poorer. She retired to bed in the hope that the medication would take effect in time for her trip up to London with Charlie.

From two o'clock onwards the shop was busy with the non-stop traffic of clients arriving and departing with ball dresses sheathed in polythene so I kept out of the way, in my room. I was pleased for Auntie Jackie because customers meant money, which she never seemed to have enough of. I wondered what she would do if Charlie did find a flat in London and move out. He would be difficult to replace; the set-up at Cliff Street might not be to everyone's taste, and Auntie Jackie had said herself that she was very particular about the sort of lodger she would tolerate.

At five o'clock, after the last of the clients had departed, Auntie Jackie left to meet her friend's flight, with final instructions to me to help myself and have a wonderful time, not to drink intoxicating liquor or consort with men of low character, or otherwise bring the House of Stenning into disrepute. Five minutes later, Charlie and Rachel set off for London, Rachel looking rather subdued and woozy from her prescription painkillers. Charlie had been unable to borrow a spare crash helmet so they were taking the train and were not expected back until Sunday morning.

Rachel didn't seem to know that I was going to the ball and for some reason I didn't want to tell her. It didn't occur to her to ask what I was going to be doing while everyone else was out; it was Charlie who said, "Are you sure you'll be OK by yourself, Ronnie?" I just smiled and said I had other plans.

Then, in a matter of seconds it seemed, they were gone and the house was quiet and mine. I went into the kitchen and found all the dishes from the morning still unwashed and that someone, presumably Charlie, had posed Mr Elkington on his stand in front of the sink in a flowery apron and a pair of rubber gloves.

I left him to it – there was no way I was going to waste valuable minutes of the two and a half hours I had to get ready. I may be sensible, but I'm not a martyr. Instead, I had a long, lazy shower until the water started to run cold and then blow-dried my hair properly, a section at a time, aiming the nozzle "down the hair shaft from root to tip" like they always say in magazines. It took forever and I had lost all feeling in my arms by the time I'd finished, but at least the worst of the kinks were flattened out.

Upstairs, the door to the shop had been left unlocked as promised and a little shiver of excitement ran through me as I pushed it open. Because the blinds were drawn the air in here was cooler. It smelled different too: clean and gently scented with flowers, whereas the rest of the house smelled of old carpet and coffee and dog, which was odd as Auntie Jackie didn't have a dog. The last surviving roses from Dave's bouquet stood in a vase on the coffee table, their lush white petals curled back and sweating perfume.

The silence was beginning to unnerve me – I found I was tiptoeing – so I switched on the CD player and immediately the air was full of the sobbing of massed violins. I waltzed across to the rails of dresses, overwhelmed by the choice of colours and styles. There was the champagne-silk backless number that Rachel had picked out for herself – a complete no-no; might as well be naked. There was the most ostentatious dress in the collection – a heart-shaped bodice and a full skirt in scarlet satin with a hooped petticoat, giving it a diameter at the hem of about two and a half metres. On the plus side, no one would ever see your feet so you could wear any old shoes, but on the minus side you wouldn't be able to fit in a taxi.

Some colours and styles were easy to dismiss outright without needing to be tried on.

Anything too clingy that would require specialist underwear.

Anything too pale and vulnerable to spills.

Anything liable to show sweat patches.

Anything in burgundy – colour of my school uniform, widely loathed and unflattering to all known skin types.

Allowing for these exceptions still left an awful lot of frocks in my size to be considered. I was gazing helplessly at the rails in that state of near paralysis brought on by too much choice, when my eye fell on the display cabinet containing the precious, untouchable Diana dress, and what I saw made my scalp tingle. *The door was open. The key was in the door and the door was open!* In all the time I had been at Auntie Jackie's, on the many occasions I had helped out in the shop, I had never known the door to be unlocked or even so much as glimpsed the key. It was inconceivable that Auntie Jackie would have opened the cabinet with clients coming and going all afternoon, and then gone out and carelessly left it like that, on the one night when the house was guaranteed to be empty.

I remembered her words to me in the garden: *Help yourself to anything. I'll leave the key in the door.* She couldn't have meant… could she? No, no, no, no, no, no, no.

All the same, I couldn't resist having a closer look. It really was the most beautiful colour – the deepest shade of blue this side of black, like a late evening sky in the countryside, unspoilt by city lights. After checking that my hands were clean, I carefully lifted the tailor's dummy out of the case and stood it on the carpet, so that I could walk around it and survey it from all angles. Even a fashion ignoramus like me could tell that it was no ordinary dress: the fabric was softer, finer, more luminous; the needlework all but invisible – possibly the work of elves.

I wondered if I dared to try it on. *Better not - you might damage it*, I told myself sternly, while my hands, as if acting quite independently of the rest of me, shakily undid the zip. I gently lifted the dress off the dummy, the layers of chiffon whispering reproachfully. It was lined with matching blue-black silk, so perfectly made you could have worn it inside out. Not a stray stitch or a raw edge to be seen.

*I'll just put it on for two seconds*, I decided. Just to see if it would fit a non-princess. The blinds were closed and I was alone in the house, but I automatically went into the changing cubicle and drew the curtain, and then laughed out loud at this irrational behaviour. In the long mirror my face looked strangely flushed. *This isn't like you*, I thought, as I slipped the dress over my head. *This isn't sensible.*

If only it hadn't fitted me so well! If only it hadn't made me look so grown-up and confident and been so utterly right and perfect! Nothing else I tried on could possibly measure up now. I looked over my shoulder and, trying to keep one eye on the mirror, turned round quickly, hoping to find an unflattering angle, but there were none. She must have been tall, Diana, taller than me, because although it was not meant to be a full-length dress, the fishtail almost reached the floor at the back. In the trunk I located a pair of high-heeled sandals which more or less fitted, and were about as comfy as barbed wire, but at least matched the silvery embroidery on the dress. I plucked a gauzy silver stole from one of the drawers and wrapped it round my bare shoulders.

For once, the mirror gave me back the person I wanted to be. From her framed photograph on the wall Princess Diana smiled her mischievous smile. "Go on," she seemed to be saying. "Life is short and this chance will never come again. Go on."

*Just two more minutes*, I told myself, *and then I will go and get changed...*

I was startled from my trance-like state by the ringing of the doorbell. I hobbled to open it, the silver sandals biting cruelly. Adam stood on the step, barely recognisable in a black dinner suit, a bow tie hanging unfastened around his neck.

"Hello. You look nice," he said simply. "Can you give me a hand with this tie? I knew I should have got one of those ones on elastic."

"Sure," I said confidently, taking both ends and tying them together as if doing up shoelaces. The result was not pretty. "No, that's not right. Hang on," I said, tweaking and pulling until I was back where I'd started. "There must be a knack to this."

Ten minutes later the cab rolled up outside and I had still produced nothing resembling a bow. "Charlie!" I said, struck by sudden inspiration. "I bet he's got an elastic one. He wears evening dress all the time when he's playing in the West End."

Adam made apologetic delaying gestures at the cab driver and bounded upstairs to raid Charlie's wardrobe. I took advantage of the extra minute or so to limp down to my room and apply another layer of lipgloss and mascara, and snatch up a twenty-pound note, which I had to tuck inside my bra for want of anything suitable that would do as a bag.

Adam returned triumphant, with an electric blue clip-on tie, which was rather frayed – nibbled in fact – around the edges. It looked like the sort of thing you might find in a joke shop, and Charlie being Charlie, this wasn't out of the question. I wouldn't have been altogether surprised if it sprayed me with water.

Casting a last guilty glance at the empty display cabinet, I carefully closed the door to the shop and followed Adam out to the cab, my heart galloping with exhilaration and panic at what I'd done.

# Twenty-five

# I Could Have Danced All Night
## (But not in these shoes)

"I hope we've been put on a table with some people I know," Adam said, shooting his cuffs, tugging at his jacket and looking generally ill at ease as we stood in the lobby of the Grand Hotel. There were other couples in evening dress emerging from taxis and greeting each other, milling around, so we didn't look too out of place, although everyone else was much older and no one else had quite our air of hesitancy.

"What do you mean 'on a table'?" I asked. "We don't sit at tables, do we?" It occurred to me for the first time that I didn't have a clue what actually went on at a ball. All my expectations were based entirely on what I had absorbed from fairy tales and Disney films, and amounted to no more than an image of women in crinolines being whirled around in the arms of men with tailcoats and big moustaches. I was painfully underprepared for reality.

"Well, we sit at tables for the meal, I guess," said Adam.

"Meal?" I said, horrified, wondering how many napkins it would take to completely cover my dress from an almost certain drenching with gravy or custard... "I didn't know there was going to be proper *food*."

Adam looked at me strangely. "For £200 a ticket there'd better be."

The lobby was becoming congested with new arrivals, and uniformed staff were trying to direct people, so we followed the general drift down some steps and along a wide corridor to a vast room with a crazily patterned blue carpet and a sprung wooden dance floor at one end, beside a temporary stage set up for a live band. On the carpeted area were twenty or so round tables, laid with white cloths and sparkling cutlery and crystal, and identical vases of purple freesias.

Eighties pop was piping faintly from the speakers, almost drowned by the babble of conversation. All around us, groups of friends, colleagues, acquaintances were forming closed circles which we couldn't hope to penetrate. Adam scanned the room feverishly for a familiar face. Were we the only people here who knew nobody? I had a sudden premonition that this was not, after all, going to be the fabulous red-carpet rave-up I had imagined, and that the highlight of the evening might very well be taking my sandals off in the taxi home.

Waiters with precarious trays of champagne were weaving through the crowd, dangerously close to The Dress. There didn't seem to be any issues with my age, so it seemed an ideal opportunity to develop a taste for the stuff.

"Cheers," said Adam, and we clinked glasses.

"Do you think champagne flutes were invented by someone without a nose?" I wondered aloud, as the rim of the glass dug into my septum every time I took a swig. "Or am I just a weird shape?" The taste wasn't too bad. Somehow the explosion of bubbles at the back of the throat provided a distraction from the metallic flavour, and made it much easier to drink than wine. It probably gave you a better class of hangover too.

A plump woman in frilly bronze taffeta rustled across and gave Adam a crushing hug. "So glad you could come!" she cried, beaming at us. She had an American accent, which for some reason made her seem friendly and approachable.

"This is Val, who I did that website for," Adam explained, when he'd been released from her grasp. "This is Robyn, my... er... next-door neighbour."

Val looked me over. She was one of those big, flirty women who have no concept of personal space and can't talk to someone – even a complete stranger – without grabbing a handful of their flesh. "I love your dress," she said, pinching the fabric of the skirt between her fingers, while gripping my arm with her free hand. "Such gorgeous material. Did you have it specially made?"

I was burning to tell her, but instead said, "No, I just borrowed it."

"Make the most of your figure while you got it," she advised me. "I was a size four – maximum – till I had kids, and now look at me." I didn't know how to reply to this, without acknowledging that she was, indeed, enormous, so I just simpered. And then someone across the room claimed her attention and she was off, only letting go of me with extreme reluctance and at the last possible minute, running her hand down the length of my arm to my fingers. It was almost as bad as having my feet molested by Charlie. Perhaps this sort of thing was normal in America.

I looked down, surprised to find I'd finished my

champagne. Not for long. Waiters were circling like lions round a pack of gazelles; at the sight of an empty glass, one of them sprang forward and refilled it.

Adam had wandered off to look at the seating plan which was on a kind of easel by the doorway. I resisted the temptation to follow him because I didn't want to seem clingy, but it is hard to look purposeful and engrossed standing on your own for any length of time. Another waiter came past with a large platter of tiny, delicate nibbles – stuffed baby tomatoes, club sandwiches the size of sugar lumps, miniature pastries topped with piped rosettes of green mousse and what looked like tiny jet beads – microscopic offerings that wouldn't have looked out of place in a doll's house. I took a couple of the pastries, for something to do. The jet beads exploded on my tongue, leaving a fishy aftertaste that had to be washed away with champagne. The waiter – who was about the same age as Adam – as if sensing my inadequacy, gave me a wink, to which I replied with a glare, before he peeled off into the crowd, smirking.

Through the mêlée, I noticed another woman wearing the exact same dress as Val and I was pierced by sympathy for them both. I had never given the conventions of evening dress a second thought before, but now it struck me as utterly bizarre and unfair how differently the sexes were treated. For men, the object was to look as similar as possible to all other men, whereas for women the opposite was true; any duplication was a social disaster. It was while I was gazing after Val's double, and pondering this injustice, that I caught sight of a familiar face some distance away through the throng. Dave! My excitement at recognising even a passing acquaintance among this crowd of strangers – effectively doubling my circle of contacts at a stroke – must have sent ripples of energy across the room, as a second later he glanced up and saw me.

I grinned manically and took a step towards him, then froze with embarrassment as he responded with a jolt of nervous recognition and a flicker of dismay, before turning his back. My face flamed at this dismissal. The blush spread across my bare shoulders and down my arms, and I had to concentrate hard on the contents of my glass to subdue the feeling that everyone in the room had witnessed my humiliation. Something was very, very wrong. What could I possibly have done to make Dave blank me like that? When I looked up, of course, no one was paying the slightest bit of attention to me and Adam was back again, saying, "We're on table F. They didn't put us next to each other though."

"Oh no."

"So I switched the place cards over."

"Oh, well done."

People were starting to move towards their seats now and as the crowd thinned out I caught sight of Dave again, and the reason for his hunted expression became clear. He was with a woman. She had her arm cosily linked through his and with her free hand was brushing fluff or crumbs from his jacket lapels. It was the sort of intimate grooming gesture that women often did to their partners, to signal to a watching world that they were a couple. I had seen Auntie Jackie do the very same thing to Dave herself. Poor Auntie Jackie. Evil Dave. No wonder he was so keen to avoid me.

It was with huge relief that I saw them take up their places on the far side of the room, comfortably out of the line of sight of my seat at table F.

I was between Adam and Val's husband, who was introduced to me as "Rajah". This seemed an exotic name for a bald, paunchy Englishman who looked like a typical bank manager. "Don't let Rajah get too tanked up before the auction," Val instructed me. "Last time he won me a balloon flight. This time he's got his eye on a Formula One driving lesson."

Rajah grinned and helped himself to a large glass of red wine. He had obviously forgotten my name already as he picked up my place card, patting his pockets helplessly for an absent pair of specs, before holding it at arm's length. "*GUEST OF ADAM HARRIS*," he read aloud.

"It's a bit of a mouthful, but my friends just call me Guest," I replied.

"Sorry?" he said, cupping his hand to his ear. "You're on my deaf side."

I didn't think my remark worth repeating at a raised volume, so I just smiled. He was in any case distracted by the woman on his right, who asked for the wine and soon engaged him in conversation. On my other side, Adam had turned away from me to talk to Val, so there was nothing for me to do but read the menu card and wonder which side plate and bread roll were mine: left or right? I was feeling light-headed from the alcohol and those microscopic nibbles had done nothing but rouse and madden my appetite, but a wrong move on the bread would set up a domino effect round the table resulting in social death so I would just have to be patient. Why had no one ever taught me this simple rule? What use was a GCSE in Food Tech if I died of starvation here at the table for lack of this crumb of wisdom?

My stomach let out a wolfish growl which caused Rajah to glance under the table in alarm as though expecting to see some ravenous beast lurking there. Not that deaf evidently. To cover my embarrassment I poured myself a drink of white wine, just for something to do. I didn't intend to drink it; I would have preferred something soft because I had quite a thirst by now, but the water jug was out of reach, on the other side of the freesias. Ice cubes crunched unyieldingly as I tried to force the bottle back into its tin bucket.

The menu, though apparently in English, still contained at least one word on every line that I didn't understand. *Ballotine, velouté, confit, ganache.* They all sounded runny, sticky, messy and likely to cause devastation if spilt. As discreetly as possible, I swathed my dress in the silver stole, spreading out the stiff damask napkin across the skirt to cover any gaps. *It'll be fine, fine,* I told myself, champagne-confident. *I'll put it straight back on the dummy when I get in and no one will ever know. What the hell is the point of a dress you can never wear?*

A skinny woman directly opposite me succumbed to the bread and the riddle of the side plate was solved at last. (The left!) When the food finally arrived, I could hardly enjoy it – I had passed through hunger into a trance-like state of nausea. In any case, it was more like Art than Food: exhibited on the plate, carved, piled, sculpted, garnished, drizzled. It was the culinary equivalent of the Diana Dress: too beautiful to be used. The background noise of dozens, perhaps hundreds of separate conversations blended into a roar, like waves churning on a pebbly beach. My glass was empty again. Rajah must have been swigging from it when I wasn't looking. Drunkard.

At one point Adam said to me: "The IRA bombed this hotel back in the 1980s. They were trying to kill Margaret Thatcher, but she walked out without a scratch."

"Someone tried to bomb my house in Oxford," I said dreamily, unable to remember why this was supposed to be a secret. The threat seemed so remote now and I, myself, invincible as Margaret Thatcher. "They wanted to blow up my dad."

"I know," said Adam. "Rachel told me."

"She wasn't supposed to tell anyone!" I said indignantly.

Adam laughed. "Have some water, why don't you?" He filled a tumbler from the jug, ice cubes and wedges of lemon becoming trapped in the spout and then flopping into the glass. It was the best thing I'd tasted all night – perhaps ever – so cold and pure.

Waitresses appeared with silver coffee pots and dishes of chocolate truffles. Since I'd broken myself into champagne so successfully, I thought I might as well do the same with coffee, but no luck. This particular brew was black and oily and must have been made by boiling up a pair of men's leather brogues in a stock made of old bicycle tyres.

I escaped to the loo for a breather, stepping with great care in my barbed wire shoes, and surrendered to the carpeted hush in the Ladies, pressing my burning face to the silvered surface of the mirror. Such a relief to be alone. Even though it was silent in here, the clamour of voices still echoed in my skull. There was an easy chair in the corner of the room, piled with plump satin cushions. I was tempted to throw off my shoes and curl up in it for a while, but there was a real danger I would doze off. Then the outer door opened and a woman came in: Dave's partner.

I recognised her dress before I recognised her: it was the emerald-green taffeta which Auntie Jackie had persuaded her to take instead of boring old black. I had even made her a pot of tea, and listened to her and Auntie Jackie discussing the merits of long gloves and little lace shrugs. I felt a surge of resentment on Auntie

Jackie's behalf at this double betrayal. The woman approached the mirror, checking her appearance, and produced a lipstick from a velvet evening bag, applying it with confident, sweeping strokes. Our eyes slid towards each other's reflections, but she showed no sign of remembering me. Then she paused in the act of dusting her nose and cheeks with a powder brush and looked at me more closely. "I know that dress, don't I?" she said. "I saw it only this afternoon in a glass case. I didn't realise it was for hire."

"It's not," I said, hoarsely. "It belongs to my aunt. She let me borrow it."

"Wow. Lucky you. Do you feel like a princess in it?"

"Not really. Just scared of ruining it mostly."

"I can imagine. I'm finding it pretty difficult to let my hair down, all tarted up like this myself." She'd finished her repair job on the make-up and was now tweaking at her hair.

"The shoes are the worst thing," I said, looking down at my strangulated toes, now purple from the biting silver straps. I felt a twinge of disloyalty, chatting away like this to Auntie Jackie's rival, but the disquieting fact was that she seemed perfectly nice.

"I'll let you into a secret." She lifted her full skirt a

couple of centimetres off the floor to reveal a pair of scuffed trainers. "I figured if no one can see them, why suffer in agony? My husband was *horrified*." She gave me a conspiratorial, woman-to-woman grin and then left.

I waited a minute or two before following, my head still spinning from this revelation. Inside the ballroom the auction had just come to an end, and members of the band were taking their positions. Banks of coloured bulbs pulsed beside the stage, and a slowly revolving mirrorball sprayed drops of light over the walls and floor.

I scanned the seating plan for confirmation. Table B: Mr David Barber. Mrs Louise Barber. Oh dear, oh dear. I remembered the day she had come for a fitting. Dave's mysterious behaviour, lurking in the back garden until the coast was clear, now made a (shoddy) form of sense. So did his brief, snatched visits and unavailability at weekends. And I had thought he was there to protect me!

Music erupted from the speakers as the band launched into a faultless cover of the Scissor Sisters' 'I Don't Feel Like Dancing'. Within a few bars, half a dozen eager couples had advanced on to the floor and were writhing and jerking and jabbing the air in the distinctive way of middle-aged people who have sunk too much wine and lost all sense of rhythm along with their inhibitions. They were soon joined by more of their kind. Not Dave though. He was keeping his head down somewhere, the rat.

I felt a slight pressure beside me.

"There you are," said Adam. "I thought you'd done a runner. You missed the auction. Roger bid for a set of golf clubs. Like he hasn't already got one."

"Oh." *Roger.* Not Rajah. Of course: that made sense.

Adam's lips twitched as he surveyed the dance floor. "Do they know how tragic they look?" He peered at me. "Are you all right?"

"I've just found out something. See that guy over there talking to the woman in green – don't stare. He's Auntie Jackie's boyfriend. You might've seen him. He's always coming round to the house. Well, I've just found out that he's married. To that woman. He saw me earlier and just totally blanked me."

"Don't take it personally," said Adam. "He was probably worried you were going to come rushing over and he'd have to introduce you. That's all."

"Yes, but, I mean, what a bastard. Poor Auntie Jackie."

"Poor wife more like. Jackie probably already knows he's married, but his wife probably doesn't know about Jackie."

"But… Auntie Jackie would never do a thing like that. Try and steal someone's husband." That would make her as bad as Dave.

"Maybe she's not trying to steal him. Maybe she's just *borrowing* him." As he said this, he looked very pointedly at my dress.

Suddenly the heat and the noise were unbearable. "Can we go out and get some fresh air?" I asked.

"Don't you want to dance?"

"I don't feel like dancing," I replied – almost perfectly in time with the music.

"Good, neither do I. Let's go."

We scuttled out guiltily, as if from the scene of a crime, along the carpeted corridor, the music growing fainter and fainter, and out through the lobby into the cool of the night. The lights of the town were strung out along the coast as far as the eye could see. Above us a shiny half moon balanced in the sky like a coin in a slot. The tide was in, as high as I had ever seen it, black as ink and with a rolling swell that sucked and seethed against the shingle. Even though it was nearly midnight, people were still strolling along the promenade; no one raised an eyebrow at our appearance. When I commented on this, Adam said that Brighton was a town of nudists and cross-dressers, and that we would have to try a lot harder if we wanted to stand out.

Without any discussion, we started heading east, the opposite direction to home. The sleeve of Adam's jacket brushed my arm lightly as we walked side by side, and now and then more firmly as I swayed into him. I hitched up my dress, leaving an attractive spare tyre of fabric around my waist, to raise the layers of chiffon in the fishtail clear of the ground, and took off my sandals. The pavement was a carpet of feathers beneath my unbound feet. Now I understood why killer heels were so popular. It was nothing to do with looking taller, fitter, slimmer, but simply that there was no pleasure on earth to equal taking them off.

The ruined hulk of the old pier squatted in the darkness, abandoned and decaying. For some reason it made me think of ghosts and I gave an involuntary shiver that brought me out in goose pimples.

"Are you cold?" Adam asked. "You can have my jacket if you want."

I shook my head. I found I had to plan my words carefully in advance, as though speaking a foreign language. If I launched straight into a sentence unplanned, I wasn't sure where it would end up.

"I can't believe Auntie Jackie would do that," I said at last, having satisfied myself that I'd included a subject, object and verb. "She's a really moral person. She wouldn't do something that was just Plain Wrong."

Adam shrugged. His whole demeanour suggested a policy of non-involvement in the lives of others.

"For instance," I said, warming to my theme. "She was really mad at Rachel for blowing you out at the last minute and going off with Charlie. She thought that was terrible."

Adam's expression darkened a shade and I clamped my teeth shut to stop any more tactless remarks slipping out.

"Oh, she's out with Charlie, is she? I didn't know that."

"Well. I don't know about 'out with'," I said, trying to backtrack. "She's gone to see his show up in the West End. So she'll be in the audience and he'll be in the orchestra pit. I mean, technically, they're not even together."

Adam looked sceptical. I tried to lighten the atmosphere by relating the incident of the tooth-whitening fiasco, but he remained unconsoled. "I should have known she wouldn't be interested in me for long," he said glumly.

"The problem is everyone fancies her so she never has to try. Even when she's really mean to blokes they still fancy her." I thought of poor old Todd, desperate for inside advice on how to shape up.

Adam smiled at me regretfully. "The thing is, you're actually a much nicer person…" he said.

"Thanks," I said, my eyes misting over to blot out the vast bleak landscape of that unspoken *but*…

Just ahead of us on the beach a movement caught my eye. A lone figure of a girl was standing, balanced on the breakwater, while the sea heaved and swayed below. It looked a precarious place to stand, only just out of reach of the water. If there had been anyone else around, you would have suspected her of showing off. The half moon rolled out from behind a cloud and lit up her pale features.

"That's her!" I said, turning to Adam, who had bent to tie his shoelace. "That girl I was telling you about who was in Cliff Street."

"Eh?"

"You know, I asked you the other day if you'd noticed her hanging around."

But when I turned back to look again, she had vanished. She couldn't possibly have had time to get back on to the beach. Could I have imagined her? My heart was racing with that sense of anxiety that her appearance always seemed to trigger. And then I saw something moving in the oily water, breaking the surface and sinking again.

"She's fallen in!" I screamed. Where minutes ago there had been no shortage of other pedestrians around, now there was no one. Cars swished by along the road, oblivious.

"Where? Where?" said Adam, who hadn't quite caught up with the emergency. "Don't!" he called after me as I dropped my shawl and sandals and ran, slithering and crunching over the pebbles, towards the water. It was no time for modesty: my fingers scrabbled at the zip of my dress, but it refused to budge.

"Don't go in. I'll get a lifebelt!"

But I couldn't have stopped if I'd wanted to: the beach shelved steeply into the water and the momentum of my run, greatly accelerated by an avalanche of sliding stones, propelled me into the waves.

*Auntie Diana's dress!* was my last mangled thought before I went under.

Icy water poured into my ears, eyes and mouth and I was rolled over and over before being flung up to the surface again. The shock of the cold drove all the air from my lungs. I could see the girl floundering just a few metres away from me, her face and hands white against the bottomless darkness of the sea. A wave bore me up like a cork and flung me on top of her, knocking her under, but I was able to clutch at her wrist – to save myself as much as her – and we clung together, gasping for breath each time our faces broke the surface. I was determined not to let her go, but her struggles to keep afloat kept pulling me under. We were just metres away from the shore and yet all our efforts seemed to take us further out.

*We can't drown here!* I thought desperately. *Not so close to land.* The drag was too powerful; every fresh wave took us down, battering us with churned up stones. Then the girl seemed to grow limp, which made it easier to hold her. I got an arm around her chest and over one shoulder so that she couldn't slip down. My chiffon fishtail had torn away, leaving my legs freer to kick.

And then Adam was there at the water's edge, braced against the breakwater with a lifebelt. Now I could see him, now I couldn't, as I rose and sank with the swell. He threw it wildly and it landed just feet away, but as unreachable as if it had been a mile. He hauled it in and tried again and again. The fifth or sixth time it hit me on the head and I was able to get my free arm over it. I felt the tug as the rope tightened and began to pull.

I was so weak, and so tired and so sick from all the water I had swallowed, that when I was finally dragged clear, I couldn't even feel relieved or saved. I just lay face down on the warm stones and hoped that all the people clustering round and talking in such urgent voices would go away and let me sleep.

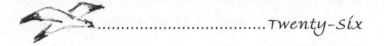 

# Alice

I was sitting on a bed in one of those curtained cubicles in A&E, wrapped in a foil sheet like a giant toffee, when Auntie Jackie burst in. A nurse had taken my temperature and blood pressure and stuck a clip on my finger to measure my heartbeat, and I had answered dozens of questions about my medical history and the professional opinion seemed to be that I was in tremendous shape. The only injuries I had sustained were a few grazes across my legs, back and shoulders, from being bowled over and over in the surf with half a tonne of pebbles, and even the resulting bruises wouldn't reveal their full glory until the morning.

Over the swish of trolleys and the squeak of rubber shoes on vinyl I became aware of a commotion in the waiting room and a familiar voice saying, "No, I won't bloody calm down. You were supposed to be looking after her," and then the curtain opened and Auntie Jackie stood there.

"Oh, Robyn, darling, thank God you're alive," she said, falling on me and hugging me fiercely. "What would I have told your dad if you'd drowned?"

She had obviously come straight from her bed in a tearing hurry, because she was wearing the T-shirt with pigs on it that she used as a nightie, tucked into her grey "housework" joggers and a pair of flip-flops. Her hair stood up in tufts and her face, so defenceless-looking without make-up, was shiny with night cream and tears. *She must love me*, I thought in wonder.

"How did you know I was here? Did Adam call you?"

"No. I only saw Adam in the waiting room just now. I gave him a bit of an earful for not taking care of you."

"Is Adam all right?"

"He's fine. His shoes and socks are a bit wet, that's all. He didn't jump in the sea like some people."

"I had to. There was this girl. One minute she was there on the breakwater and the next she was in the water. And it was so deep and black." I started to tremble at the memory of it.

"Don't think about it," Auntie Jackie advised. "You've been so brave."

"Auntie Jackie, I'm so sorry." I pointed to the remains of the dress, hanging over the back of an orange plastic seat, still dripping. A few shreds, looking and smelling like seaweed, were all that were left of the chiffon fishtail. "I shouldn't have taken it. I was so careful with it all evening. I never spilt a drop down it. And now it's ruined."

Auntie Jackie gave a dismissive wave. "Oh, don't worry. It's just a dress. People are more important than things."

This casual reaction to the loss of her most precious possession made my eyes fill with grateful tears. Then a worrying thought occurred to me: she didn't realise which dress it was. This was not surprising: in its current state it was unrecognisable. "But… but… it's not just any old dress. It's Princess Diana's dress."

Her eyebrows shot up. She went across and had a closer look, holding up the soggy, salt-stained material for inspection, swearing softly. She dropped it back over the chair and her shoulders shook. *Oh, God*, I thought. *She's crying*. She put a hand to her eyes. I shrank a little further inside my toffee wrapper. "I'm really sorry. How can I ever make it up to you?"

A strange, snorting sound was coming from Auntie

Jackie. She turned to face me and I could see that she was laughing. "Oh, you poor little darling," she said, wiping her eyes. "I bet you were even more scared of telling me than you were of drowning."

I nodded. "About the same," I admitted.

She seemed about to say something more, but at that moment there was a flapping sound of someone trying to knock politely on a curtain. "Come in," said Auntie Jackie.

Dave stepped into the cubicle, still dressed in his evening suit, his bow tie now undone and hanging around the open neck of his shirt. He looked haggard and old.

"Hello," he said. Auntie Jackie didn't seem the least bit ·surprised to see him, but even so, electric currents of awkwardness almost crackled in the air between them. *She won't like him seeing her all scruffy*, was my first, irrelevant thought. It was a moment or two before I realised it was me he had come to see.

"I just wanted to say thank you," he said.

"What for?" I said. Did he mean for not spilling the beans to his wife? If so, I didn't want his thanks. It was too sordid.

"For saving Alice's life. That was my daughter you just rescued."

"She's your *daughter*!" I said stupidly, too tired and slow-witted to understand anything new and surprising.

"Yes. I don't know what she was doing out on the beach at that time of night, but if you hadn't come along, and risked your own life… I don't know…" The big rat-catching policeman was too emotional to say any more.

"It was Dave who told me you were here." This was Auntie Jackie, her voice sounding flat and small. "He got there just in time to see you go off in the ambulance. He recognised you straightaway and rang me."

"I didn't know she was your daughter," I said. "I thought…" What *had* I thought exactly? That she was an Animal Rights fanatic who had stalked us all the way from Oxford. The idea sounded absolutely barking now of course, and I was just thankful that I hadn't shared my insane fantasies with anyone else. I had at least been right about one thing: she had been watching 29 Cliff Street. But not on my account. It was her dad and Auntie Jackie she had been spying on. It wasn't about me at all.

"Well anyway, thank you for what you did," said Dave, mastering himself. "We won't forget it."

The other half of that "we" had appeared at his side, still in her emerald ballgown, her eyes red with recent crying. Beside me, Auntie Jackie had gone very, very still.

"So this is the heroine of the hour," said Dave's wife,

smiling at me in recognition. "You did the most amazing thing tonight," she went on. "You and your boyfriend."

"He's not my…"

"I know we can never repay you," she rolled on, "but if there's ever anything we can do for you…" Her generous smile included me and a frozen Auntie Jackie.

"It's all right," I said, embarrassed by the vague vastness of this offer. "I'm glad she's OK. That's enough."

Dave's wife caught sight of the ruined dress and her eyes widened as she remembered our earlier conversation. "My God," she said to Auntie Jackie. "You will forgive her, won't you?"

"I already have," Auntie Jackie replied. "There's nothing to forgive."

"We'd better get back to Alice," said Dave, who was understandably not enjoying this encounter.

"Yes… yes," agreed his wife, without making any move to leave. There seemed to be something else she wanted to say. She hesitated. "Did you see… I mean, it was probably all a blur, but we can't understand what she was doing there in the first place. We don't even know why she was out at that time of night."

Dave looked so stricken, I couldn't help feeling sorry for him, even though I could see very well why his daughter might have been feeling unhappy enough at home to make a desperate gesture.

"I don't know," I said truthfully. "One minute she was standing on the breakwater, and when I looked again, she'd gone. A wave must have swept her off. That's what I thought."

Dave's wife nodded non-committally. "Well, thank you again. So much. Goodbye," she said to Auntie Jackie.

"Goodbye," said Dave, failing to make eye contact, but instead addressing a poster on the wall between us, which proclaimed that assaults on NHS staff would not be tolerated.

"Goodbye," said Auntie Jackie with great dignity. There was something firm and resolute in her tone of voice that told me this parting was permanent.

Husband and wife went out, their arms around each other for support and comfort. Auntie Jackie turned her face away and for a while her sniffs and gulps of breath were the only sounds to break the silence of our separate thoughts.

# Twenty-seven

# The Gambler

It was nearly three before I got to bed. Assuming that I would be staying overnight in hospital, Auntie Jackie had brought in my Mad Cow pyjamas and I had no choice but to wear them home. Adam, who had been sitting patiently in the waiting room all this time, looking after my silver wrap and sandals, lent me his dinner jacket for the walk across the car park. I couldn't help thinking that wearing pyjamas in public places was getting to be a habit with me.

"Well, thanks for a great evening," I said, as Adam and I made our parallel way up to our separate front doors.

"Yes, we must do it again some time," he replied in the same overenthusiastic tone. "I'm sorry it was a bit uneventful, but maybe next time we'll find a way to liven things up…" We both began to laugh. Auntie Jackie had bolted out of the car and into the house ahead of me as though she would otherwise be in the way of a passionate doorstep farewell. You would have thought the events of the evening might have dented her faith in romance. Anyway, there was no way I was kissing anyone: I hadn't cleaned my teeth since being sick on the beach.

"It was you who told me to stop being sensible and do something reckless for a change," I reminded him.

"Did I? God. That was bad advice."

"Well, goodnight," I said, hardly opening my mouth. "Oh, and thanks for rescuing me. I seem to have got all the credit so far."

"You deserve it," he said. "You were the brave one. I was just sensible."

My hair had dried, stiff and salty, and when I took my bra off, I found the soggy twenty pound note inside and a ghostly purple print of the Queen's head just below my left nipple.

*I don't feel at all tired any more. I'm wide awake*, I thought as I got into bed and pulled the duvet around me. And then sleep came down like a sledgehammer and laid me out, and I didn't move – or even dream – for the next twelve hours. It was only the sound of Charlie's trumpet bubbling away in the attic that woke me, and when I looked at the clock, it was the middle of the afternoon.

Rachel, who had been given strict instructions from Auntie Jackie not to disturb me, was waiting impatiently for me to surface so that she could interrogate me about my little adventure. She had heard the general outline from Auntie Jackie, including the Dave connection, and was eager for details, so we sat in the kitchen, drinking banana smoothies and exchanging accounts of our nights out. (Auntie Jackie had bought a blender off the Shopping Channel on Three Easy Payments and was pulping everything she could lay her hands on.)

Rachel's trip up to the West End hadn't been quite what she'd hoped. As I'd pointed out to Adam, for most of the evening she was in the auditorium watching the show, while Charlie was in the orchestra pit. "It would have been so much more fun if you'd been there with me," she said at one point, which just shows what depths of loneliness she must have reached.

She had been unable to throw herself fully into the atmosphere of the closing night party afterwards because of the pain in her gums, which the pills hadn't quite dulled. The whole cast was there, kissing and hugging each other goodbye and getting overemotional, but they hadn't shown much interest in her or even in the musicians, who tended to form a separate clique at the bar. Charlie, she said, had been networking like crazy, and she knew she was being a drag and looking miserable, but smiling was so damn painful. Eating was out of the question and the pill packet said AVOID ALCOHOL, but it was intolerable being the only sober person among a bunch of boozy old luvvies, so she had two vodkas to try and jolly herself up, then found she was too tired to stand.

At about the time I was floundering in the English Channel, she, Charlie and a couple of his friends had got a taxi to a flat in Pimlico where a serious poker game was under way. Rachel couldn't join in because she had only the foggiest recollection of the rules, and these didn't look like the sort of players who would appreciate being asked whether two pairs was better than three-of-a-kind halfway through a hand. Besides, she didn't have anything like enough money.

"They weren't playing for matches like we do at home. There must have been three hundred quid on the table," she said, enjoying my scandalised expression. I thought of that brown envelope in Charlie's back pocket, stuffed with notes.

There were a couple of other bored wives-or-girlfriends there in the flat watching the TV in a back room, but they didn't talk to Rachel so she sat in an armchair and fell asleep. When she woke, it was morning and she found someone had put her to bed, fully clothed, in the spare room, which seemed to be furnished with various items belonging to Charlie. She didn't know where Charlie had spent the night, or if he had ever got to bed at all: she found him in the kitchen, still in last night's concert gear, frying bacon and mushrooms as if he owned the place. The poker players had all gone, but one of the wives-or-girlfriends was flitting about in her dressing gown.

"It was like a weird dream," Rachel said. "Charlie never explained anything – like who people were or what we were doing there. I thought this woman must be the London equivalent of Auntie Jackie, a sort of landlady. I asked him about it when we were on the way home and he said he paid her for the use of a room when he was up in London. He's a bit like the cat in that book we used to read who lives in all these different houses."

"I loved that book," I said, pleased to be reminded of it. "*Six Dinner Sid.*"

"Yeah, that's it. He goes from house to house getting meals and everybody thinks he's their cat, but he's not."

I couldn't help laughing. Rachel had certainly nailed an aspect of Charlie.

"I wouldn't be surprised if he's got another room somewhere else," I said. "Why stop at two?"

"He even asked if he could stay with us next time he's in Oxford," said Rachel.

"And what did you say?"

"I said yes," she admitted.

Dad rang that afternoon. While I was asleep, Auntie Jackie had phoned to tell him about my Aquatic Exploit, as she termed it. In this version, my role as heroic rescuer was played up while my role as potential corpse was very much played down. "I didn't want to freak him out," she explained. "You were supposed to be safe here with me. When he finds out you nearly drowned, he'll probably come storming down and take you back home." This possibility seemed to cause her genuine distress.

"I'll have to go back soon anyway," I reminded her. "School starts in less than two weeks." Even as I said this,

I couldn't quite picture myself anywhere but Cliff Street. The possibility of returning home to Oxford with any kind of confidence seemed remote. Rachel would be all right at university in far-off Newcastle, but where would Dad and I go? The prospect of dossing down among the dog hairs and organic muesli at Mark and Kathy's filled me with gloom.

Auntie Jackie looked aghast. "Everyone's deserting me," she wailed. "You, Rachel, Charlie…" Dave's name hung unspoken in the air. "What will I do without you?"

"You could get a whole new bunch of lodgers," I said. "People like us, only much more fun and less trouble."

Dad's response to the crisis represented by my near drowning – he hadn't been fooled by Auntie Jackie's account for one moment – was to tell me how proud he was of me and in the next breath to say that if I ever put myself in reckless danger like that again, he would kill me.

"But that's why you made me have all those swimming lessons," I reminded him. "So that I'd be able to look after myself in an emergency."

"Have you any idea how many people drown each year trying to save someone else?" he demanded.

"But I didn't drown, did I? Which proves it was the

right decision," I replied. "And if I hadn't, then that other poor girl…"

"But I don't love that other girl. I only love you," he protested.

Once he had extracted a promise that I would do a careful risk assessment before performing any future sea rescues, he moved on to his next area of concern. Publicity. "We don't want your name and address to get in the papers," he said. "After we've been so careful."

"It won't get in the papers," I said dismissively. "Girl Gets Wet. No one Drowns. It's not news."

"We'll see. Anyway, I'm coming down. It feels like I haven't seen you for ages so I'm going to take Thursday and Friday of this week off before the bank holiday and come down for a long weekend."

"Oh, brilliant," I said. "You can have my room and I'll go in with Rachel."

I had so much to tell him – and so much that was maybe better left untold. Perhaps he could come and see me play at the Indigo Club. Or not…

"Book up a nice restaurant for Friday night and I'll take you all out," he promised. "Better ask this boyfriend of yours who pulled you out of the water. I owe him a drink – at least."

"Adam's not my boyfriend," I said. "He actually fancies Rachel."

"Oh. This is the trombonist guy?"

"No, that's Charlie. It's a trumpet actually. We're not sure who he fancies. Rachel calls him Six Dinner Sid. Auntie Jackie put Mr Elkington in his bed – he's not a real skeleton by the way. It was the funniest thing ever…" I realised I had lost him.

"Are you sure all that seawater hasn't affected your brain? I didn't understand a word of that."

"I'll explain it all when I see you."

Auntie Jackie obviously took to heart my remark about finding new lodgers as I found various draft advertisements in her handwriting on the kitchen table. *Room to let in fashionable, convenient area of Brighton, close sea front/shops. No pets, non-smoker, references required. Non-musician preferred. Tolerance and good humour useful.* Several sarcastic corrections/insertions had been made by a different hand – presumably Charlie's.

"I haven't even given notice yet and she is trying to replace me," he grumbled to me. "She barged in while I was getting dressed and asked if I would mind keeping my room tidy for the next couple of weeks, as she might be showing new tenants around and she doesn't want to create a bad impression!"

"It's not you she's trying to replace: it's us," I said. "And anyway, you did tell her you were looking for a flat."

"Well, I am sort of, but not with any urgency. It could take months. Anyway, it's given me a brilliant idea for how to pay her back for that skeleton."

"Oh dear."

"It was when she said she'd be showing prospective tenants around. I could just imagine her pushing open my bedroom door and saying, 'This would be your room,' and…"

"Don't tell me!" I interrupted. "If I know what you're planning, I'll have to warn her." There was no way I was getting drawn into their crazy game. If Auntie Jackie found out I was in on the joke, I'd be next in line for revenge. "Especially if it's going to put off any new lodgers. That would be too mean."

"But that's the beauty of it," Charlie insisted. "It's like a vetting process. It'll just weed out the sort of boring, respectable types with no sense of humour who wouldn't fit in here anyway. I'll be doing her a favour."

"Hmmm."

He had sought me out in my room to tell me that Ollie's "bust" arm had made a miraculous recovery and that I wouldn't be needed at the Indigo Club that night after all. "Sorry to let you down," he said, making himself comfortable in my armchair.

"That's OK. I haven't had a chance to practise much since last week anyway," I admitted. This had been my opening remark at every music lesson for the past eight years so the words tripped out more or less automatically.

"Well, I've warned Ollie that his understudy was a big hit with the punters so he'd better shape up if he wants to keep his place in the band," Charlie assured me. He seemed to take some persuading that I wasn't in the least bit disappointed.

"Surely no one as brave as you were last night could admit to suffering from something as feeble as stage fright?" he demanded.

"It was the other way round," I explained. "Compared to playing with your band, jumping into the sea was easy."

After breaking what he imagined to be his bad news with so little opposition, he didn't appear to be in any hurry to leave. He asked me how much longer Rachel and I would be staying in Brighton, and from this we had progressed to talking about Auntie Jackie's advertisements for new lodgers and his cunning plan for revenge.

Having made him promise that it didn't involve snakes

or crocodiles or anything else likely to endanger life, I turned the conversation to his evening out with Rachel. For the first time ever, Charlie looked guilty and uncomfortable.

"Oh, it was all right. I don't think Rachel enjoyed it much though. She wasn't her usual cheerful self. I could hardly get a smile out of her all night."

As I was still sworn to secrecy about the tooth-whitening fiasco, I couldn't enlighten him.

"I thought she was supposed to be a real party girl, but she just kind of sat in the corner and went to sleep."

"She usually is," I said, feeling bound to defend her hard-won reputation. "She's normally the one ordering tequila slammers and dancing on the bar when everyone else is ready to leave. I think she was feeling a bit... er... off-colour last night." I congratulated myself silently on the aptness of this pun.

"I suppose I didn't look after her very well," Charlie conceded. "I'll have to think of a way to make it up to her." He sighed as though this was a great personal inconvenience, and I felt a pang of sorrow for Rachel because I knew that she had let herself fall for Charlie, while he was already looking over her shoulder.

# Twenty-eight

# The Visitor

On Monday morning I got up early to help Auntie Jackie with the returns from the ball. The first caller, knocking promptly at 9.00 a.m, was Louise Barber, carrying the emerald-green dress and a bouquet of yellow roses.

"Would you do the honours?" Auntie Jackie said to me, peering through a chink in the blinds to observe her approach. "You just have to take the dress and give her back her deposit. I don't think I can face it."

"Did you already know Dave had a wife?" I asked her.

"Oh, I knew. But it was only when she came here to hire the dress, and I actually saw her in the flesh, that it hit me that she was a real person – not just an inconvenience. I'm not proud of myself."

"Have you broken up with him?"

She nodded. "This thing with Alice has shaken him right up. He thinks it's his fault – well, it probably is. So anyway, he's sorted out his priorities, as he put it, and family's got to come first."

Sighing, she withdrew to the kitchen and left me to play shopkeeper.

The flowers, it turned out, were for me. I didn't want to put them in the bucket by the back door, even temporarily, because of the unhappy parallels with Dave's bouquet, so I hid them in the sink in Rachel's room for later.

Louise Barber was just as friendly and grateful as she had been at the hospital, scrupulously pointing out a microscopic pulled thread hidden among the folds of the skirt and insisting she should forfeit her deposit. "I wanted Alice to come with me to meet you properly," she said as I put the dress to one side for cleaning. "But she wouldn't. She's shy, I suppose. And stubborn."

"That's OK," I said, thanking God for Alice's stubbornness. I wouldn't enjoy a reunion any more than she would, both of us knowing what we knew about her dad and my aunt, but too embarrassed or ashamed to mention it. We could never be friends with that dangerous secret, like a sleeping dragon, always between us, so what was the point?

There was one thing that I would have liked to talk to Alice about, if it wasn't for the presence of the dragon, and that was her appointment at the photo studio. I wanted to know if she had noticed anything suspicious, and also to reassure her that any images of her would have been destroyed just minutes after she'd left, by Adam and his lethal Lucozade.

I made a note of their address from the paperwork in Auntie Jackie's file and when Louise had gone, I wrote the following letter:

> *Hi Alice*
>
> *My name is Robyn – we met on Saturday night although I'd seen you before on a few occasions.* [A tactful way of putting it, if I say so myself.] *I hope you are OK. I'm only writing this note because I remembered seeing you at that photo studio in Balrudry Street and I wanted to tell you something that happened there in case the same thing happened to you. My sister Rachel went to have some pictures taken there because a woman who said she was a scout for a modelling agency stopped her in the street*

and told her she could get her photos done for nothing.

When Rachel went along she had to undress in this cubicle and she discovered that there was a hidden webcam in there filming her undressing and recording the pictures on a laptop in the office next door. Our friend Adam and I went back there (that was when you saw us) and he poured a bottle of Lucozade (!) all over the laptop to stuff it up (so if there were any pictures of you on it they've been destroyed). Next time he went past the shop it was all boarded up and empty, so we think the photographer guy, whose name was Gundry, had done a runner. It's probably not his real name anyway. (The modelling agency in London didn't exist either by the way. It was a flat above a kebab shop or something.)

I'm only telling you all this because I keep thinking that this guy has probably set up somewhere else and is doing the same thing to other girls, and it bugs me. I know your dad is in the police and if he knew this had happened to you, he might do something about it, but it's up to you if you tell him or not.

Best wishes

Robyn Stenning

In the ten minutes I was out posting this letter, the phone had not stopped ringing, I was informed on my return. The *Brighton and Hove Argus* and *The Leader* and one news agency had got hold of the story of the rescue and called to check details, and a researcher from Breakfast TV wanted me to ring her back urgently. Auntie Jackie had had to resort to the extreme measure of turfing Rachel out of bed to help in the shop while she fielded calls. "God, she's grumpy in the mornings," each of them separately complained to me.

"What sort of details did they want?" I asked anxiously, remembering Dad's paranoia about security and also Auntie Jackie's tendency to embellish the facts. "Did you give my real name?"

"Well, of course I gave your real name," Auntie Jackie said impatiently. "I wasn't going to make one up, was I? They wanted a picture of you so I said they could have that one of you and me at Arundel. Your hair looks a bit straggly, but at least you're smiling. If it's no good they're going to send a photographer round."

"You'd better get some make-up on," Rachel advised, looking critically at my naked face. "I'll switch on my straighteners."

"You've got to ring this TV woman back first," Auntie

Jackie said. "They want you to go on *Good Morning* or something."

"What for?"

"To talk about your heroic rescue. You know. They might nominate you for one of those Children of Courage awards."

"Yeah, right."

"You might get your picture taken with Carol Vorderman," Rachel said, and folded up laughing.

"I'm not ringing some woman I don't know."

"You must," Auntie Jackie insisted, passing me the phone. "If you don't hurry up, they'll fill that slot with something else. Instead of you on the couch, it'll be some kid with ADHD who can play 'Bohemian Rhapsody' on the handbells."

"Don't you want to be on TV?" Rachel demanded.

"I suppose. But if they're that keen, they'll ring back..."

"They might not," Auntie Jackie said. "You can't trust these media types."

As if to rebut this slur, the phone sprang to life in my hand, trilling, flashing and throbbing all at once. Rachel and Auntie Jackie looked at me expectantly. "It's probably Dad," I said, but as soon as I heard the breezy, overfriendly voice on the other end, I knew it could only be a media type.

The woman introduced herself so quickly that I didn't catch her name – it sounded like Felicity Trout-Spanky, but surely can't have been – and said she was a researcher for the BBC programme *On the Sofa*? They'd heard all about my adventure and would love me to come on the show and talk about it? She had one of those accents that go up at the end of the sentence so that everything sounds like a question? "We're especially interested in the dress you were wearing?" she bubbled. "It used to belong to Princess Diana, right?"

I confirmed that this was the case. "And you'd borrowed this off your aunt, without telling her, to wear to a ball?"

"Sort of."

"And then on the way home you jumped into the sea *in that dress* to rescue someone?"

"Yes. I would've taken it off, but the zip stuck."

"Wow. That's amazing. Did you feel Princess Diana's *presence* while you were in the water? I mean, did you feel that the dress was kind of keeping you afloat in some way?"

"Er… I can't really remember what I was thinking. I was just trying not to drown really." Far from buoying me up the dress had in fact done its best to drag me down – that is until the skirt ripped off, but I sensed that this wasn't the answer she was after.

"What did your aunt say when she found out what had happened to her dress?"

"She swore a bit under her breath and then she started laughing."

"Wow. That's amazing. Do you think your aunt would be happy to come on to *On the Sofa* as well? It's such a lovely story."

"I don't know. She's pretty busy," I said, looking at Auntie Jackie who started making urgent gestures of denial. *I'm not busy*, she mouthed.

This distraction caused me to miss Felicity's next remark, but the gist seemed to be something to do with a parent-or-guardian. "She's just here. I'll put her on," I said, as Auntie Jackie lunged for the phone.

"What was that all about then?" asked Rachel, only to be silenced by an imperious wave from our parent-or-guardian, who swept out of the room with the phone still clamped to one ear to continue her conversation in private.

"*On the Sofa* want me to go and talk about how I ruined Princess Diana's dress."

"You mean they're not the least bit interested in the fact that you saved someone's life," Rachel snorted.

"Not really, no. I don't think they'd be bothered if I'd just been wearing my jeans."

"God, that programme is such crap, it's unbelievable." Rachel's face was a picture of utter disgust. "The people who watch it must be total saddos."

"Absolute losers," I agreed.

"Are you going to do it?"

"Yes."

"Cool… Can I come?"

# Practically Famous

This is how the local paper reported the story of my midnight swim.

Two fourteen-year-old schoolgirls were pulled from the sea near the West Pier in the early hours of Sunday morning. Robin Stebbings (left) was walking home from a charity ball at the Grand Hotel when she noticed a swimmer in difficulty. Plucky Robin, 14, from Cambridge, jumped into the waves in full evening dress to rescue Alice Barber (below, right). Fortunately for the teenage twosome, passer-by Andy Harris, a full-time student at Sussex University, saw their struggles and was able to throw them a lifebelt. Alice, of Mercer Road, Brighton, had already lost consciousness and was revived by paramedics at the scene. Paramedic Gary Thrower said she was lucky to be alive. "Without the intervention of these two young people, we would have had a tragedy on our hands." Both girls were treated in hospital.

So many errors in such a short article! It was bad enough being downgraded to fourteen, but it was being renamed Stebbings that really hurt. Typical of my luck that my moment in the limelight should have to take place under an alias.

The *Daily Mail* had a slightly different angle:

An off-duty policeman who stopped to assist at the scene of a dramatic sea rescue discovered that it was his own daughter who had been pulled from the waves. David Barber, of the East Sussex Constabulary, was on his way home from a ball at the Grand Hotel, Brighton, with his wife Louise when the incident occurred. Alice Barber, 14, was swept off a breakwater on Brighton beach by a freak wave. She was pulled from the water, unconscious, by two other ball-goers just minutes before her parents arrived on the scene. She was given life-saving resuscitation by paramedics and is expected to make a full recovery. "It was the shock of my life," said Barber, 42. "I thought she was tucked up in bed at home."

*Do you know what your teens get up to while you're out? See Penny Pringle, p. 6.*

And this is the story that got picked up by the Associated Press Agency and syndicated around the world before any of us could stop it:

# DIANA DRESS PROVES A LIFE-SAVER

*UK.* A fifteen-year-old schoolgirl, wearing a dress once owned by the late Diana, Princess of Wales, jumped into the sea to rescue a drowning teenager off the south coast of England, *writes Ed Newby*. Robyn Stenning of Oxford had borrowed the dress – valued at £65,000 – without permission from her aunt's costume-hire shop in Brighton to attend a charity ball. She was walking home along the coast road with her boyfriend when she noticed a female swimmer in difficulties. Brave Robyn kept the girl afloat in rough seas until rescue arrived. "I think the spirit of Princess Diana was giving me strength," she said. Her aunt was unavailable for comment.

Of course, I never said that or anything like it. I wouldn't even have thought anything so wet. No one called Ed Newby ever spoke to me and I didn't mention the Diana dress to anyone – except Auntie Jackie of course. Journalists just make things up!

# Charlie's Revenge

Auntie Jackie responded to the prospect of Dad's arrival with a storm of cleaning and household repairs, as though she was expecting a visit from the environmental health officer, the Queen and Social Services all rolled into one.

"It's only Dad. What's the big deal?" Rachel protested, as Auntie Jackie traipsed back and forth to the car with sacks of junk for the tip. Out went old Wellington boots, broken tennis racquets, dead house plants, lumpy pillows, singed lampshades, the slimy shower curtain and Gunter the pig. In came new rugs, pillows, towels, duvets, bath mat, a couple of women called Winnie and Bunny from a domestic cleaning agency, and a bloke with a giant machine for shampooing the staircarpet.

"We've got to get this place in shape by Thursday. Your mum always kept such a tidy house. I don't want your dad thinking I'm some sort of slut who can't cope," Auntie Jackie said through gritted teeth, scrubbing at the blackened interior of the oven.

"Have you seen the muck on them skirting boards?" I heard Winnie mutter to Bunny when she thought no one was listening. Bunny responded with a low whistling sound, as though she'd been punctured.

There was an added urgency to this war on dirt as a couple of prospective tenants were coming to look around on Thursday evening. Most of that day was going to be taken up with our visit to the television studios in Shepherd's Bush, which left even less time for housework.

By Wednesday evening, thanks largely to the efforts of Winnie and Bunny, who seemed to have a mania for hygiene that went far beyond their contractual obligations, the communal areas of 29 Cliff Street were transformed. Even Rachel had been seen to steer the hoover around the little islands of clutter on her bedroom carpet.

A minor upset was caused by the disappearance of Mr

Elkington from his regular perch by the larder, which he guarded with what seemed to me a hungry expression. Auntie Jackie was at first convinced she must have accidentally carted him off to the dump with the rest of the trash. Later she changed her mind and began to harbour suspicions about the carpet-man, who had made several unsupervised visits to the kitchen to fill his water tank and drove off in a Ford transit van – an ideal vehicle for body-snatching, in her view.

Rachel and I knew where Mr Elkington was, but were sworn to secrecy for the next forty-eight hours. In spite of my determination not to get involved in Charlie's prank, I had been unable to resist investigating the peals of laughter coming from his room while Auntie Jackie was out on one of her trips to the dump.

I found him and Rachel giggling together over the prone figure of Mr Elkington, who was face down on the bed, dressed in some of Charlie's old clothes. They were in the process of scattering him and the bed with chunks of plaster, builder's rubble and wooden laths, which Charlie had raided from a skip at the end of the street. Directly above him, stuck to the ceiling, was a large poster of sunshine breaking through clouds. The edges had been roughly torn so that at first glance it gave the impression of a patch of sky visible through a ragged hole in the roof.

"Jackie's always cheerfully talking about the roof collapsing on top of me so I thought her new lodger might like to see the possible fate that awaits him," said Charlie, disposing of the last few flakes of dried plaster. "Wouldn't you love to see her face?"

The final touch was to rig up a crow-scarer across the doorway so that it would let out a terrific bang as the door opened, not only scaring Auntie Jackie and the prospective tenant half to death, but giving the impression that the roof-fall had just that second occurred.

I thought this last detail was going a bit far, but Charlie insisted it was no more sadistic than the removal of the lightbulb from his lamp in Auntie Jackie's original stunt.

"Where are you going to sleep tonight then?" Rachel asked in as neutral a voice as possible, as we surveyed the carefully trashed bed.

"I'm going back up to London tonight for a poker game," Charlie replied, glancing at his watch. "But I'll be back tomorrow afternoon. In plenty of time."

"Don't forget to watch *On the Sofa* at 9.15," Rachel said, hiding any disappointment that she was not included in his plans. "Rob's going to be on it talking about what it's like to be a teen superhero."

"Are you, Ronnie?" asked Charlie, with great interest. "Well, I'll definitely watch it then." He then went on to qualify this by adding, "If I'm awake at that unearthly hour."

"Don't worry, we'll record it," Rachel assured him, with an evil smile in my direction. "We want to be able to give copies to all our friends."

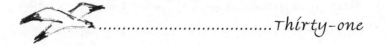

# On the Sofa

It seemed as though Rachel might have second thoughts about accompanying us up to London when I went to wake her at 6.00 a.m. as agreed. As I twitched the curtain open, she groaned and tunnelled further under the duvet, in temporary denial, so I left her and went to get dressed. If she wasn't ready when the car arrived to collect us at 6.30, she could stay behind and stuff herself.

Auntie Jackie had been up for ages, blow-drying her hair and putting a fresh layer of purple polish on her nails. She had offered me the freedom of the frock shop again, and even Rachel had said I could borrow her white jeans since it was a special occasion, but I had learnt my lesson and was determined to stick to my own clothes, however unglamorous. The only advice offered by Felicity on the matter of dress was to avoid bright red as it didn't film well and tended to clash with the sofa, which I took as permission to wear my star print skirt with the Sellotaped hem, polka-dot (skulls) vest and striped converses. Auntie Jackie raised a critical eyebrow at this combination, but I faced her down with a particularly uncompromising stare and she backed off without a word. Rachel wasn't nearly so tactful. "You're not actually going to wear that, are you?" was her reaction.

At about 6.29, just as the driver was pressing the broken doorbell, she had emerged, yawning, her eyes half shut as if she was not fully committed to being out of bed, but at least dressed and ready to go. In spite of her unhelpful remark, I was glad she was coming with us and, by the end of the day, so was she; though she couldn't have imagined it at the time, it was a decision that might just have saved her life.

Because of the events that followed, my memories of that brief TV appearance are slightly fragmented. Something to do with shock I expect. Certain impressions remain with perfect clarity: the disorientating walk down endless curving corridors in the wake of Felicity and her clipboard, with the occasional glimpse into offices where even at this early hour, media types were already at work. The long table in the hospitality suite laid out with tea, coffee, fresh orange juice, sparkling water and vast platters of Danish pastries, buns and croissants, and bowls of fresh fruit. Who on earth, I wondered, could manage a whole mango at eight o'clock in the morning? For a moment I wished it was Rachel not me who was going in front of the camera because now I was too queasy and nervous to eat, while she was helping herself with complete abandon.

I remember being led away to be made up in a small white room full of mirrors, like a hairdresser's. A youngish woman all in black held my hair off my face with what seemed to be a section from an old pair of tights, and proceeded to paint me with beige foundation. She had a whole tool kit of make-up and brushes, all of which looked rather tired and well-used. I couldn't help wondering whose eye sockets had last been gouged by this same eyeliner pencil, and whose lips had last been smeared with this same sticky gloop.

"I did already put some on this morning," I managed to squeak when the woman had finished with my mouth. My lips felt heavy with jam; my skin prickled.

"You need more than you think under studio lights," she

said kindly. "Or you'll look washed out." She twirled a fat brush in some bronzing powder and dusted my cheeks and chin. I think I might have had more confidence in her artistry if her own face wasn't completely free of make-up. When she was satisfied that I was a match for the most powerful studio lights, she plugged in a hot brush and began tweaking at my carefully straightened hair. I couldn't quite see what she was doing because she had a cunning way of standing between me and the mirror, but occasionally she'd lean out of the way and I would get a heart-stopping glimpse of a tangerine-faced drag queen with a mullet. As soon as she let me go, I raked my fingers through my hair to flatten it all down again.

"Don't you like it?" she said, not troubling to conceal her disappointment.

Of my five minutes on the sofa I remember very little; it was over before I had even begun to start processing the experience and all my concentration was focused on trying to look normal in spite of the Rocky Horror makeover. The studio was small and cluttered with equipment and crew, and I wasn't sure whether I was supposed to face the camera or the presenters, Tracy and Bill, when I was speaking. I realised I was sitting rigidly upright, while Auntie Jackie, beside me, was lounging comfortably, but it was now too late to rearrange myself. There was a blown up photo of Diana wearing the Dress in its full glory, and beside this was a mannequin in a blonde wig displaying its sorry remains – tattered, shrunk and rippled with salt stains.

Tracy invited me, in a voice full of professionally modulated eagerness, to tell the viewers my story and then proceeded to keep interrupting with expressions of amazement. I had the feeling I was all the time being prompted by her and Bill to claim that I had felt "the spirit of Diana" at work in the water, but to their immense frustration I couldn't and wouldn't. Finally, I conceded that I had looked at her photograph while I was contemplating my unauthorised borrowing of the dress and been influenced by the thought that tragedy could strike any of us at any time. This much was true.

I only knew it was over when Tracy suddenly dropped her bubbly TV persona and began talking in a normal voice, and then Auntie Jackie and I were back in the hospitality suite and I was hungry at last, but all the Danish pastries had now been cleared away or perhaps eaten.

Rachel, who had been watching it all on a monitor, said I hadn't stuttered at all, hardly, and my make-up didn't look too bad on screen, and if she had one teensy-weensy criticism, it was the way I was sitting bolt upright like a ventriloquist's dummy, but apart from that it was fine.

There was a form to be filled in so that we could claim the payment of £120 each which Auntie Jackie had discovered was our due for appearing. "Not much for the best part of half a day," she sniffed, whereas to me it seemed easy money for so little effort – even better than an hour at the Indigo Club.

Felicity thanked us and took us as far as the lift to reception, where she said a driver would be waiting to take us home.

"Oh, look, it's the same guy from this morning," said Auntie Jackie a little too eagerly. She had sat in the front with him all the way from Brighton and had his entire life story before we even reached the M25. He was another dodgy charmer in the Dave mould and I could just see where this was going if we didn't keep an eye on her.

"My three lovely ladies again," he said smoothly. "I've really hit the jackpot today."

Behind his back, Rachel and I mimed puking, while Auntie Jackie leapt into the front seat before anyone could object. She'd been in a slightly manic mood all morning and kept smiling to herself as if at some secret joke.

We had had our phones turned off while we were in the studio, and on switching them back on, Rachel and I found that between us we'd had six missed calls from Dad. "What's that about I wonder?" said Rachel. She tried calling his work and mobile numbers, but there was no reply from either.

"I texted him on the way here to remind him to watch the TV," I said, "so perhaps he was phoning to say he saw it."

"He was probably ringing to tell you you were wearing too much make-up," Rachel said and we both laughed. That reminded me that I was still in full stage paint so I wiped as much of it off as I could with a dry tissue. There was a pot of dashboard wipes on the parcel shelf behind us and I was sorely tempted to finish the job with one of them, but some of the ingredients looked a bit caustic.

Auntie Jackie chatted to the driver all the way out of London and by the time we hit the M25, he was her new best mate. "Are you in a hurry, Tony?" she asked him as we approached Gatwick. Rachel and I exchanged sideways glances. *Tony*.

"Would you be able to do a twenty minute detour? I want to show these girls something."

"Sure," he said.

"I don't want to get you into trouble."

"No trouble. After all, it's not surprising if I'm a little late back – the traffic's terrible," he said, smiling at the open road ahead.

"What are you going to show us?" Rachel demanded.

"You'll see in a minute. Be patient," said Auntie Jackie mysteriously. On the outskirts of Crawley she began to issue directions, around the ring road, across half a dozen roundabouts away from the town and through increasingly insalubrious areas until we came to a grim industrial estate of low rise units, warehouses, car dealerships and cash-and-carry stores – boxy grey islands in a sea of asphalt. At her instruction we finally pulled up outside a massive storage facility the size of an aircraft hangar, and she jumped out of the car with a thoroughly unconvincing, "Back in two ticks," and disappeared around the side of the building.

"What the hell's she up to?" Rachel wondered.

Minutes passed. Eddies of dust and litter whirled across the expanse of empty car park. Rachel and I shifted in our seats in embarrassment. Tony looked at his watch, surfed the radio channels for a while, and finally got out of the car and lit a cigarette. And then another.

Rachel wound down the window. "Sorry about this," she said. "Shall I go and find her?"

Then Auntie Jackie appeared around the corner, beckoning urgently. *The minute we're out of sight*, I thought, *he is going to jump in the car and drive off and abandon us. And I don't blame him.* But, as if drawn by the force of Auntie Jackie's personality, he obediently followed us and a moment later we were standing in the entrance lobby of the vast storage facility.

Auntie Jackie was standing beside a sort of conveyor belt which emerged from a hatch covered by thick rubber flaps. In front of her was a large, solid trunk with a combination lock. She twirled the dials and snapped the catches open. I don't know what I expected to see inside – in my bewildered state of mind a dead body didn't seem entirely out of the question – but I still gave a gasp of surprise when Auntie Jackie parted the layers of polythene and tissue and lifted out the midnight-blue Diana dress, with the chiffon fishtail and the silver stars, pristine, undamaged and perfect in every detail.

............................

# Thirty-two

# A Genuine Fake

"For my Christening my godmother gave me a string of real pearls," Auntie Jackie said. "I was never allowed to wear them when I was young because they were too precious, but every so often I'd get them out of their red velvet box in Mum and Dad's room and look at them. That's just how I feel about this dress." She stroked the fabric reverently. "About once a year I have to come up here and have a look, make sure it's all right." She laid it carefully back in the trunk in its tissue paper wrappings.

"So if this is the real dress, that one I wore was just a fake?" I said, having taken an inordinate amount of time to reach this simple conclusion. I couldn't – yet – say why I was so thrown by this. My principal feeling was one of embarrassment at being the victim of a bizarre practical joke.

"Not a fake. A replica," said Auntie Jackie reprovingly. "Lovingly reproduced by hand down to the last stitch. It took me about six months to make."

"But you told us it was Diana's actual dress. When we first looked round the shop."

"I didn't actually. You saw the photograph and just assumed. I told you I bought Diana's dress at auction, which is true. You didn't really think I'd just leave something that valuable on show, with customers trooping in and out all day? I'd never get insurance."

"Did you leave the door of the cabinet open before the ball deliberately?" We were back in the car now, doing ninety down the fast lane of the M23. Tony had to make up the missing half hour somehow.

"Yes. I wanted to see if you'd take it. I so wanted you to be a princess for a night. But I didn't want to give you permission because that takes away the pleasure. It's the forbidden things that we want most."

"But you let me think I'd destroyed your precious dress! That's why you were so laid back about it! You could have told me then," I protested.

"I swear I would have if you'd been inconsolable!"

Auntie Jackie protested. "But you seemed to get over it pretty well once you realised I wasn't going to murder you. I thought a little bit of remorse wouldn't go amiss given that six months' handiwork went down the pan."

"You could have told me later on."

"But once the TV people and the papers got hold of it, it was too late."

"But you must have told them about it."

"I didn't! I never mentioned the dress," Auntie Jackie insisted.

"How did they find out then?" Rachel wondered. "I never said anything."

"Neither did I," I said, remembering, even as I said the words, that there was someone I had talked to about the dress, as we stood side by side at the mirror, in the loos at the Grand Hotel. "Oh…."

"The point is," said Rachel, who hadn't taken sides up to that point, "you just went on TV in front of millions of people and made Robyn come out with a load of crap that isn't even true." This aspect of the matter had only just occurred to me, and I was feeling duly dizzy.

"But it was true for her," said Auntie Jackie. "She thought it was the real dress. It could have been the real dress. And since I own the original, no one will ever know it wasn't."

"I'd never have agreed to go on the TV if I'd known it wasn't real," I said in dismay.

"That's precisely why I didn't tell you," said Auntie Jackie triumphantly. "You know that idiot Felicity would have spiked the story straightaway if we'd told her the dress was just a replica. I didn't see why you should have to give up your fifteen minutes of fame just because they are too stupid to recognise the really important thing, which was you saving someone's life."

"Have we just done something illegal?" I asked weakly.

"No, of course not. It's not as if I'm trying to pull off an insurance fraud." For a second Auntie Jackie sounded almost wistful at this missed opportunity. "It's my dress. If it ever comes out of its box, I'll say it's a replica. OK. No one outside this car need ever know." She turned to the driver, who had been listening to this discussion blank faced, without comment. "I'm sorry, Tony," she said, patting his arm. "We're going to have to kill you."

# Ruth

"They said there'd be storms," Auntie Jackie said, as a distant thunderclap broke the silence just outside Brighton. "I didn't think the weather would hold."

The funny thing was, the sky was still quite blue.

Tony pulled into a garage to fill up with petrol, and came back to the car with four dark chocolate Magnums. He ate his while he drove, holding it just out of the open window between mouthfuls so as not to drip ice cream on his leather upholstery. On my first bite the entire chocolate shell fell off into my lap in two pieces and began to melt.

We smelled the smoke before we saw it, drifting in on the warm breeze, mixed with city smells of cooking and drains and exhaust. The traffic leading up to Cliff Street was unusually congested; ahead of us drivers, sensing defeat, were beginning to make three-point turns in the road and head back the way they had come. There was a moment of near chaos as an ambulance, sirens whooping, tried to nose down the wrong lane, forcing the oncoming cars up on to the pavement. Then, as we rolled another twenty metres or so down the hill, we saw it: a funnel of smoke billowing from the rooftops.

"That's coming from Cliff Street," said Rachel uneasily. "Isn't it?"

A policeman in a bright yellow tabard was trying to keep the traffic flowing and stop people slowing down to have a gawp. "Straight ahead only," he kept barking, making sweeping gestures with his arm. "No left turn."

Tony leant through his window and called him over. "What's going on, mate?"

"Next turning's blocked; there's been some sort of explosion. You've got to go straight on."

Auntie Jackie was out of the car and running before he had finished speaking. Under the astonished gaze of Tony and the policeman we jumped out and chased after her, Rachel stumbling in her high shoes and both of us, absurdly, still holding the remains of our ice creams. The entrance to the street was cordoned off. I had been here before: the sideways-on police car, the fluttering tape, the spectators. Two fire engines blocked the middle of the road.

"Keep back, love," one of the policeman said to Auntie Jackie as she ducked under the tape. "There could be another explosion."

"That's my house!" she wailed, pushing past him and then stopping helplessly as she watched the unfolding chaos.

At the word "explosion" Rachel and I looked at each other in sheer horror. We both knew what the other was thinking. *They* had tracked us down and come for us after all, and if it had been any other day than today, we would have been there in the house. In the drama and excitement of the past few days we'd forgotten why we'd left Oxford in the first place, but the threat had never gone away. Rachel was shaking violently and I tried to hug her, but my hand was wet with melted Magnum. For someone who had nearly died twice in one week I felt weirdly calm and detached. It was as if I was watching everything from above – I could even see myself as part of the scene, which was one of complete confusion.

Two firefighters in breathing apparatus ran into the house, dragging a black rubber hose. On the doorstep, another was holding a big plastic clipboard; he took something from the men as they passed, like an usherette collecting tickets. Two more, in yellow helmets, seemed to be trying to gain admittance to the houses on either side. A ladder was slowly extending from one of the engines up to the top of the building, towards the gaping hole where the roof had once been from which smoke still pumped thickly. An ambulance stood ready, back doors open. Adam burst through the crowd of spectators and hurried towards us in alarm, his face white with shock. "Thank God you're OK," he said. "I thought you were in there."

"What happened?" Rachel said, wiping her eyes.

"I don't know – there was this massive bang. Like a bomb. I came out the front and saw the roof had blown off, so I got Gran out quick and then dialled 999."

"How did they find us?" I said, and my voice sounded far away and strange.

Adam had gone across to talk to one of the firemen who seemed to be in charge. He was the only one wearing a white helmet, and was standing by the pump supervising proceedings. "They don't know for definite, but they're saying it looks like a gas explosion," Adam said on his return. "Leaky boiler – they've seen it all before. Was the boiler in the attic room?"

I nodded, remembering Charlie's regular headaches and his complaints about dead mice under the boiler, gassed to death, poor things.

"You mean it wasn't deliberate?" said Rachel, not quite believing him.

"No. Dangerous, but not deliberate," Adam replied.

Not terrorism then, not a murder plot, just an everyday domestic disaster. A little carelessness, a little bad luck and *boom*!

I seemed to float back down and rejoin my body. I didn't know what to believe.

One of the policemen had come over to talk to Auntie Jackie. "Are you the householder? How many of you are still inside?"

"There's just us here," Auntie Jackie said, pointing wildly round at me and Rachel. "And my lodger who lives up at the top." We looked in horror at the demolished attic. None of us had given Charlie a thought. The policeman went to confer with one of the firemen who had come out of the building.

"They're bringing out one male casualty," I heard him say, and the paramedics sprang into life, bringing a stretcher on a folding trolley from the back of the ambulance up as far as the front steps. A few minutes later the two firemen came out, carrying between them a lifeless figure, covered from head to foot in grey plaster dust, and laid him on the stretcher. The crowd of bystanders went suddenly still. I felt Rachel's fingernails digging into my arm and then everyone seemed to exhale in one sigh, as the figure on the stretcher moved slightly, passing one hand over his eyes as he was loaded on to the waiting ambulance.

"Charlie!" Rachel gave a sort of choking sob and broke away from us in her skittering high-heeled run, and just made it to the ambulance before they closed the doors.

We watched as she was swallowed up inside, and then a familiar voice behind me said, "Ronnie! What the hell's going on?" Charlie stood there in his motorbike leathers, crash helmet under one arm, gaping up at the wreckage of his former room. The exposed and shattered beams of the roof looked naked and terrible through the smoke, like the skeleton of the ruined pier.

"Oh, Charlie, thank God you're all right." Auntie Jackie collapsed against him and they clung to each other for a moment, swaying. "I thought you were dead in there."

"But if Charlie's here," I said, pointing to the ambulance from which Rachel was now emerging in a trance-like state, "then who's that in there?"

# The Jealous Guy

I watched Rachel take a few steps and then sit down suddenly on the low wall, where once Alice Barber had watched and waited, and put her face in her hands.

I left the other two, still hugging, and went across to Rachel, squatting down in front of her and trying to see whether she was crying. She looked at me with a face full of fear and confusion.

"It wasn't Charlie on the stretcher," she said, as if she had only just understood the implications of what she had seen in that ambulance.

"I know – Charlie's OK. He's over there."

She shook her head as if this was now irrelevant. "It was him. It was him all along."

"Who? What was?"

"He must have broken into the house. He was lying in wait for me."

"Who?" I was really afraid that the shock had affected her brain.

"If I hadn't come with you today, I'd have been in there." She looked at me as if I was the one who was mad. "Todd," she said. "It was Todd."

There are two ways of dealing with a narrow escape, Charlie reckons. The pessimist says, *Poor me, I nearly died.* The optimist says, *Lucky me: I'm still alive.* Auntie Jackie, as might be expected, took the optimist's route. In fact, once the initial shock had passed, she reacted to the destruction of her property in much the same philosophical way as she had to the loss of the Diana dress, which made me wonder if 29 Cliff Street wasn't just a replica house and she had another, better one hidden away in a trunk somewhere. Once it was established that the damage was almost entirely confined to the upper storeys, and that her business, down on the ground floor, was intact, she was even able to see a silver lining through the clouds of smoke.

"I suppose I'll get a new roof on the insurance now,"

she said brightly from the comfort of her temporary accommodation in the Travelodge opposite Preston Park. "So it's not all bad news." Her main source of regret seemed to be the ruination of Winnie and Bunny's efforts, not to mention the freshly shampooed staircarpet, now devastated by fallen rubble, litres of water and heavy-footed firemen. "Typical bloody luck. It was first time in two years that the house had been properly clean."

Charlie too chose to be stoical in the face of losing half his possessions, including a brown envelope stuffed with poker winnings. (The other half of his belongings, most importantly his precious trumpet, were safe in the London flat, which just showed, he said, the importance of having more than one residence.)

Rachel was the one who suffered the most; the discovery that all this time she had been the object of Todd's violent revenge fantasies left her traumatised for a long time to come. The fearless, reckless Rachel we all loved changed almost overnight. She began to have nightmares and anxiety attacks, and became nervous in crowds and even more nervous when she was on her own. She couldn't help reimagining the incident with alternative tragic endings, dwelling on all the terrible things that didn't happen, but might easily have done if she hadn't come to

London with us that day. It wasn't surprising that she felt more personally victimised than the rest of us – she had much more to lose than her possessions – but it was horrible, horrible to see her so shaken.

Todd didn't prove a particularly tough nut for the police to crack: they already had his fingerprints on the inside of the box of chocolates, and if we had answered any of those missed calls from Dad on the morning of *On the Sofa*, we would have already known that. Under questioning, Todd readily admitted the prowling and the phoney bomb. He was adamant that he intended no serious harm and utterly denied any Animal Rights agenda, which the police were keen to pursue, since recent legislation meant a serious sentence was a real possibility. His story, which I believe, sort of, was that he had been hurt and depressed by Rachel's rejection, and was trying to find a way to make her want him again. He thought that a campaign of minor harassment might make her turn to him for protection or comfort. What a sad loser! Any girl could have told him that the very last person you would ever want to be grateful to is the person you have just dumped. I should have known all along that he was a dangerous weirdo the minute I caught him peeing in the washbasin.

He had bumped into Rachel quite by accident, as she had said, at Paddington, the weekend of Frankie's party, and although they had spent the afternoon together, Rachel had deliberately failed to follow up his suggestion that they meet up. He had seen her board the Brighton train at Victoria and decided to try and track her down. This had proved harder than he'd imagined until my name appeared in the paper, along with a mention of Auntie Jackie's dress shop. He had come down to Cliff Street and climbed in through my bedroom window – like so many before him – not with anything criminal in mind, he insisted, but just to give Rachel a "surprise".

This part I didn't believe: the discovery of his fingerprints *inside* Rachel's wardrobe suggested his plans were much more creepy. It was while searching through the house to check that he was alone that he had opened Charlie's bedroom door, setting off the crow-scarer, which had ignited the build-up of gas in the closed room. The blast had knocked him down the stairs on to the first landing and half buried him in rubble.

The police were confident that he would get a custodial sentence – there were so many different offences to charge him with, but the one that really excited them was the phoney bomb; especially if they could prove that its harmlessness was down to Todd's incompetence rather than his gentle, peace-loving soul.

In spite of what he had done and may have been planning to do, Rachel didn't seem able to summon up any hatred for Todd and it gave her no pleasure to imagine him in prison. Instead, bizarrely, she said that in her bleaker moods she felt guilty. Perhaps she had handled their break-up badly; perhaps she had been a bit cruel. She hadn't thought the male heart such a fragile thing. She would be more careful in future. Auntie Jackie was appalled by this response. "You're not to blame!" she blazed. "He's the guilty one. Ever since Adam and Eve men have been trying to wriggle out of trouble by saying 'it's her fault'. Well this is *not your fault.*"

But later, when I asked Rachel if the Todd thing had put her off guys in general, or made her worried about starting new relationships, she said: "No. Just worried about ending them."

Another of Charlie's sayings: for every loser there's a winner. If the losers in this case were Auntie Jackie and Rachel and Charlie himself, then who were the winners? Dad, certainly, since he could now go to work and do the job he loved without fear, and the Institute, who could relax security in the knowledge that there had never been any threat to them. And me too I suppose, in a way, because now I could go back home.

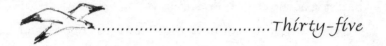 

*...................................Thirty-five*

# A Roof Over Her Head

Rachel and I sat on the station in the early evening sunshine, awaiting the 16.51 from Paddington and watching the commuters flowing from the ticket hall on to the platform to catch their homeward trains. West to Long Hanborough, Charlbury, Moreton-in-Marsh; north to Nethercott, King's Sutton, Banbury; the names on the departure boards were as familiar to me as the Lord's Prayer, and yet I'd never had any reason to visit a single one of them.

September in Oxford is the loveliest month. The summer tourists have started to thin out and the students haven't yet returned to the colleges, and always, reliably, as soon as school restarts, it stops raining and

345

there is a week of scorching sun and turquoise skies pressing at the classroom windows.

"How was your summer then?" various friends had asked in those first few days of term. "What you been up to?" I would take a deep breath and wonder where to start, and how to abbreviate everything that had happened into two sentences, which I knew from experience was the maximum amount of information it was possible to convey before the questioner interrupted or lost interest.

"I've been staying with my Auntie in Brighton," I would say, "How was Florida/Cornwall/Center Parcs?" And they would launch with relief into an account of their holiday, full of unfamiliar names and places, and my mind would drift off along channels of its own. Fishy ham, mice, rats, Dave, jazz, Charlie, Lucozade, macaroni-no-cheese, white teeth, champagne, the Diana dress, Alice, hospital, Breakfast TV, Mr Elkington, smoke and flames, Adam.

It was Adam that my thoughts returned to most often. There had been no opportunity to say goodbye or ask for his phone number or email address before leaving Brighton. Dad had driven down on the afternoon of the explosion, looking forward to his long weekend break, and found us still out on the pavement while the house smouldered. He had taken us all off to a hotel, and we had only been back to Cliff Street briefly to pick up our belongings. I had knocked next door, but there was no reply and the windows looked blank and dark.

"Here we go," said Rachel as the London train shimmered into view through the heat haze rising from the tracks. She had spent the whole day while I was at school packing up her belongings into boxes and moving them into the dining room. Until she went off to university at the end of the month she would be bedding down in my room on the foam cushion from the sunlounger. There was a time when this sort of sacrifice on her part would have been unthinkable: now, strange to report, Rachel herself had suggested it. "I might as well move out of my room since I'll be going away soon anyway. As long as Robbie can put up with me coming in late at night and disturbing her."

"As long as you can put up with me getting up early for school and disturbing *you*," was the obvious reply.

After two weeks, Auntie Jackie's boxy single room in the Travelodge had started to lose its appeal. 29 Cliff Street had been cleared of debris and made safe, and now the builders had moved in to begin the complicated repair job on the top storey, and she needed somewhere to stay until the work was complete.

"Come and stay with us," Dad had insisted. "Stay as long as you like." It was no less than she had done for us and besides, after a lonely summer in a college room, he was glad of some extra company, especially with Rachel's departure looming.

I was looking forward to showing her around, and seeing how she would transplant from landlady to lodger, and then I remembered that of course she knew the place already – she had lived here once before.

The train pulled up, whining, and the crowd on the platform began to divide and cluster, shuffling one way and then the other as they estimated where the doors were likely to come to rest.

Passengers streamed out and as soon as the last had set foot on the ground, the waiting crowds swarmed forwards as though being sucked through the doors by a powerful vacuum.

"Don't say she's missed it," sighed Rachel, checking her phone to see if there was some message to that effect. The train had been Dad's suggestion. "No point bringing a car to Oxford. There's nowhere to park." The guard was just raising his hand to signal the off when a suitcase came toppling through the open door in one of the front carriages and landed with a thud on the platform. It was followed, in a more stately style, by Auntie Jackie, dragging another large case on wheels and a leather bag. She looked up and down the platform expectantly, as though porters, chauffeurs and maids might suddenly materialise to assist her, and then tossed her head with annoyance and began to stagger along with her baggage. We ran to meet her, laughing.

"Don't they have people to carry bags any more?" she asked, when we had been properly hugged.

"You're getting confused with the Orient Express," said Rachel, taking the heavier of the two cases.

"Round about 1930," I added, taking the other.

In the cab ride home she started to rummage through her leather holdall in a state of mounting panic. "I saw Adam this morning," she said, at last finding what she was looking for. "He asked me to give you this." It was a paper dart – a proper precision-engineered feat of origami, guaranteed to glide for miles, if only it hadn't been so crushed in transit. Through the paper I could see the impression of his handwriting.

I smiled to myself and put it in my pocket for later.

# *Mr Elkington's Revenge*

*Hi Robyn*

*I can't quite believe that in the 21ˢᵗ century, and with a third of a degree in IT I am still reduced to this primitive method of communication. What next? Carrier pigeon? Smoke signals? Please let me have your email address – mine is adam@gardenofeden.co.uk*

*It has been strangely quiet here since you went away. Mum and Dad came down and took Gran back to Telford with them. Things in Cliff Street had been getting a bit too exciting for her. I went back home with them for a few days, and that was enough. They plan to sell the Brighton house so I will be homeless and destitute, living in a cardboard box under the arches, unless of course you know someone who is looking for a new lodger...*

*I'm sorry I didn't get to see you before you went. I noticed that we went past Oxford on the journey to Telford, so perhaps next time I go back home I could stop off on the way. We could get dressed up in expensively hired clothes and go for a walk along the River Cherwell, and see if we can find anyone who needs rescuing.*

*Anyway, must stop rambling now. Got to give this to Jackie before she goes.*

*Email me!*

*Adam x*

*PS I enclose a cutting from the local paper that might make you laugh.*

---

Red-faced police were forced to call off a murder investigation yesterday when it emerged that a human skeleton found in a partially destroyed building was in fact an acrylic model. Emergency services had been called to the house in Cliff Street on Thursday after a gas explosion tore the roof off. It was only when a pathologist began to examine the remains that the error came to light.

The skeleton's eccentric owner, Jackie Joseph, made the headlines last week when her £65,000 dress, once owned by Diana, Princess of Wales, was destroyed by her niece during a night out.

Mrs Joseph, 39, said, "It's been an eventful week."